Not Quite a Bride

Not Quite a Bride

KIRSTEN SAWYER

KENSINGTON BOOKS.

http://www.kensingtonbooks.com

KENSINGTON BOOKS are published by

Kensington Publishing Corp.
850 Third Avenue
New York, NY 10022

All Kensington titles, imprints and distributed lines are available at special quantity discounts for bulk purchases for sales promotion, premiums, fund-raising, educational or institutional use.

Special book excerpts or customized printings can also be created to fit specific needs. For details, write or phone the office of the Kensington Special Sales Manager: Kensington Publishing Corp., 850 Third Avenue, New York, NY 10022. Attn. Special Sales Department. Phone: 1-800-221-2647.

Kensington and the K logo Reg. U.S. Pat. & TM Off.

ISBN 0-7582-1663-7

First Kensington Trade Paperback Printing: January 2007
10 9 8 7 6 5 4 3 2 1

Printed in the United States of America

To David:
Without you, this book could
have been an autobiography.

And

To Jenny:
Without you, this book
couldn't have been.

Acknowledgments

A big thank you to:

Hilary Rubin for taking a chance on me and working so hard to make this book happen . . . I forgive you for abandoning me and am so grateful to Kimberly Whalen for taking me on.

Audrey LaFehr for being an amazing editor, and Amanda Rouse for patiently answering my countless questions.

And, of course, many thanks to my wonderfully supportive friends and family.

Prologue

Always a bridesmaid, never a bride. Not just cruel words that older relatives and married friends love to throw around at functions where you are in some pastel monster called a bridesmaid's dress and a friend, sister, cousin, etc., is in something magnificent and white. These are painfully true words that I believe drove me over the edge.

Thirty is not that old . . . it's a perfectly acceptable age to still be single. It's a good time for a woman to focus on finding herself and building her career. Unfortunately, no matter how many times I told myself that, I still didn't buy it.

When I was in high school, I truly believed that by the time I was thirty I would be married, the owner of my own home, and the mother of a couple of children. Instead, after three decades of pursuing this life, I was still a single, childless renter, while everyone around me was living my dream. So I decided to take matters into my own hands, and that's how I ended up where I am today.

Today is my wedding day . . . it should be the happiest day of my life. It should be the day that at long last all my dreams are realized and I embark on the love boat to the island of happiness and bliss that everyone else has already been living on. That couldn't be farther from the truth. Instead, this day is worse than I ever imagined it could be. I'm standing in a suite at The Plaza hotel . . . no expense has been spared in pursuit of matrimonial perfection. I am wearing my dream—a white (at last!)—Vera Wang strapless wedding gown. My fantasy wedding is minutes away and I'm finally realizing what I have done.

Okay, so I mentioned that I was driven over the edge . . . let me take you back and explain the whole thing.

One Year Earlier

I'm sitting alone on the subway . . . it's Sunday, so there are hardly any other people. The few people in my car—a woman who looks like she may live there, an athletic couple in workout clothes, and a man with a cranky little girl—are staring at me. I close my eyes and lean my head back . . . why wouldn't they be staring at me? I must look like I came from *The Night of the Living Dead* prom.

I'm wearing one of the ugliest bridesmaid's dresses I've ever worn . . . and that's saying a lot, because I've worn a lot. It's lavender and chiffon and huge. I think my friend, Maggie, was going for some sort of *Gone With the Wind* theme . . . for her bridesmaids; of course, her own gown was sleek and sophisticated and amazing.

I've been in the thing since 2:00 P.M. yesterday when we began the marathon three-hour photo session. My makeup is no longer where it started . . . it's all streaked down my cheeks. My fancy hairdo that I thought had enough spray to go through a wind tunnel looks like some squirrels took up residence and then had a domestic disturbance. And one of my adorable lavender Hype sandals, the only thing about my ensemble that didn't nauseate me, is missing a heel. I can only imagine what a sight I am.

I'm sure you're wondering why someone who looks as bad as I currently do would opt for the public humiliation of the subway and not take a private, less shameful taxicab? Well, I had some problems . . . let me explain. I guess all the problems can be traced back to one big problem—namely, alcohol. I had too much of it. Then, at 11:00 P.M., the open bar ran out and switched to a no-host bar . . . meaning: buy your own booze. At that point I'd already had too much alcohol to accurately judge that a) I didn't need any more drinks, or b) spending my cab money on rum and Cokes was a really dumb idea. The second problem, and the reason I'm on the subway during daylight hours with other human beings and not in the dead of night, is Kevin (I think it's Kevin), the extremely handsome (I think extremely handsome) groomsman.

Too much rum and not enough Coke allowed me to think for a brief, blurry moment that perhaps Kevin was "the one" (a common problem for single girls . . . every human with a Y-chromosome could be "the one"), and so I joined him in his hotel room for a high-school-caliber make-out session that would have gone farther had another groomsman not been kind enough to pass out in the same room (I am a strong believer that after college it's wrong to have sex when other people are asleep—or awake, for that matter—in the same room). I ended up passing out in the room as well and didn't wake up until the pounding in my head got too loud at the crack of dawn this morning when I crept out (without disturbing Kevin, the other groomsman, or the third guy who I didn't even know had come in) to do the walk of shame.

Thankfully, we arrive at my stop just as I feel the chunks of last night's "wedding chicken" start to rise in my throat. You know what I'm talking about, right? The standard hotel chicken, in sickening sauce with smaller-than-usual vegetables to make them fancy and creamier-than-usual potatoes to ensure stomach problems, particularly for anyone in a hoopskirt. I get out of the station as quickly as a girl with a missing heel can and take a deep breath of fresh air. Well, as fresh as Manhattan air gets in July.

As I arrive at my apartment—an apartment I've lived in since I graduated from college—I feel enormous relief. It's only 8:45 A.M., but I think I've sweated one or two pints in the three-block walk. I climb up the three flights of stairs and I am living proof of Dorothy's wise words, "There's no place like home!"

I absolutely love my apartment, and although it might not be as fancy as some with elevators or doormen, it really is a Manhattan gem. It was my grandmother's for as long as I can remember. She passed away shortly before I graduated from college and left the unit to my dad. He and my mom agreed that a two-bedroom in a great Upper East Side location was the perfect place for my sister, Jamie, and me to live upon graduation. The plan was that I would live alone until Jamie graduated three years later; then she would move in with me. Only Jamie graduated from college madly in love and got engaged and then married and never moved in. Thankfully, I was able to keep the place all for myself.

The apartment wasn't the only thing left behind by my beloved grandmother when she died. She left me an extremely generous "wedding fund," which has been cruelly burning a hole in my pocket. Nana and I had an extremely close relationship, and we both shared a passion for weddings. Nana really started it all. She was a hopeless romantic, married to her high-school sweetheart from the day after their graduation until the day he died. Up until the very end, she still put her wedding dress on every year on her anniversary. According to her, this was so she could relive the happiest day of her life. When questioned by my father why his birth wasn't the happiest day of her life, all she could do was shrug. She loved weddings. Nana could describe all eight of Elizabeth Taylor's weddings (and wedding dresses) in detail. She was up at the crack of dawn to watch every second of coverage of Princess Diana's marriage to Charles, she kept me up late to watch Joanie Cunningham marry Chachi Arcola, and she talked my mother into letting me stay home from school when Luke and Laura were wed.

Ever since the day she presented me with my first Barbie bride doll clad in a miniature white lace gown, she and I had been planning my special day. With Nana, no wish was too indulgent. Together, we planned for five-foot trains and six-foot cakes. All through my adolescence, I believed that these plans could and would come true. I was certain that, like Nana, I would marry my high-school sweetheart. It didn't turn out that way . . . instead I found him having sex with my best friend in the girls' bathroom at our prom. As I entered my twenties, still alone, I started to have my doubts, but Nana never did. *He's out there, Molly, so you'd better think about these plans now so that you're ready when you find him,* she'd say.

I believed her, and kept planning. As my friends started to marry off, at first it gave me hope. I saw how it was happening to people around me—dreams were coming true—so my day in the sun must be just around the corner. The block kept getting longer and longer, though, and the corner was still nowhere in sight. When my grandmother passed away, a significant portion of my devastation was that she would not be around to share the day that she and I had planned for so many years.

Then my father informed me that Nana had specifically left me an inheritance to be spent on my dream wedding. While I knew the day would never be the same without her physically there, her gift made me feel like whenever Mr. Right came along, my wonderful grandmother would still play an important part in what she promised would be the happiest day of my life. My father was kind enough to help me invest my wedding fund until the day came when I was ready to use it. Thanks to him, what was an extremely generous gift to begin with had grown into what I was quite sure would afford me my dream-fantasy wedding. The only thing missing, of course, was that dream-fantasy guy . . .

2

Hangover Pains

I struggle through the door trying to juggle the mail, the hoopskirt and my cat, Tiffany, greeting me with the excitement that only a cat can have toward a massive amount of lavender chiffon. I drop the stuff onto the table and add some kibble to Tiffany's dish before I drag myself to the bedroom and remove the pastel monster that has been strangling me for twenty-six hours (but who's counting?). I kick it into the back of my closet where there is a pile of pastel puffiness in a variety of disgusting shades and materials. My cat loves this bridesmaid's-dress graveyard, so I haven't had the heart to heave them down the garbage chute or start a bonfire—yet. I've been fantasizing about doing it, though.

Other than the "graveyard," my apartment is adorable. I really love it; it kind of looks like Monica's apartment on *Friends*, but less funky and more feminine. I am so happy with it . . . the only problem is that if I could ever get a man to want to come upstairs, he'd probably take one look at my pink-and-green Pierre Deux couch and run for his masculinity.

Okay, so now you know my secret . . . I'm one of those

women. I live alone in an overly feminine apartment with a cat.

I pull a tank top and boxer shorts on (so much better!) and collapse on my bed, not even bothering to pull my Ralph Lauren quilt back or remove the seventy-five bobby pins poking me in the skull.

I don't stir again for many hours, and by the time I finally do manage to heave my body off the bed it's starting to get dark. I head back out to the living room, where I am faced with an angry white cat (cats don't like to be ignored for two days straight) and a stack of mail, which I flip through, only halfway paying attention.

"Wedding invitation, wedding gift thank-you, shower invitation, baby shower thank-you, engagement party . . . what?!? When did *she* get engaged?!?" That gets my attention because it's the story of my life.

Oh, I should tell you at this point . . . I talk to myself, sometimes under the guise of talking to my cat, but sadly, she's not always in the room. As I'm flipping through the mail, rubbing salt on my wounds, I notice the answering machine blinking and hit the button.

"Time of call: 6:57 A.M.," the friendly, computerized voice tells me.

"Jeez, who called *that* early?!?"

Okay . . . I also talk to the answering machine man . . . and occasionally—all right, often—to TiVo.

"Good Golly Miss Molly . . . it's hard to believe . . ."

My mother . . .

" . . . that thirty years ago at this time my first baby was born. Daddy and I love you . . . we will see you next weekend for your birthday dinner? I hope you had a lovely time at Maggie's wedding. Did you meet a man?"

I can hear my father grumbling something in the background, and then my mother hissing something with her hand over the receiver.

"It doesn't matter if you did or not, 'cause we love you very much, Molly." CLICK.

Ugh . . . I'd kind of forgotten . . . and I was kind of trying to keep it from you. Today is my thirtieth birthday. So now you know the rest of the secret . . . and I'm sure you have a clear picture of me in your head. Oh, wait . . . and did I mention I'm a schoolteacher? There you have me: a single, thirty-year-old schoolteacher who lives with a cat. It's not what you think, though. I'm not a spinster or old-maidish at all . . . at least, I don't think I am.

"Time of call: 12:04 P.M."

"Happy Birthday to you! Happy Birthda—" a voice sang. CLICK.

My sister, Jamie . . . she sings every year. I don't need to hear it and *you* definitely don't need to hear it. Jamie is wonderful, but she's always happy and upbeat and that can be exhausting. She's also a schoolteacher (maybe that helps explain why she's not opposed to leaving musical messages for people?) and so is our mom, just so you understand the genealogy. Jamie and I are exactly the same in some ways and couldn't be more opposite in others. The similarities mean that we are really close but sometimes that can cause us to bicker like we are still little kids . . . plus she has some middle-child issues. Jamie is three years younger than I am, she's much trendier, and she's way more "cutting edge." I'm so uncool that I say things like "cutting edge." People are always shocked when she tells them she teaches third grade, whereas they look at me and nod like it's an obvious fact. The biggest difference, though, is that she's married to her college sweetheart. They were together five and a half years before they tied the knot, and if I didn't love Jamie and her husband, Bryan, so incredibly much, I'd hate them both to death.

"Time of call: 2:42 P.M."

"Molls, it's me . . ."

"Me" is my best friend, Brad.

"I hope you don't feel as bad today as you looked last night. Hahaha . . . just kidding! Be ready at seven tonight . . . I'm coming by to pick you up." CLICK.

Brad Lawson has been my best friend since the first weekend of rush parties our freshman year of college. We both had bad first experiences with something called jungle juice—it's a highly potent fraternity concoction that tastes suspiciously like Kool-Aid. Anyway, Brad and I ended up puking our guts out on the same bush outside the Phi Kappa Psi house. He ended up pledging there, and many of our happiest college nights finished up on that same poor hedge. When we met, we were both awkward freshmen, but by senior year my sorority sisters were both thrilled and confused by our strictly platonic relationship. I cannot count how many girls begged to be fixed up with him, thinking he was some kind of California surfer stud. He did grow up in Southern California and has blond hair and blue eyes . . . but actually he's from somewhere called Tarzana in the San Fernando Valley, and he's never been on a surfboard. He made me swear to keep that a secret, though.

But really, once you learn to ignore his West Coast good looks, he has an amazing soul. Brad is the kind of friend you can count on to come pick you up in the middle of the night when you're driving home from a boyfriend who has just dumped you and it's raining and you get a flat tire. He'll show up at your door with an Egg McMuffin when he knows you are nursing a hangover. He'll even send you a dozen long-stemmed roses on Valentine's Day when you're sad and single. A better friend could not be found . . . honestly, he has done all of these things (and more) for me.

I glance at the clock on the microwave and can't believe

it's practically 4:30! I only have two and a half hours to re-cover from last night and be ready to go, looking twenty-five years old, to celebrate my thirtieth birthday! Perhaps I should have checked my messages sooner?

First stop: bubble bath.

3

The World's Worst Birthday

Somehow, and don't ask me how I did it, only two and a half hours later I am ready to go and looking adorable—I really am—except for the slightly funky tan line from the hour we spent outside taking pictures in the lavender curse. And even with the strange stripes around my shoulders, the hours I have spent with the free weights have left my arms looking anything but thirty. I'm telling you, prepare to watch me get carded tonight. I'm also working really hard on my positive attitude. I will not let turning thirty make me bitter.

At 7 P.M., practically on the dot, my front door buzzes. I'm in the final stages of the getting-ready process . . . final sprays of perfume, buckling of sandals, lip gloss, etc.

"Crap . . . who is that?" I ask Tiffany . . . as if a cat knows who's at the door. "Hello?" I holler into the intercom.

"Molls, it's me . . . buzz me up."

"Brad?" I question Tiffany, who looks at me, confused. "Why is he so early?"

Brad enters my apartment carrying a single chocolate (my favorite) cupcake with a burning candle in the shape of a three.

"You bought a new candle for me?!?"

The birthday cupcake isn't a complete surprise . . . it's more a tradition, really. Since my 21st, Brad has always "surprised" me with a cupcake. What *is* a surprise, though, is that the wax candle in the shape of a two that was used to celebrate the past nine birthdays (he never bothered to specify where in my twenties I was, which was always appreciated) has been replaced.

"Nothing but the best for you. Happy Birthday, Molly. Make a wish."

I blow the candle out . . . we all know what I wished for.

"It's going to come true, I promise," he says as he kisses my head.

I smile at him as I take the cupcake and start peeling off the paper. Whoever said, "Life's uncertain, eat dessert first," was definitely onto something.

"You're so early—thank goodness I'm dressed!"

Brad looks at his watch, "I'm not early—it's seven on the dot."

"Exactly—who's on time? On time is today's early."

He starts to laugh, and I can't help but look at him fondly because his whole face twinkles when he laughs as the buzzer buzzes again.

"Huh? Is this a birthday surprise?!? (Into the intercom) Hello?" I say, looking suspiciously at Brad.

"Molly, it's Claire. What is taking Brad so long? I'm holding a cab, you know."

The happiness, the joy, and the anticipation of a nice birthday celebration come to a screeching halt. Brad has brought the human equivalent of nails on a chalkboard: Claire Reilly. Now I know I said that I personally don't find Brad attractive; however, based on the reaction he gets at every bar, club, and dental office I've ever seen him in, all other women do. Okay, I'm lying . . . I mean, I'm not blind;

even I can see how good-looking he is. I have just convinced myself that he's not, because I never want to jeopardize our friendship. But why he has chosen Claire Reilly to be with for the past year is beyond me. She's truly awful and evil. She doesn't work because her grandfather invented whatever thing it is in pacemakers that makes them pace and then died (ironically) of a heart attack shortly after, leaving her with an enormous trust fund. The really annoying thing is that she genuinely doesn't understand why everyone doesn't live off their trust fund and often acts like Brad's job, as a writer for an extreme-sports magazine, is a hobby. She is insanely uptight and the exact reason why Brad was ringing my doorbell at 6:59 P.M.

"Molly . . . are you ready? Come on, we've got to go."

Oh, and did I mention that Brad is completely pussy-whipped?

I grab my bag and buckle the left sandal strap as I hop out the door. I finger my hair as we literally run down the stairwell and secretly curse Claire for preventing me from doing one last mirror check.

Out on the street, she's holding open a cab door and tapping her little Jimmy Choos on the curb while she keeps time on her Cartier watch.

"Sorry, baby. Molly wasn't quite ready."

I open my mouth to protest, but what do I care? Let her hate me. The feeling is definitely mutual.

"You know, Molly, when people say seven, they mean seven."

She ushers me into the cab and I feel like an eight-year-old who is late for the school bus. Actually, worse . . . I teach eight-year-olds, and I never talk to anybody like that! Claire is one of those people that you would probably be compelled to hate even if she was an angel, because she is physically flawless. She has skin that looks like porcelain, lavender-blue eyes, and pale blond hair without a single dark root or a moment of frizz. She has a great figure and a wardrobe to match. Everything is perfect. The fact that she's evil just makes it that much easier to wish her dead.

We get to my favorite restaurant in Little Italy where I have been coming for years and everyone knows me. I'm never sure if this thrills me or embarrasses me. A long table is set and waiting. And guess what? We're the first of our party of nine to arrive.

We sit down and get to work on a bottle of Chianti. Well, Brad and I do . . . and about fifteen minutes later my very timely sister and her husband show up with arms full of gifts. (Ooh, hooray, I forgot there would be presents!)

"Molly! Happy Birthday!! I can't believe you're thirty!"

Ouch . . . did someone just drop an anvil on my heart?

"Jamie, can we please celebrate without using the word or any references to the number thirty?"

Jamie laughs . . . does she realize I'm serious? They look around the empty table.

"You guys are so early! We thought we'd be the first ones here and could set this stuff up (meaning the stack of presents hiding Bryan). Didn't you say 7:15?"

Claire has to cut in. "Actually," she says, pointing to that stupid watch, "it's 7:30."

Jamie looks confused, but she's never one to rock the boat, so she shrugs it off.

Over the next half-hour my friends slowly show up. It's a good thing looks can't kill, or Claire would have murdered my two best girlfriends from college, Alex and Lauren, and their husband and fiancé, respectively, Steve and Rob.

Lauren and I were pretty inseparable until a year and a half ago when she met Rob. We were the lone single girls from our group of core college friends and could always count on each other. Then she met Rob while interviewing for a job . . . he was actually the one interviewing her. He called to tell her that she couldn't have the job because she was just too cute, and instead of being upset (as a normal person who'd been out of work for seven months would), Lauren thought this was just the sweetest thing in the world, agreed to go out with him . . . and one thing led to another. Honestly, when I have to hear them tell the story, I throw up in my mouth, just a little bit. After Rob came into the picture, Lauren forgot about our sisterhood and all the humiliating bouquet tosses and lonely Valentine's Days we shared. Rob is great, but I still constantly have to remind myself not to be bitter and jealous . . . I know it's not intentional.

Alex is the opposite of Lauren and me . . . I don't think she's spent a total of five boyfriendless minutes since I met her my freshman year. Although, everyone was completely shocked when she announced her plans to marry Steve, the rebound from a three-year relationship that left her completely crushed . . . but he fell so head-over-heels in love with her that she was convinced by it and vowed 'til death do them part only seven months into their relationship. Because Alex was always busy with one (or two) guys, we were never as close as I was with Lauren, but I still consider her a "core" friend.

Once everyone is settled and happy (except Claire, of course) and drinking, I can't help but look around the table: married, married, engaged, relationship, and me. I'm not sure which hurts more . . . that or thirty. I push the thought out of my head, though; I'm determined to have a good time . . . and I do. Lots of food, lots of wine, and the world's largest slice of tiramisu later, I'm thoroughly enjoying myself. I'm definitely having a glass-is-half-full evening. I have wonderful friends, I have a favorite restaurant I can always count on, arms that rival Jennifer Anniston's (when making muscles at the bathroom mirror after six glasses of wine, anyway). Life is SO good.

Don't start thinking this is a birds-singing-in-the-meadow story. The proverbial shit is about to hit the fan.

"Okay, everybody, gifts! Gifts!" Jamie's teacher skills are strong. She's standing with one hand in the air and the other motioning to the pile of gifts at the end of our table.

"Oh, yippee!" I exclaim as Alex passes the first package down to me. Generally, when I open presents, people want to murder me. I always save ribbon, and if paper is especially nice, I'll save that, too. The only person who doesn't go bonkers is my sister because she does the exact same thing.

The first gift is from Alex and Steve. It's a scented candle: generic, but thoughtful nonetheless. A single-gal staple, and it will get put to good use.

"You guys, it's perfect. I have a spot right beside my bathtub that this will be perfect in," I gush, and they look pleased.

"I know that you used to love that scent . . . I hope you still do," Alex says.

"Definitely," I lie . . . I haven't used cucumber-melon in a few years, but it does smell good, so I'm sure I'll enjoy it.

I'm working on the paper on Brad and Claire's gift, secretly annoyed that my best friend got me a joint gift with the evil one, when my sister grabs it from me and thrusts another package at me.

"I can't wait any more. Open ours!"

"Okay . . . sorry I'm so slow . . . you know how I am."

"I know, I don't care . . . just open mine."

Jamie and Bryan's is quick and easy to unwrap . . . they took the gift bag route (obviously I will be keeping the gift bag . . . unless Jamie swipes it back like she did with my Christmas gift bag). Inside is a T-shirt that says, WORLD'S GREATEST AUNT. What am I missing?

"Huh? I don't get it."

"*World's Greatest Aunt*," Jamie emphasizes.

"I can read it, I just don't get it. Is this, like, a new fad?"

Like I said, Jamie is a bit trendier than I am . . . if something is about to be the hottest thing, she already knows about it. Like she totally brought the Laverne initial monogram back before everyone else did. She sewed a hot-pink "J" on an old black cashmere sweater and I told her she was crazy for ruining her sweater, and before I knew it, people were paying hundreds for the same look! But honestly, I'm wondering if she's losing her touch, 'cause everyone at the table looks as confused as I feel.

"I told you she wouldn't get it." Jamie's husband, the practical one, says. Bryan appreciates and adores Jamie, but it's definitely a case of opposites attracting.

"Shut up, Bryan—it's an awesome surprise . . . she'll get it."

"Molly, don't you get it? (A little louder and slower than before) *World's Greatest Aunt.* (pause) Oh Jeez . . . you're going to be World's Greatest Aunt because I'm going to be World's Greatest Mom," she says as she squeals with delight.

Everyone around the table starts buzzing with conversation but it takes me a minute to catch on . . . then I realize. This is a prank. It's a roast. It's a big, cruel joke on me because I'm single and thirty and live alone with a cat that I talk to. Maybe I've had too much wine, but truly I think it's the brutality of the situation that causes my eyes to fill with tears. Jamie glows as she informs everyone, "She gets it! She gets it!!"

"Yes, I get it, Jamie . . . and it's the meanest thing I've ever seen," I say, trying, fruitlessly, to hold back tears. "I asked you all to be sensitive that today is my thirtieth birthday . . . and of everyone here—no offense, everyone else—I thought you, my sister, would be the most sensitive. Haha . . .

I get your joke. It's hysterical. 'World's Greatest Aunt' because I'll never get married, I'll never have children, and I'll never be 'World's Greatest Mom.'"

Jamie's face looks stricken . . . apparently her little joke isn't going off like she planned. Good!

"No, Molly . . . you will be World's Greatest Mom one day. I'm trying to tell you that you are going to be World's Greatest Aunt in six months. I'm pregnant!"

Suddenly, everyone at the table starts shrieking and cheering. It's all kind of a foggy haze to me. Lauren jumps up and hugs my sister, and Rob and Alex both congregate on Bryan. Everyone is rejoicing—even Claire cracks a smile. My younger sister is pregnant? It's bad enough she got married before I did, but now she's having a baby before I've even met someone?!? I am cruel. I am selfish. I am jealous. And I am drunk. Also, I think I'm hyperventilating. I honestly cannot breathe. I feel like that girl on *The Bachelor* who had some sort of an attack when he didn't give her a stupid rose. Only this is a legitimate reason to have an attack. As I sit there, struggling to breathe, the world goes on around me in slow motion. Everyone is toasting and congratulating. They have forgotten about me, so I get up to leave.

Jamie tries to stop me, but her voice is distant . . . it almost sounds like it's underwater . . . probably the same as it sounds to her fetus. I stumble out of the restaurant, calling over my shoulder something about needing air—possibly calling over my shoulder something that sounds like Daryl Hannah saying her mermaid name in *Splash*. I get in a cab and by the time it pulls up in front of my building, I'm sobbing. The walk up to my apartment is a blur, and without even taking off my adorable outfit I get a fresh bottle of Jack Daniel's from a high cupboard and a pint of Ben & Jerry's Phish Food from the freezer. There, alone on my floor (well, my cat is there, but even she looks a little frightened), I try to eat and drink my sorrows away.

You're thinking this must be it . . . I must have hit bottom. Well, sadly, you are incorrect. It's going to get worse. Buckle up.

4

The Meltdown

I wake up early—well, it feels early—to the sound of the door buzzer. I am on the floor in a fetal position cuddling the empty Ben & Jerry's container. The almost-empty bottle of Jack isn't too far away. My cute outfit has chocolate, caramel, and drool . . . actually, it looks like chocolate-caramel drool, all over it. I try to cover my head with a pillow from the couch, but the buzzing won't stop. I catch a glimpse of myself in the hall mirror and hope that if the buzzing is to tell me that the building is on fire that I am burnt to a crisp before any cute firemen reach my door.

"Who is it?" I moan into the buzzer.

"Molls, it's Brad—buzz me up."

"I'm sorry, wrong number . . . go away. Come back at a decent hour."

"Molly, It's 11:30."

"No. Go awa—"

"Oh, never mind . . . your neighbor just came out and held the door."

"What? No! Damn neighbor. See if I ever lend you a cup of sugar!" I yell through the intercom.

I'm not completely distraught, though, because Brad

might be in the building, but it doesn't mean he's coming in here. I'd have to open the door for that to happen. Ha!

A few seconds later there is a knock on my door and I completely ignore it. The bastard keeps knocking, which is really killing my head, but I'm strong and I don't give in. Then there is a key turning in the door and Brad walks in.

"What are you doing? That's breaking and entering!"

"No, it isn't—I have a key. You gave it to me to feed Tiffany when you were at Suzanne McNally's wedding."

"Damn."

I hated Suzanne McNally for making me wear a peach taffeta dress with a bow on my ass and now I hate her even more for making me give Brad a key.

"Look, can you leave? I think I have food poisoning."

"You don't have food poisoning."

He glances at the chocolate-caramel drool and me and then to my nest on the floor.

"Come on, Molly, let's get you cleaned up. We're going to go for a run."

"No! The only place I will run is away from you."

"The only way you're gonna get over this hangover is to sweat it out."

I protest a bit longer without getting anywhere, and then, like a four-year-old who has been denied a cookie, I throw a tantrum. I'm screaming and crying and pounding my fists . . . but I can assure you this, I'm not leaving this apartment. When I finish, I look up smugly, positive that Brad will have gone running for his life, but the bastard is still there, in my apartment, and now he's laughing at me!

"Okay, fine, you don't have to go running, but you do have to take a shower. I have something I need to talk to you about."

Crap. The thing about Brad is that he always calls me on my shit. I know that he is here to tell me how awful I was to my sister last night. I know a lecture is coming . . . all I can do is postpone it, so I agree to the shower as a way to put it off. I retreat to my bathroom for the longest shower in the history of showers with hopes that I'll be in for so long that Brad will give up and have to leave, or die of starvation, before I return.

By the time I exit the shower I am pruned to within an inch of my life and certain that I am alone . . . but I'm not. I watch him for a second, sitting on my floral couch . . . he is the only guy I have ever met who can sit on it and not look like he's afraid the flowers will crawl up and devour his heterosexuality. I have to suck it up . . . he was right about the shower making me feel better and he'll be right about everything he says regarding how awful I was to my wonderful sister. I wrap myself in my pink robe and go out to the living room.

"Okay, you were right about the shower. I feel better. Now, let me have it."

Brad solemnly turns off the TV and turns toward me.

"Molly, come here and sit down."

He pats my shabby-chic chair-and-a-half as I cross the room and settle myself into it as a brace for what is to come.

"I'm not going to tell you how awful you were to Jamie, because you know that. You know that she is not malicious and that her decision to have a child now has nothing to do with where you are in your life and everything to do with where she is in her life. And you know that you need to call her and apologize today."

I nod in agreement . . . but I'm a little confused. That was so easy. Could we really be done?

"What I actually need to talk to you about is something different."

Huh? What's going on here?

"Molly, Claire and I got engaged."

There is no chair on earth sturdy enough to brace me for this.

"What?"

"We're going to get married. I asked her on Saturday and she said yes."

Okay, so remember the fog from last night. Imagine it much, much thicker and that's sort of where I am right now.

"But she wasn't wearing an engagement ring. Are you sure you're getting married? To Claire?"

"Yes . . . I'm sure. She didn't like the ring I got her, so she's exchanging it today. She'll be wearing it the next time you see her."

And then the weirdest thing happens. I've heard people who have cheated death in the nick of time say that before you die, everything becomes very clear and calm. Well, that's what happens to me. I emerge from the fog with a whole new view of the world. I feel like I have put on glasses that allow me to see clearly for the first time in my life.

"Congratulations," I say slowly and deliberately. "I'm sure you will be very . . . prompt."

I said the glasses helped me see clearly . . . I didn't say they were rose-colored.

"*Happy*, Molly—you're sure we will be very *happy*. Thank you. And we're having an engagement party on the sixth. I want you to be there . . . you are my best friend . . . I want you to be the best man . . . best woman—whatever—we'll think of a name for you."

I sit there and stare blankly at him like I've never seen him before in my life. It's one of those moments where you know you have to say something, but the seconds are ticking by and nothing is coming to you. One . . . two . . . three . . .

"Aw, Molly, I know what you're thinking."

He knows what I'm thinking? Well, thank goodness somebody does because I certainly haven't got a clue.

"Always a bridesmaid, never a bride. I promise it's going to happen for you, sweetie."

Oh my gosh . . . that definitely wasn't what I was thinking, but now that he said it, I am. It's true! Now I can expand my wedding résumé to include best man . . . best woman . . . whatever, but still not the bride. I nod like an idiot, hug Brad, and wave cheerfully as he walks down the hall. I cannot believe this. It's bad enough that my *younger* sister is married and pregnant before I'm in a serious relationship, but now my best friend and practically my only single friend left is not only getting married, but to the devil herself . . . and I have to stand up at their wedding.

Yet, despite these crushing blows, I am not freaking out. I am not hitting the bottle (or the pint). I am doing what any pathetic old spinster would do . . . I'm sitting in my apartment talking to my cat.

"I'm okay, Tiff, really, I am . . ." Even the cat isn't buying it. "This is pathetic," I tell her. "No offense to you." She meows and walks away . . . I'm not sure if offense was taken or not. "I've got to get out of here."

I grab the *Village Voice* off my coffee table and flip to the page with the movie times. I am aware that going to the movies alone is yet another pathetic thing to do, but it's got to be better than sitting here. A good chick-flick will help me forget my miserable life—at least for a couple hours. I scan the page and am excited to find that a theater not far from my apartment is showing the old '80s classic, *Can't Buy Me Love*. A dorky Patrick Dempsey (pre-*Grey's Anatomy* hottie days) should cheer me up a bit. As I check the movie times, my eyes wander to the next page where the personal ads are, and that's where I see:

Male Escort—NOT MAN WHORE
Handsome, well-mannered gentleman
to escort/entertain males or females.
NO SEX. Nightly or weekend rates.
Call Justin: 212-555-6373

I look at the ad and then back to the page with the ad for *Can't Buy Me Love*. My eyes go back and forth, back and forth, back and forth . . . lightbulb . . . I pick up the phone and dial . . . it rings . . . I wait. Finally a machine answers.

"Hi, Justin, my name is Molly Harr . . . just Molly. I saw your ad in the *Village Voice* and I have a proposition for you. Don't worry . . . I don't want sex. Well, I do, but not yours . . . well . . . never mind . . . just call me—212-555-7543. 'Bye."

And there you have it: rock bottom. It's not as dramatic as you expected, I'm sure . . . but this is it. I have figured out a way to live my dream without any of my dreams actually coming true. At thirty years old, I have decided to give up on love, give up on romance, and settle for marriage . . . or at least a wedding . . . My day will finally come and I will finally be the one in the white dress—it's just going to take some white lies to get there.

5

When Molly Met Justin

The next week, I find myself sitting in a Starbucks drinking a Caramel Frappuccino and waiting for Justin to arrive. I am early . . . truly early, not just on-time early. I get there fifteen minutes before our scheduled meeting time! At two o'clock on the dot (so he was early, too . . . points for being prompt), Justin walks in. I know it's him because he'd described himself quite accurately on the phone. I must have described myself accurately as well because he waves as soon as he looks in my direction and comes over to the table. I guess there's no turning back now.

"You must be Molly!"

He extends a hand enthusiastically and his friendly attitude and natural warmth calm my nerves. And his ad was right; he is handsome and he definitely seems well mannered. He's tall and athletic-looking with dark hair and dark brown eyes. Actually, he's exactly my type. This could work.

"I'm going to grab a cup of coffee real quick . . . you want anything else?"

"No, I'm fine, thanks," I answer, giving him even more points in the courtesy column.

I study his butt as he approaches the counter . . . really

nice. He's friendly with the Barista. He puts money in the tip jar, and not just his change . . . very generous. I start to get excited. What if he actually *is* the one? Wouldn't that be a hilarious story to tell our grandkids? How Grandma hired Grandpa as an escort but their love couldn't be denied . . . and obviously he didn't charge! We're ninety and in side-by-side rocking chairs by the time he returns with his latte.

"So," he says, "you said you had a proposition for me. You don't seem sketchy—tell me what you were thinking."

I'm so entangled in my fantasy that I'm not ready to get to business.

"Why don't you tell me a little about yourself first . . . let's get to know each other."

He smiles and it's one of those great smiles where the whole face actually lights up.

"Okay, I'm thirty-three years old. I'm an actor . . . well, right now I'm a waiter, but I want to be an actor. I grew up in the Midwest but came to New York to attend NYU, and I've been here ever since. I always knew I'd come to New York, though . . . people like me don't exactly fit in in the middle."

"People like you?"

"Gay people. They are much less homophobic on the coasts."

"Oh, you're gay?"

"Yeah . . . that's not a problem for what you had in mind, is it? My ad said no sex . . . you sounded like you understood that in your message."

"Oh gosh! No! No sex—I definitely understand that."

And I guess no fiftieth anniversary party where our grandkids sing songs and put on little skits to reenact our romance, either.

"Okay, phew! So anyway, I needed to earn extra money, so I started this escort business and it's been going okay. Some of the people are a little creepy and some of them make me a little sad . . . not that you are creepy or sad. I'm actually kind of confused by you, so do you want to tell me what's going on now?"

I take a deep breath. Here comes the moment of truth— the moment that I share my grand plan with another human being. The moment that it grows wings and flies away or crashes and burns in a fiery grave.

"Okay, Justin . . . here's my plan. Have you ever seen the movie *Can't Buy Me Love?*"

"With Patrick Dempsey? Absolutely!"

"Good. I want to rent you," I inform him.

"Seriously? Look, it's a great movie and all . . . but I don't think renting an out-of-work, gay actor is going to make you more popular."

"Well, that's not exactly my plan. Let me tell you a little about myself. I'm thirty. I'm a teacher . . . I teach third grade. I'm the oldest of three . . . I have a younger sister who is married and pregnant and a younger brother who is in Europe 'finding himself.' I grew up in Connecticut; my parents are still there and happily married. And all of my friends are either married or engaged."

"It's nice to know about you. I don't get it, though . . ."

"Justin, I want to rent you for one year. Not full-time . . . don't worry. I want to stage a whirlwind romance, an engagement, and a wedding. I want the experience of being a bride and I want all the fun and celebration that brides get, but so far that hasn't happened, so I'm revising my fantasy and going with Plan B. This way I'll get the engagement party, the bridal shower, and the wedding before I die alone."

Justin looks at me in utter disbelief for a second, and then breaks into laughter, and then looks at me again and realizes I'm dead serious.

"It's like an acting job," I continue, "and I'll pay you well."

"Let me get this straight . . . we're going to fake a romance . . ."

"A whirlwind one," I break in, "since we only have one year."

"Okay, a whirlwind romance, an engagement, all the wedding planning, engagement parties, showers, etc., and then a wedding . . . but then what happens?"

"You'll leave me at the altar. I'll act devastated but put on a strong face, and everyone will feel so sorry for me and stay for the reception of my dreams to cheer up my broken heart, and let me keep the gifts."

"Are you on any medication?"

"Medication? Me? No."

"Molly, I just don't get it. I'm looking at you, and although you're not my type, I can see that you are beautiful, you seem nice and smart, you have a good career, and it doesn't sound like you have any huge family problems . . . stable and not abusive or anything. Are you sure this is what you want to do? Thirty isn't old . . . wait for the fairy tale to come true."

"I've tried—I've been waiting my whole life and I'm tired of waiting. I want an engagement, I want to register, and cake taste, and try on dresses, and have hair and makeup run-throughs. What if Mr. Right isn't out there for me? Why should I have to miss the whole experience?"

"But what if he is? Won't the experience be better shared with someone you love?"

"I'm not willing to take the risk. I'm tired of waiting. I want a French whisk."

"Maybe you *are* a little crazy. What is a French whisk?"

"You know, it's one of those fancy little whisks they sell at Williams-Sonoma that nobody buys for themselves because it's ridiculously expensive for a glorified fork, but everyone registers for it and then swears by it. Anyway, it's not the whisk itself that I'm talking about, although we will register for one—it's a metaphor for the whole picture."

"Do you cook?" he asks me, completely missing the point.

"No, I don't cook at all."

"Then why do you need the whisk?"

"'Cause it's just one of those things that you get . . . that you *need* to get and never use, like espresso machines and ice cream makers."

"So buy yourself the whisk," he offers as what should be a logical solution.

"You're not getting this. I want to be a bride. Everyone else in the world gets the experience of a wedding. Why shouldn't I, just because I don't happen to have a soul mate?"

"I'll never have the experience, either," Justin counters, but I'm starting to sense a breaking point in his voice, so I work this angle.

"Then this would be an opportunity for you to!"

"No offense, but you aren't exactly what I picture standing next to me in my fantasy."

"But Justin . . . we're in the same boat. People like us, gay people and people without soul mates, are both expected by society to go without all the experiences of a wedding."

At first he laughs kindly at me, but then I can see him think a little more and I can tell by his slow nodding that he is coming around, "Yeah, I guess in a way we are."

"You'll get to register for stuff, too!" I throw in as an additional sales point. "Haven't you always wanted Egyptian cotton towels?"

"Yeah, I guess I have. What gay man hasn't?"

"This is our chance," I tell him with the fervor of a TV preacher.

"Okay, Molly." Justin takes a long pause with a deep breath, and I fear he is going to run out of the coffee shop or scream to get a straightjacket because I need committing, but he finally says, "I must be crazy, because I'll do it. Let's have this experience that society is denying us!"

He extends a hand over the little table and my smile doubles as we shake on it. I can't believe step one is secured! Here we go.

6

World's Worst Sister

Before I can throw myself into the details of my plan, I have to deal with my sister and make amends for my behavior. I know it's pathetic that it's taken me a week to work up the courage to apologize for ruining her wonderful surprise, but I said I hit rock bottom . . . obviously people at rock bottom are pathetic.

Jamie and I both live for chocolate chip cookies, so I know that showing up at her apartment with a dozen from her favorite bakery all the way across town will win her over. I stand at her door with my best mea culpa face and the pink box she immediately recognizes.

"Jamie, I'm sorry. I am 'World's Worst Sister.'"

"No, you're not. I should have been more sensitive . . . it probably wasn't the night to spring it on you. I'm sorry."

We hug and we cry, just a little . . . it's genetic. Finally I pull back, wipe a final tear from my eye and smile at her. I follow her inside the beautiful brownstone she and Bryan have to their cozy family room where I can see she has been sitting, knitting a blanket for her unborn baby.

"Oh my God . . . you're having a baby!" I exclaim.

I put my hand on my sister's normally washboard stomach and realize that there is a little bump. She REALLY is pregnant!

"Nice bump, huh? We call the baby 'Bumper,' but we'll probably find out next month if it's a boy or a girl."

"Really? Wow! Oh my God. When are you due?"

"December 25—Christmas!"

"A winter baby! It's going to be so wonderful. I didn't even realize you were trying!"

"Well, it actually happened really fast. We decided that I would go off the pill for a few months and then we would really start trying . . . but we must be really good at it, 'cause we got pregnant right away!" Jamie says as she laughs at her own, somewhat tasteless, joke.

She's always had kind of a raunchy sense of humor, which is even funnier coming from someone so petite and feminine. Jamie and I are very similar-looking sisters. We are both on the shorter side, with medium brown hair and blue eyes, from our dad's side of the family. I wear my hair in a neat, shoulder-length bob, but Jamie lets hers grow down her back and often gets golden blond highlights through it. As I watch her giddy-with-pregnancy excitement, I realize her blue eyes are twinkling just a little more than usual.

"What names are you thinking about?" I jump right in with the tough questions.

"Well, I really love Jane for a girl."

"I LOVE Jane, too!"

"And maybe Harry for a boy . . . like Harrigan, so he will have my name."

"James . . . that is so cool."

"Yeah, I just have to get Bryan to like it. He thinks Harrigan Hope sounds like a soap-opera character. And the problem with Jane is if we call her Janie. Jamie's daughter Janie seems a little too confusing."

Jamie and I both love names . . . as little girls we would sit around thinking of more original names for our Barbies than "Barbie" and always came up with very bizarre choices like Naomi and Yolanda . . . I'm so glad her taste has improved.

"But, you'll be Mommy, so it won't be as confusing." I remind her.

Jamie squeals, "That's true! I'm going to be Mommy! I didn't even think about that . . . she wouldn't call me Jamie. Maybe I should think of something cooler than Mommy . . . or spell it with an 'ie'?"

Oh yeah, we also loved spelling regular names with irregular spellings. For example: I remember one doll we fought viciously over named Stefany. Don't ask me why.

Jamie and I spend a good part of the afternoon talking about her pregnancy. It really is such an exciting thing. And I'm still jealous, but not *as* jealous . . . especially after she throws up the cookies. By the time I leave, I am excited to be World's Greatest Aunt . . . but I remind myself that I cannot get too caught up in that because I have a lot of planning of my own to attend to.

7

The Whirlwind Romance Begins

Justin and I agreed that we would meet again in a week to devise the game plan for our "relationship." It'll be important to bring him to strategically placed events with the proper mixture of family and friends so that the fast engagement seems legitimate and doesn't come as a complete shock to anyone. Thankfully, there are a few such events coming up.

A week later I am at the same Starbucks with Justin to finalize the details. Stuff like how affectionate I want him to be, what is the story about how we met, what he does, etc. Also how and when he will be paid. We decide that sticking as close to the truth as possible will make it harder to mess up the lie. So, his name is still Justin Blake. He's still thirty-three and working as a waiter until his acting career takes off. We had a good laugh about what would happen if we said he was a neurosurgeon and then someone went for dinner at the restaurant where he works.

Obviously we decided to skip the whole escort and me answering a *Village Voice* ad thing and say that we met at the Starbucks where we had our first "date." It's actually a romantic little story. It's basically how it happened in real life sans the business side of our meeting. We also agree that he will not escort anyone else during the year because if someone saw him out with another woman (or man) it would be bad . . . but he can continue his own dating life as long as he keeps it discreet. I will pay him, in cash, for each event that he attends as my date/boyfriend/fiancé. I will get a slight discount on his usual evening rates since I will be such a good customer, but I also have to give him a sizable "down payment" to make sure that he will not escort any of his other clients for the year.

He asks about what would happen if I really did meet "the one" during this year, but I assure him that it hasn't happened in the previous thirty years, so there is no way it will happen in the next 365 days. We even set an engagement date (eight weeks after our first "date") and our wedding date, June 30, as kind of an inside joke since the whole scheme is kind of my thirtieth birthday present to myself.

The first order of business is making our "love" known to the world. Brad and Claire's engagement party is the obvious place to begin. But before I can just show up with him, I need to plant seeds to those around me that he is in my life.

First, I decide, will be my brother, Logan, who is "finding himself" in Italy. It feels easier to lie on a long distance call, so it seems like the ideal warm-up. Logan is the youngest Harrigan—and the much-anticipated son who will carry on the family name. Really, our dad isn't as ridiculous as that sounds, but I think he always had dreams of raising a son, and when his first two children were girls he began to fear it would never happen. But the third time's a charm and he finally got his boy.

I think Logan has always been a bit of an enigma to Dad, though. I still remember Logan's nursery—a major league sports theme. There was even a brand-new mitt in his crib waiting for him, but Logan was never too into sports. He's brilliant and creative and sensitive—and not at all the jock that Dad had been waiting for. Luckily, Jamie turned out to be a little bit of a tomboy, so Dad still had someone to use the mitt. Logan graduated from Yale (I told you he was brilliant) with a degree in art history, and went to Italy to travel and explore.

I wander into the park and find a shady bench to dial Logan from my cell phone. Of course, no answer . . . he's impossible to get hold of. I take the wimp route and leave a message.

"Logan, it's Molly. How are you? I miss you. I have exciting news! I met someone. His name is Justin—he's great. Come home so you can meet him. I love you."

Hooray! The first lie is always the hardest and now it's behind me. The catch about starting with Logan, though, is that I have to tell the rest of my family immediately so that they hear it from me, because he's an enormous gossip. Nobody is perfect, right?

I decide to walk home and make the rest of the calls from the comfort of my own couch. When I walk in the door, the light on my answering machine is blinking "2." Shoot . . . I must have walked too slowly.

"Time of call: 3:06 P.M."

"Jeez!" I called Logan at, like, three o'clock. I realize he must have been screening his calls, listened to my message, and immediately got on the horn.

"Good Golly Miss Molly!" My mother's voice screeches her annoying pet name for me through the machine. "Why am I always the last to know? Logan told me you met someone. Call me. Share with your mother." CLICK.

"Time of call: 3:10 P.M."

"Molly, it's Jamie . . . I just talked to Logan. What's the dillio? I *just* saw you! Call me." CLICK.

Okay, here we go . . . the plan is now in action . . . let's go full force. I take a deep breath, pick up the phone, and dial my sister. I'm saving my mother for last because I have NEVER been able to lie to my mother. She sees right through me like a plate-glass window, and I inevitably crack under the pressure. I figure warming up on Jamie might ease me into my mom. Jamie answers immediately.

"Hello?"

"It's me."

"What's going on? Logan called and told me that you met someone! Why did you tell him first?!?"

Now is probably a good time to explain that Jamie has a slight middle-child complex when it comes to family stuff. In real life she's extremely confident and centered, but when it comes to the Harrigans, she's a complete Jan Brady.

"Jamie, I'm sorry. I hadn't talked to Logan in a while and I just happened to be calling him." GOD, I hate lying!

"Well, tell me more than you told him to make up for it. He said all you said is you met someone named Justin."

"Okay, he's right . . . I did. Justin is thirty-three. He's an actor—well, he's a waiter who wants to be an actor. He's wonderful . . . at least he seems wonderful. It's only been a couple weeks."

"A couple weeks?!? Why didn't you tell me sooner?"

"Sooner? It's only been two weeks! I didn't want to jinx it."

"Fine. Tell me more. Where did you meet him?"

I launch into the planned story, "We met at Starbucks, actually. I was there, he came in, he asked to share a table, and we started talking." Shoot, it seemed a little rushed. I hold my breath.

"That sounds awesome!" Phew . . . she must be buying it! "I'm so excited for you. When can I meet him? I'm free tonight." Slow down! I'm definitely not up for that.

"Jamie, relax . . . you'll meet him at Brad and Claire's (gag) engagement party (double gag)."

Justin and I decided that we would make that our grand

entrance because it would give us some more time to "get to know each other," and I thought it would piss Claire off. After a brief description of her, Justin thought that pissing Claire off sounded like a lot of fun.

"Okay, (beep) I'll wait (beep)."

"That's my Call Waiting . . . I'll call you tomorrow."

"Okay, maybe it's him!"

I click over . . . I was definitely ready to get off that call. Thank goodness for Call Waiting.

"Hello?"

"Molly! I called you. Why didn't you call me back?"

"Mom, hi, I just got home." (Mental Side Note: I should look into that Call-Waiting Caller-ID thing.)

"Logan said you met someone. Who is he? Does he have a good job?"

"Yes, Mom, he's an actor . . . actually, a waiter to pay the bills. His name is Justin Blake. He's thirty-three. You will like him—he has excellent manners."

"An acting waiter?!? You call that a good job? Forget it, Molly, he's not the one," my mother says, her tone immediately shifting from hope and elation to that of a person who has been severely let down.

My mother has a dream for us to marry doctors, lawyers, CEOs, or independently wealthy people. She's an equal-opportunity pain in the ass . . . it's not just her daughters she tries to impose these limits on; she's always trying to fix Logan up with women doctors she goes to or women lawyers she meets in elevators. Don't ask . . . my mom is a character. She was skeptical about Jamie's husband, Bryan, being a computer consultant, but when she saw the ring he bought Jamie she lightened up. (Oh, shoot . . . another Mental Side Note: I'm gonna need a ring.)

"Mom, he's a really good actor. And he's a kind soul." Those two words, *kind soul*, always win over my mother. The truth is that she herself is a kind soul and has a soft spot for all other kind souls. And he could be a really good actor . . . I have no idea.

"Oh my God, Molly, maybe you're falling in love," she exclaims as the optimism her voice held before she learned of Justin's profession returns.

"Yeah, maybe I am." I smile at the idea. It would be wonderful to fall in love, and maybe I am starting to, a little . . . obviously not with gay Justin—I'm not self-destructive like that—but with the idea of the romance of getting engaged and planning a wedding and having someone by my side for the next year.

"Mom, I've gotta run . . . I've got cookies burning in the oven." My God . . . it's true what they say—once you tell one lie, you open floodgates.

"I thought you said you just got home?"

Shoot . . . this is why it's bad to lie.

"I did . . . I did just get home. I put some break-and-bakes in the oven—I was really craving chocolate chip cookies— and then I dialed you." I really need to watch myself!

"Craving cookies? Are you pregnant? Jamie said you brought cookies to her house, too!"

"What?!? Mom! NO!! I haven't even slept with him." And yuck that I just told that to my mother. "I'm hanging up now. I love you, good-bye." CLICK.

I bang my head on the wall a few times and dial one final number for the day. Of course, that person doesn't answer.

"Logan, you are lucky I love you because you have a big fucking mouth." CLICK.

I flop down on the couch and Tiffany makes herself comfortable next to me. I'm going to need to get in shape for all this! It's exhausting.

Many hours later, I'm in my comfy sweats (not to be confused with my cute sweats that I could actually leave the house in, thanks to JLo) with take-out chopsticks in my hand. I jump a foot when my buzzer buzzes.

"Who is it?" I frantically screech through the intercom while chow mein hangs out of my mouth.

"Molly, it's me. Buzz me up."

I am totally confused as to why Brad is at my house, but I buzz him up. Literally seconds later—he must have run up the stairs—Brad is at my door, slightly out of breath.

"Brad! What's going on? Is everything okay?"

"Jamie called me . . ."

"Oh my God! Is everything okay? With the baby??" I interrupt.

"What? Yes. She's fine. She said you met someone."

Hang on, back up. What is wrong with these people? Don't they have lives of their own?!?

Brad is standing in my doorway, staring at me expectantly. I have no idea what he is doing there.

"Yes, I met someone. What's the problem?"

A strange thing happens . . . when I confirm that there is someone in my life, Brad gets this look of deep hurt for just a split second and then quickly replaces it with a look of fake enthusiasm.

"That's fantastic! That's what Jamie said, and I just wanted to get the details from you. I guess I'll go now."

Huh?

"Brad, you (from the looks of it) ran all the way here to 'get the details,' which you didn't actually get, and now you're leaving? Why didn't you just call me?"

He looks confused by my question.

"I dunno . . . I guess I just wanted to see you." He pauses for a second. "Why didn't *you* call *me*?"

Now I realize . . . I've hurt him. He's supposed to be my best friend, and he had to find out from someone else that what I've been complaining to him about not happening for most of our friendship finally happened and I left him out. God, I feel awful.

"I'm so sorry . . . I should have called you. I just thought it would be better to tell you in person."

The truth is that I thought I would be better not to tell him at all because more than my mother and sister combined, Brad is able to see right through me. His bullshit meter is very finely tuned.

"Oh, okay. So, here I am. What are the details?"

We are still standing in the doorway and I still have the container of chow mein in one hand and the chopsticks in the other.

"Come in. Let me grab another pair of chopsticks."

Suddenly he's totally on edge again.

"Actually, I can't. Claire's waiting for me—I told her I was going for a run."

A rush of anger overwhelms me . . . God, I hate Claire. My best friend has to sneak out to visit me?

"Okay, I don't want you to get busted."

Brad smiles a pathetic half-smile.

"When do I get to meet this mystery man?"

"Actually, I was hoping to bring him to your engagement party. What do you think?"

"Definitely. Well, let me just check it with Claire, but I'm sure it won't be a problem."

Let him just "check it with Claire"?!? What is she, his mother?

"Great, let me know."

"I'll call you tomorrow to get the specifics. I've gotta go now."

Brad pecks my forehead and runs off down the hall before I can respond.

As I watch my wonderful, smart, handsome friend run down the hall like a trained poodle, the overwhelming anger and hatred of Claire is replaced by deep sadness. I shut the door and return to my spot next to Tiffany, sad that it feels like the deterioration of my friendship with Brad is beginning. If he isn't allowed to visit me just weeks after their engagement, by the time they are married I'll never get to see him at all. I'm so glad my engagement to Justin won't be anything like that. It might be fake, but at least it will allow me freedom.

Needless to say, Brad does not call me the next day, or the day after that, or the day after that. I talk on the phone to him *once* between the night at my apartment and the night of his engagement party when he calls to tell me that Claire said it would be okay for me to bring Justin, but he couldn't even chat then because she had him so busy with all the party details.

8

Introducing Justin

Their engagement party is actually a huge deal for me and I'm bubbling over with nervous anticipation. Unlike Brad and me, Justin and I have seen each other very often and talked on the phone at least once a day. We have our story straighter than an arrow.

Like we agreed in the beginning, we stick to as much truth as possible, and only shift things slightly to make our relationship a romance, not a business deal. Each time we had a "meeting," we chose a different romantic restaurant so that if questioned about where we have gone on dates, we had good answers, experiences, and food comments on hand. The truth is, I'm having the best time!

Justin is a fantastic person. He is smart and funny and has led a really interesting life . . . and having a gay man as a boyfriend is really ideal in every way except that you never get sex. He isn't at all distraught by the hours of shopping and was instrumental in helping me pick out the perfect dress for the party, plus he totally understands why I need to look better than Claire. It's like we are back in junior high school, creating our very own secret club . . . we have deep, touching conversations and are so silly that I laugh until I cry talking about everything from Justin's "coming out" to the awfulness of Claire Reilly to the wedding (of course). And again, his flawless taste is going to be extremely helpful in planning the wedding. This fake relationship is better than any real one I've ever had!

The night of Brad and Claire's engagement party, Justin and I are dressed to the nines and ready to make our grand entrance. Most of the important people in my life will be there (except big-mouth Logan): Jamie and Bryan, my parents, Alex and Steve, Lauren and Rob, and, of course, Brad. Justin looks amazing in his black suit, and the black strapless dress he insisted was the one to steal Claire's spotlight really does look like it will be able to do the trick. Don't get me wrong—we are both nervous (Justin calls it stage fright) but we're also excited.

The party is at a restaurant supposedly owned by a friend of Claire's family. Justin and I arrive just fashionably late and the party is beginning to get going. I take secret joy in how angry Claire must be that half an hour after the time on the invitation the room is only half full. Justin and I clasp our hands and enter the room, where we are almost washed over by the wave of my family and friends ready to pounce on him. Jamie reaches him first . . . either she's fast for a pregnant lady or the others felt uncomfortable shoving a woman with child out of the way.

Justin looks at me and smiles his dazzling smile; under his breath he says, "Here we go." Before I realize what hit me, I'm standing behind a mob of people crowded around poor Justin . . . I can just see the top of his head. I figure I'm not needed and make my way to the bar in hopes of being able to say hello to Brad.

From the bar I have a good view of the party. About 95% of the guests are Claire's family friends. The few guests Brad was allowed to invite are our good friends from college, and my family. Brad really is an honorary Harrigan.

Since his family is across the country and he's not that close to them (they didn't even come "all the way to New York for one weekend" for the party). Beginning back in college, he would always come home with me for holidays and long weekends, and to this day, he still shows up for these events. My mother thinks he is adorable, my father loves talking sports with him, and both Logan and Jamie treat him like a brother. I think in some ways, it means more to him to have them here than his own parents. Besides the hive of people I know who are buzzing around my poor hired beau, almost everyone else at the party is a stranger to me.

Claire looks stunning, but there is something icy about her bleached-teeth smile. Maybe I am starting to imagine her evilness being more obvious than it is, but I swear, it shows through. Far across the room, I finally see Brad, trapped in conversation with two older men in three-piece suits. He has his polite smile on and I watch him fake-laugh four times before I can catch his eye. I raise my glass of champagne to him, and he excuses himself from the group and makes his way over to me. Maybe I am imagining this the way I am imagining Claire's visible horns, but there seems to be a sadness to Brad tonight that I've never seen before. When he reaches me he smiles his normal, twinkling smile and hugs me.

"So, where's Mr. Wonderful?"

"See that group of women huddled over there?" I point in the direction of the mosh pit assembled around Justin. "He's somewhere in there."

Brad laughs . . . he knows my family well enough not to be surprised by their behavior, only amused.

"Well," he says, "I'm the guest of honor here tonight and I want to meet him . . . so let's break up the ladies."

He extends his arm to me and I take it (keeping my glass of champagne in the other), and we make our way over to rescue Justin.

Brad is good with my family and good with rowdy crowds (the spectators at the extreme-sporting conventions he usually covers for *Extreme Outdoor* magazine have prepared him for anything), so he thinks nothing of arming his way to the middle of the circle and extending a hand toward Justin.

"Great to finally meet you."

Justin is amazing; he doesn't miss a beat. "Brad Lawson. Molly swears I shouldn't be jealous, but she sure speaks highly of you."

Brad beams at Justin and then at me for a moment. It's not hard to win him over . . . he's truly such a softie.

"Let's go get you a drink. I want to hear all about you . . . and in return, I'll tell you all about Molly's college days."

"Sounds like a plan. Ladies, I will be back."

The girls moan like teenagers at a rock concert, but hardly give the boys a chance to cross the room before they turn their attention on me. Oh jeez! I liked it better when Justin was in the firing line!

My mother jumps in first. "Molly, he's wonderful!"

Jamie seconds her emotion. "He really is, Molls. I'm thrilled for you!" And she actually squeals.

And then, before I can believe it, all my friends are saying how great he is. They actually all love him! I am beyond thrilled. Step one of the plan is going off without a hitch!!

I relay the story of how we met and all the wonderful dates we've had so far. It's so much fun . . . and I even catch Claire throwing an extremely annoyed look at our somewhat noisy corner of the room, which only adds to my joy. After sharing every single detail (and even making up some new ones—I decided our song should be, "Just the Way You Look Tonight"), I excuse myself from the crowd to go find Justin and congratulate him on an exquisite performance.

I spot him at the bar, still with Brad, and make my way over. I walk up and slide my arm around Justin's waist. It feels slightly strange to do this, because in a lot of ways he's still a stranger, but I know it's little details like this that will prevent any doubt from forming in anyone's head. I notice Brad look at my arm around Justin's waist for a second before greeting me.

"Hey there, we were just getting to know each other a bit. Don't tell me you were having separation anxiety?"

I laugh at his joke, albeit a strange joke. "Nope . . . just wanted to be certain you weren't divulging too many secrets."

"Don't worry," Justin assures me, "Brad has only had the nicest things to say about you."

I beam at Justin for a moment, thrilled at how well this is going, and he beams back . . . we're actually having fun. It's like performance-theater for him, and it's like a dream come true (again, minus the sex) for me.

"Justin, could you get my champagne refilled while I find out what Brad really thinks of you?" I say with a wink.

We all have a good chuckle and Justin turns toward the bar while Brad and I head onto the dance floor. Brad and I dance in silence for a few minutes; Brad is a fantastic dancer . . . his mother forced him to attend cotillion as a kid and it really paid off. Finally I can't stand it anymore.

"So? He's awesome, right?"

"Shhh . . . I love this song."

I'm a little dumbfounded, but okay. I listen to the music and—wouldn't you know it?—it's "Just the Way You Look Tonight." Crap. I look over at Justin and he's talking to my mother and sister again. Shoot . . . please let nobody notice that this is the song I proclaimed to be "ours." When the song finally ends and some other danceable tune begins to play, Brad finally starts talking.

"I think he seems fake, Molly."

My heart skips a beat, "You do? Everyone else loves him."

"I dunno. Something doesn't feel right about him. There is something I can't put my finger on."

The sincerity and concern in his voice causes a moment of extreme guilt on my part that I am telling this lie, but it is quickly replaced with a feeling of panic because Brad really likes everybody. I mean, obviously he's not super picky about personalities if he's marrying Claire.

"Maybe you're just being overprotective because you've seen me get hurt before," I say, trying to convince him.

"It could be. Just be careful. Really keep your eyes open and watch your back."

"I will, I promise," I say as I settle back in the comfortable rhythm of Brad's lead.

We dance the rest of the song and my mind is racing about what Justin could have said to tip Brad off. I'm thinking so hard I don't notice Claire come up and physically pull Brad's arm off my waist. When I look up and see her, she looks pissed and Brad looks like a deer caught in headlights.

"We were just dancing," he explains lamely . . . which, if you ask me, is clear to anyone with eyes.

"Do you have any idea how it looks for you to be dancing with *her* at our engagement party?" She motions at me.

"Like he has friends?" I pipe in, trying to be helpful.

Claire gives me one of her death glares and I shrug and walk away as she scolds Brad. I have bigger things to worry about at this point. As I'm walking off the dance floor, I hear Claire reprimanding Brad. He's such a weenie when it comes to her . . . he doesn't even try to defend himself. It's no surprise that he can't put his finger on something wrong with Justin . . . he can't seem to see Claire's faults at all!

I walk up to where Justin is chatting with my mother and sister.

"Hey, sweetie," he says as he hands me my champagne and kisses my head. Damn . . . the guy is good. My mom and Jamie look at each other like they are about to melt.

"That Claire is a pistol, huh?" he asks, looking out onto the dance floor where Brad and Claire are now dancing. She's leading and still telling him off.

"She's the devil," I whisper in his ear. Since her family is hosting the party, I can't be too open about my feelings.

He nods in understanding and Jamie nods, too.

"It's sad that all of us have found such wonderful people and he is with her."

We all nod sadly and I feel a rush of warmth. I snuggle a little closer to Justin; I'm someone who has found a wonderful person—at last!

"Come on, Molly, let's dance." Justin takes my hand and leads me out to the dance floor. I look back at my mother and sister, and I swear my mother wipes a tear from her eye!

"You are an amazing actor!" I whisper in his ear.

Justin laughs a little and smiles warmly at me. "It's not really acting—I do think you're great . . . I'm just embell-ishing."

We dance quietly for a few minutes and let me tell you, Justin makes Brad seem like he has two left feet. Forget attending cotillion—Justin must have been professionally trained.

"You're an amazing dancer, too."

"Just another perk of having a gay boyfriend."

We both chuckle, just a little.

"Oh, I forgot to tell you. 'Just the Way You Look Tonight' is our song, 'kay?"

"When did we decide that? Your mom asked me why I was letting Brad steal you away for our song and I was so confused . . . I thought I remembered all the details we decided on."

"We didn't," I admit. "I just got a little carried away and told everyone."

"That's okay," he laughs, "I did that, too. I told your sister I'm into yoga, which I am, but then I added that I've been giving you lessons and now she wants to join us. So, I'll have to show you some yoga moves this week."

"Okay," I agree. "I've always wanted to try yoga anyway."

For the rest of the evening, Justin waits on me hand and foot. That is, when he's not dancing with my mother (since my father refuses) or my sister (since she complains too much about Bryan's dancing so he won't go near her on a dance floor). I dance with Bryan (he's no Justin . . . he's not even a Brad, but we have fun), hang out at the bar in the restaurant's front area with my dad where he has managed to, as always, find a television playing sports, and get to wave at Brad from across the room twice. The dinner is good, and the wine is a bit too free-flowing.

By the end of the evening, I'm quite tipsy. I kiss my family and friends good-bye, Justin kisses all the girls (on the cheek, of course), and shakes hands with all the men. It is clear that he has won everyone over . . . even my dad! I go to say good-bye to Brad while Justin makes plans to get together with everyone over the next couple weeks. I finally find Brad, totally hammered, at the bar.

"Hey, we're leaving."

"NO! Don't go. Don't leave me."

"You're smashed, my friend. When can you get outta here?"

"I dunno." His chin drops down to his chest. "I hate this shit."

"What?"

"These fake events, all these fake people."

I feel my cheeks flush as he emphasizes "fake." Little does he know, I am quickly becoming the queen of it.

"You'd better get used to it—it's preparation for the wedding."

He looks up, into my eyes, "I love you, Molly."

"I love you, too, Bradley. Drink lots of water tonight, okay? I'll call you tomorrow."

"No, Molly . . . wait."

I giggle for a second at his drunken slurring. "It was a lovely engagement party," I lie through my teeth.

For a second I think Brad looks crestfallen . . . I swear, that woman is squashing his spirit. I kiss him on the head and head toward the door.

"Molly!" he calls after me and I turn around, "Just be careful."

"Don't worry, silly."

I turn back and Justin is waiting for me at the door, waving at Brad. Brad gives him a kind of drunken wave/send-off and Justin and I leave the party, holding hands.

In the cab on the way home, Justin can't stop talking about how great everyone is. And he has made plans for us to go out with just about everyone in the coming weeks! He bonded with my mom over dancing, Jamie over teaching prenatal yoga, and even Bryan over eating paste in third grade! I can't help but beam at him.

I've never had a straight boyfriend that my family loved so much!

We laugh and recount all the funny anecdotes of the evening all the way back to my apartment. When the cab pulls to the curb, Justin asks the driver to wait a minute and I get the cold reminder that he isn't a real boyfriend and that I have to go upstairs alone. He walks me to the door and gives me a warm but purely friendly hug. Then he stands back and looks at me with a slightly uncomfortable face. It takes a second for me to realize what it is . . . duh . . . he wants to get paid. I open my purse and hand him the money.

"Thanks," I say, "you were perfect."

"I think we're in great shape, Molly. After all the plans we have made to see your family and friends, I don't think anyone will object to our quick engagement."

I smile at him and agree, then give a little wave as I make my way through the door and he heads back to the cab.

Upstairs, alone in my apartment . . . well, alone except for my loyal Tiffany, I start to feel really sad, but I'm really surprised at what I am sad about. Not being reduced to hiring a fake fiancé, not lying to my beloved friends and family, but sad that I am losing Brad. Seeing him miserable and wasted at his own engagement party had more of an effect than I realized while I was in the cloud of excitement over Justin's success.

Brad and I have shared everything for over a decade, and now I see that I won't have him. I mean, I assume Claire will allow us to remain friends . . . at least acquaintances . . . I hope, but there won't be any more middle-of-the-night calls, or watching *Survivor* over the phone, or going out for pancakes for dinner. This isn't right! It's an injustice!! I bawl myself to sleep and vow to try to rescue Brad in the morning.

9

Rescuing Brad, Part One

When I wake up I have a plan. Don't worry! It's not another crazy scheme . . . I won't be hiring anyone I saw advertised in the paper. I am going to be mature and adult . . . and convince Brad to see the truth about Claire and call off the wedding. I call his apartment and immediately a glitch is thrown into my strategy when Claire answers his phone.

"Jeez, Molly. It's the morning after our first engagement party. Can't you give us some privacy?" CLICK.

"What the fuck?!?" I ask Tiffany.

Did that seriously happen? Number one: they aren't married yet . . . should she be answering his phone? Number two: their *first* engagement party? How many do you get? Seriously . . . how many? (Mental Side Note: I must look into how many engagement parties a couple gets . . . I'm not completely objecting to more than one.) And number three: who is rude enough to hang up like that on someone? Answer to number three is: Claire. Number two I'll have to do some research about. Number one baffles me. So, I call Justin.

"Good morning, Girlfriend," he greets me . . . calling each other Boyfriend and Girlfriend is kind of an inside joke that also happens to increase the validity of our romance, since people in love tend to invent stupid pet names and call each other stuff like that.

"Hey there, Boyfriend. What are you up to today?"

"I was going to call and see if you wanted to meet for a low-fat muffin at 'our place.'"

We also started calling Starbucks "our place," which follows the same strategy I explained above.

"I can be there in twenty minutes looking crappy or one hour looking fabulous. Which will it be?"

"I'll see you in twenty." CLICK.

See, I'm not totally sensitive to people hanging up on me. "'Bye" isn't always necessary—this hang-up didn't bother me one bit.

I throw on sweats and head over to Starbucks. When I walk in, Justin is waiting at "our table" with my nonfat latte in hand.

"You are the best," I inform him.

We spend a good part of the morning sitting in Starbucks people-watching and outfit-critiquing. It's always been one of my favorite things to do, and it turns out Justin loves to as well.

Then we decide to "exercise." AKA: go for a walk through the park.

"So," I say, "I had a Claire run-in this morning."

I tell him about my decision the night before to try and break them up and my phone call to Brad's apartment and her rude hang-up. I expect Justin to share my shock and disdain and help me think of a way to get to Brad without having to go through Claire, but he railroads me!

"Molly, I think breaking them up is a bad idea."

"What?"

"I think it's too late . . . he's gotta figure it out on his own. He's in too deep."

"But he can't see the evilness!"

"I know . . . don't get me wrong—I completely agree that he shouldn't marry her, but at this point it's too risky that you'll ruin your own friendship."

"But with Claire in the picture the friendship is ruined anyway."

"Yeah, I guess that's true. You're kind of stuck between a rock and a hard place."

"Figures. What do you think I should do?"

He really isn't any help at all. We hmmm and haaa over the situation until Justin needs to go home and get ready for work.

"I'm working late tonight, so I'll just call you tomorrow."

"Okay, have a good night at work," I say as I hand him a smaller payment. Big events like the engagement party last night cost more than quick coffee runs. He silently takes the money and nods a thank-you . . . it's more comfortable than making a big deal out of it, even though it always feels a little weird. I have to fight this urge to look over each shoulder before handing him money, as though I am doing something illegal.

We part ways and I wander around the park a while longer, thinking about how to handle the Brad situation. Justin's comment that Brad is "in too deep" keeps replaying in my head. Does that mean I should help him get out or it's too late?!? I keep going back and forth. Believe it or not, dusk starts to fall and I am still not sure.

I start to head home and realize how starving I am. A low-fat cranberry peach muffin can only hold a girl so long. I stop for a slice of pizza at a favorite place that just happens to be on my way home . . . if I walk three blocks out of my way. It's worth the extra six blocks (round trip), I confirm, as I make my way home with the pizza grease disintegrating the paper bag I am clutching as if it were my firstborn.

When I get home, I am excited to see the light blinking on my answering machine. Why is it that a message is so exciting? I'm really hoping it's Brad, but I'm not totally disappointed that it's my mom . . . mostly because of what the message says.

"Good Golly Miss Molly! It's your mother. I have wonderful news. Your brother is coming home . . . at last. Logan just called to tell us that he's ready to come back to Connecticut and he's booked a flight for next week."

"HOORAY!" I screech at Tiffany who looks up, confused and annoyed at the disturbance in her busy napping schedule. I am so excited to have my baby brother back on this continent that I am dancing around my apartment. So much commotion gets the cat going and she realizes her starvation and starts howling for some kibble. I abide while I pick up the phone to share my excitement with—.

In the past I would have called Brad. He knows how close I am to my family and how much I love Logan and he would have understood and been happy. But after my exchange with Claire this morning, I feel uncomfortable calling my best friend. Damn that bitch! She is taking the joy out of everything in my life. I could call my sister, but I want to share the news as in tell it, not share it with someone who already knows, and if she doesn't know yet, that'll be a whole other conversation that I don't feel like having. Neither Alex nor Lauren would really care that much. They don't know Logan and they aren't super close to their families . . . in fact, Alex is an only child. I guess Justin is a good option, but he's at work. Darn!! I decide to bite the bullet and call Brad. He's a free man . . . he can decide who he wants to talk to. I dial his cell phone (okay, I'm still sort of a chicken) and it goes to voice mail. Would you like to take a guess whose voice is on his greeting?

Brad's voice mail used to say, "I'm not taking your call because I'm in the bathroom taking care of my scorching case of genital herpes. Leave a message; if you're lucky, I'll give it to you."

I know, it's vulgar, it's gross, it's immature . . . but it's funny. You can't help but see the humor . . . and it's not like he ever really had herpes. Well, apparently someone didn't think it was so humorous, though. Claire's voice now leaves a greeting so cold it's really not a greeting at all.

"You have reached the cell phone of Bradley Lawson. Press one to leave a message after the beep or two to leave a page." BEEP.

Not even a hello?

"Brad," I whisper to his voice mail . . . like if I'm quiet she won't hear me, "call Molly." CLICK.

I look around the empty apartment and spy my cat sitting on the kitchen counter, cleaning her foot. Super sanitary, I know.

"Tiffany!" She looks up, annoyed at the distraction. "Your Uncle Logan is coming home!"

10

Rescuing Brad, Part Two

The next morning I sleep late . . . although I don't realize it's late. I awake to the phone ringing and am really annoyed that someone would be so rude as to call so early. I make my way out of bed and find the phone.

"Hello?" I answer in a grumpy and groggy voice.

"Good Golly Miss Molly!" my mother cheers through the phone. She is, and always has been, a morning person . . . a perfect trait for a schoolteacher. I am a morning person, too, usually, but as summer vacation drags on, so does my sleep.

"What time is it?"

"It's 10:30 . . . I didn't wake you up, did I?"

"No," I lie. Now that I realize how late it is, I'm completely ashamed that I am such a lazy bum.

"Good, I didn't think I would. Listen, Molly, your brother will be home on Thursday morning, so that evening we are having a welcome-home dinner for him and we would like you to bring Justin."

"Really? Wow . . . that's wonderful. Thank you. I'm sure he would love to. Let me just check to make sure he doesn't have to work."

WOW! My family must have really adored Justin to be including him in family dinners. Things are going so well!

"Okay, let me know as soon as you can."

"I will, Mom. Love you."

"I love you, too, Molly." CLICK.

The way my mother says she loves me causes a momentary surge of guilt for the enormous lie I am concocting. Only for a moment, though . . .

"Eyes on the prize," I tell myself. "White dress, tall cake, bone china."

Okay, I'm good. I pick up the phone to call Justin.

"Hello?" he groggily answers the phone.

"You kick ass!" I tell him, ignoring the fact that I have definitely woken him up.

"What did I do?"

"You got yourself invited to a Harrigan family dinner! Few non-Harrigans have gone where you will be going. Please tell me you don't have to work Thursday night."

"Even if I'm on the schedule, I'll get someone to cover my shift. This is awesome!" he says, trying to fake enthusiasm through his sleepiness.

"And you wanna know the best part?"

"That isn't the best part?"

"Nope. It's Logan. You are finally going to get to meet Logan!"

"Ah, the infamous Baby Harrigan."

"I can't wait for you to meet him."

"Me neither!"

"So, I'll see you for dinner tonight with Lauren and Rob, right?"

We have yet another dinner with my friends scheduled by Justin during Brad and Claire's engagement party. I swear, he is a social butterfly.

"Definitely. Want me to pick you up?" I offer.

"Puh-leeze, Girlfriend. I will pick *you* up at eight . . . and don't be late."

"See you then." CLICK.

I bask in the glory of the success of my plan thus far while enjoying a snapping, crackling, popping bowl of knockoff Rice Krispies before remembering my true problem at hand. Operation: Save Brad.

I check my answering machine just to make sure I didn't somehow sleep through his callback. No blinking light— darn. Then I check my cell phone voice mail . . . just to cover my bases. Needless to say, he hasn't called me back. It's almost 11 A.M. on a Tuesday, and even though Brad is rarely in the office (he's usually out on assignment scouting people doing insanely dangerous, sports-related stunts), I decide to take a chance on catching him. I'm positive Claire won't be around there . . . she doesn't understand places of employment or why people go to them. I have to look the number up since I never dial it, and as I'm waiting for it to go to voice mail, a crazy thing happens—Brad answers.

"Brad?!?" I can't believe it.

"Molly? Are you okay?"

"I've been trying to reach you. Are *you* okay?"

"Yes, of course. What's going on?"

"I really want to get together. When can I see you?"

He pauses for a minute. Looking over his schedule, maybe?

"I think we're free tonight. Claire's friend Andrea had to cancel because of some problem with her Botox injection. Do you want to meet us somewhere halfway?"

Huh? *US?*

"No, Brad, just you and me."

He pauses again, but this one is awkward.

"Actually, Molly, Claire doesn't want me seeing you when she's not around. She says it's inappropriate."

Now my end of the line is the one with the pause. I am utterly speechless. I manage to get out the words, "Are you kidding?"

"I'm sorry," he says lamely.

"Brad. We have been best friends for twelve years. We've never even kissed. Okay, well, we kissed that one time our junior year, but we haven't kissed in ten years."

"I know—it's just her thing. Let's get together, all of us."

"Brad, this is ridiculous. I thought it was just coincidence that she answers your apartment phone and answers your cell phone, but it's all to keep me away from you, isn't it?"

More awkward silence.

"Look, Brad," I say, "I really need to talk to you . . . in person. Is there any way?"

After a pause that is so long I worry the line has disconnected, he asks if I am home right now. I say I am, and he says he will be right over.

Time for some courage . . . it's definitely now or never.

I pace back and forth across my apartment for what feels like about thirty seconds, but according to the clock it has been more like fifteen minutes, and even though I am expecting Brad, I jump a mile when the buzzer buzzes. I push the button to let him up without even talking through the intercom. A few seconds later, he's standing at the door of my apartment, looking as nervous as I feel.

Okay, here we go.

"Okay, Molly. Are you all right? Is it that Justin guy?"

"What? Huh? No. I'm fine. I'm worried about you."

"Me?!? What for?"

Wow, this is going really swell so far. I take a deep breath and realize that my hopes that this could be easy were a dream.

"Brad, I'm worried about you marrying Claire."

He takes a breath, but a calm breath, and I relax a little.

Maybe he just needed someone, a close friend, to tell him it's okay to call this off. He looks at me with eyes so full of sadness I reach out to hug him . . . but he puts his arms up and blocks me.

"Molly, no. Claire was afraid this was going to happen."

Excuse me?!? What's going on?

"That's why she didn't want me to be alone with you," Brad continues. "She had a feeling that you were secretly in love with me and would realize your jealousy as our wedding got closer and try to destroy our happiness," he answers, eyes glazed over, as if he really has been brainwashed to repeat this rhetoric.

I am speechless. I am such a combination of confusion and repulsion and hate (for Claire, of course) that I have lost the ability to form words. Finally something comes to me.

"You are insane! And so is your stupid girlfriend!"

Okay, not exactly the calm, cool, and collected approach I was planning to take. I feel tears welling up in my eyes and sting my cheeks as they fall down my face.

"I am not secretly or otherwise in love with you," I yell at Brad as he looks at me with eyes full of pity. "I am worried that you are marrying a woman who trusts you so little that she has forbidden you from seeing your best friend! She has you wrapped around her finger and you don't even care!"

Brad stiffens slightly. "I like being wrapped around her finger, Molly. This is exactly what she said you would say. She does trust me—she just saw what we've been avoiding all these years."

"And what's that?" I yell.

"How inappropriate our relationship was."

Again . . . words are escaping me.

"What was inappropriate about our relationship?!? We have never been anything but best friends!" I manage to blurt out.

"But Claire pointed out to me that it's unrealistic for a man and woman to be best friends because one of them is always thinking about sex."

"I NEVER thought about sex with you!" This is a *slight* lie . . . that one night in college that we kissed I did think about sex with Brad . . . and about changing our friendship, but it wasn't worth the risk and I completely put the thought out of my head and hadn't thought about it since (even though he was a good kisser).

"Look, Molly, we can still be friends. We just can't be in that place where we were treating each other like boyfriend and girlfriend."

I am shocked and appalled and I can't go on anymore. I realize that my fight is futile . . . I've already lost. The game is over, the fat lady has sung.

"Brad, you're making a huge mistake," I say sadly as I open the door for him to leave.

He steps through the door and looks back at me and for a split second I can see that he is as heartbroken as I am. I watch him walk down the hall and then close the door and sink down to the floor, sobbing.

11

Dinner with Lauren and Rob

The day is totally unproductive because I am too depressed to function. I even cancel the student I was supposed to tutor at 2:30, which is a pretty stupid thing for a person in my financial situation to do. It's like the pain of being broken up with, but SO much worse. I can't even describe what it's like to be dumped by your best friend.

At 7:30 I realize that Justin will be there to pick me up in, like, half an hour. I drag myself off the couch and into the bathroom where I get the first good look at my face. I look like I've been beaten, seriously. My eyes are practically swollen shut, my nose looks like a cherry, and my mouth is all goopy. I need to cancel the plans with Lauren and Rob.

I reach Justin on his cell phone. "I can't do tonight. I need to cancel."

"What? No. You can't. You're the one who said how important it is to stick to the 'courting' schedule."

"Something awful happened today and I look too terrible to go out in public."

"What happened?" I am touched to hear genuine concern in Justin's voice. A thought washes over me that maybe I don't need Brad. Maybe Justin will want to be my new best friend and I will be okay. Then reality comes back to me—I realize I'm not in the third grade and that best friends cannot be replaced like Converse sneakers. It's "make new friends and keep the old; one is silver and the other is gold." No matter what, Justin will be a silver friend and I want my gold friend! I know what you're thinking . . . you thought I said I wasn't in third grade, but you forgot I *teach* third grade.

"Brad dumped me. He said we can't be friends anymore." My bottom lip starts to quiver as I say the words out loud and I finish with a sob.

"Molly, I'll be there in ten minutes. Brew some chamomile tea and put it in the fridge."

I'm slightly comforted that Justin is coming, but a little perturbed that he is demanding food service from me in my condition.

I fiddle around with the tea and before I know it he's there. He got there faster than ten minutes.

As soon as he enters the apartment he gives me a big hug, then says, "I moved Lauren and Rob to nine, so we have some time here. What happened?"

I admit that I did what he recommended I avoid—tell Brad what I thought of Claire—but he is still shocked when I tell him the outcome.

"That's not what I expected," he says, and I whimper in agreement. "Molly, there's nothing you can do. You tried your best. Do you want to know what I would do if I were you?"

"Oh-kay," I sob.

"I would do what he asks. If the only way to be friends with him is to play by her rules, that's what I'd do. It's better to have him with restrictions than not at all, right?"

I nod.

"And sooner or later he's going to see the truth on his own."

"That's true," I agree.

"I know you're sad, sweetie. But let's get you ready to go . . . it's going to be okay."

"Oh, no . . . I really can't go. Look at me!"

"I already did . . . you're a mess, but I can fix you."

Sometimes he is so gay!

"Go get the chamomile tea," he orders.

I go to the kitchen and return with two glasses of iced tea . . . I assume that's what he wanted since he told me to put the tea in the fridge.

"Where are the tea bags?"

"In the kitchen," I answer, confused.

"Go get those. They are for your eyes. I didn't want to have a tea party."

"Oh." I get it now.

I return with the tea bags and Justin makes me lie down on the couch with the bags on my eyes. I must admit, they feel good. As I'm lying there he smears something on my face that smells suspiciously like yogurt. I take what feels like a very short rest with the snack bar on my face before I am ordered into the shower. The hot water has evidently been on for a while and the room is very steamy. As I stand in the tub, my sinuses start to clear and I can breathe again. When I emerge, Justin has an adorable outfit laid out on my bed.

As we are walking out the door I sneak a look in the hall mirror . . . it's hard to believe the transformation. Justin knows what he is doing! We're like a mini version of that show, *Queer Eye for the Straight Guy*, but we would be called, *Gay Boyfriend for the Pathetic Girl*. I silently remind myself that tonight is important and I cannot let my current situation with Brad destroy what Justin and I are working for.

"Eyes on the prize: tiara, cake tasting, bachelorette party," I say to myself. Okay . . . I'm ready.

We stand outside the restaurant and prepare to go in. I

can see through the window that Lauren and Rob are already seated. Lauren and I were pledge sisters our freshman year of college. Until eight months ago, when she and Rob got engaged, we were the ever-complaining singletons . . . together. But then the second she had a ring on her finger, she forgot our bond completely. At first I was hurt—I mean, Lauren and I had suffered through countless bouquet tosses together—but I realized that she wasn't being insensitive . . . she was just so thrilled and excited that she forgot how it felt to be, well, me. Their wedding is now two months away and I'm sure she is bouncing off the walls.

Justin and I look into each other's eyes and clasp hands.

"Ready to be deeply in love, Girlfriend?" he asks.

"Absolutely, Boyfriend. Ready to talk about their wedding all night?" I ask with only the tiniest hint of sarcasm in my voice.

"Be a good sport," he gently reprimands me. "In a few months it'll be you."

This reminder cheers me up enormously and we walk in, beaming (as a newly-in-love couple should), and immediately spot Rob (duh, we'd seen him through the window) waving us over.

"Hey, guys! Sorry we're so late," Justin greets them wholeheartedly.

They promise it's not a problem as we sit down and help ourselves to the already-open bottle of wine on the table.

"So," Lauren looks at me, "can you believe the big day is only fifty-seven days away?!?"

I steal a quick look at Justin before diving warmly into Lauren's happiness.

"No . . . time has just flown by. Tell me what else you have to do."

Lauren and I talk about dress fittings and wired ribbon versus satin ribbon, Jordan almonds, and mothers' corsages versus mini-bouquets. I realize it's in my best interest to really pay attention to all this stuff now! The boys scoff at our "wedding craziness" and then discuss wedding topics that interest them, like wine, music, and food. It is actually a fantastic evening that is only made better by how much Lauren and Rob clearly like Justin. We even have such a good time (and so much wine) that my heartbreak over Brad is out of my head.

As we walk home, Justin and I are excited to start wedding planning after all the information we got from Lauren and Rob.

"So," Justin begins, "Rob was telling me about how he and Lauren got engaged, and I realized that we need a really good engagement story."

This guy is amazing! *This* is why I'm paying him the big bucks.

"You're totally right," I agree.

"And you're gonna need a ring. What do you want to do about that?"

"I haven't completely figured that out yet . . . I thought about it a while back, but I haven't gone ring shopping yet or anything."

The truth is that it is going to take some budgeting on my end. My inheritance includes plenty of money to throw my dream wedding, but Nana had assumed that my engagement ring would be a gift from my fiancé . . . a logical assumption . . . and so the wedding fund doesn't necessarily have enough to cover the rock of my dreams, too. I am hoping that the additional money earned by my father's wise investment strategy could fill this gap. Since I have no knowledge of what wedding rings cost, besides the common saying that it should be three months' salary, some research is probably in order.

"Want to go tomorrow?"

"Absolutely!" I squeal.

Another amazing thing about a rented gay boyfriend: he's

so uncommitment phobic that he actually *wants* to go engagement-ring shopping!

"Also," he adds, "I think I should ask your father for permission. You know, be really traditional about it."

I get warm tingles all over.

"That is brilliant."

"I thought you'd like it," he says proudly, "but don't worry . . . not yet . . . we'll stick to the same time frame."

"Absolutely," I agree, "moving too fast will be suspicious."

We get to my door and Justin gives me a kiss on the head.

"I'll pick you up at 11:00 tomorrow. We'll get brunch and go to Tiffany's."

"Tiffany's," I echo.

I doubt I'll be able to sleep tonight. I've been dreaming about trying on engagement rings at Tiffany's since I realized I had fingers. I even named my cat in its honor!

"I can't wait," I tell him as I quickly shove a wad of cash, including a little extra for the way he saved me earlier in the evening, into his hand and head inside, giddily running up the stairs to my apartment.

12

Lunch Near Tiffany's

The next morning, moments before Justin will be at my apartment, I am in full crisis mode. Tell me, what does one wear to try on engagement rings at Tiffany?!? I am wishing I'd had more notice so I could have had time to get a manicure when the buzzer buzzes. Justin enters my apartment and looks slightly frightened at the sight of my closet emptied onto my bed.

"I have no idea what to wear," I frantically shout at him.

I start holding up different options.

"Do I go conservative and preppy, like Kristin Davis on *Sex and the City*? Or fashionable and trendy, like Reese Witherspoon in *Sweet Home Alabama*? Help me!"

Justin stands back for a second, eyeing Mount Gap, and then dives in. He tosses a flared pale blue skirt and pale blue tank top at me, then a short-sleeved wraparound coral sweater, and finally flat tan sandals and a tan leather ponytail holder.

"It's Charlotte meets Reese," he informs me.

"The best of both worlds."

I am, once again, blissful with the benefits of a gay boyfriend.

Moments later I'm ready to walk out the door and start the first of many upcoming "happiest days of my life."

We decide that we are way too excited to get to Tiffany to stop for brunch on the way there. Lunch afterward, to discuss what we've seen, is a much better option.

We arrive outside Tiffany on Fifth Avenue at Fifty-seventh Street, and it's like the mother ship calling me home. Justin holds the door open for me, and I swear, I can hear angels singing above the hustle and bustle of Asian tourists and rich Manhattan housewives. Justin takes my hand and leads me through the crowd to the case of engagement rings. After a short wait, which didn't even feel like a wait at all because I am mesmerized by the sparkling diamonds, a salesperson approaches us.

"May I help you?" she asks politely.

Suddenly I am shy and ashamed of what we are doing. I feel worse lying to this helpful Tiffany's employee than to my own mother! I stare at her like a deer caught in headlights. Justin steps in and calmly takes over.

"We'd like to look at some engagement rings, please."

"Of course," the woman answers.

She hands me a booklet of engagement-ring information and explains about the different clarity ratings, different sizes, different shapes, and different colors for diamonds and bands. Tiffany has three main styles of engagement rings: the "Tiffany setting," which is a round diamond with a beveled band, the "Lucida," which is a square diamond with a wider band (this is the one Reese gets in *Sweet Home Alabama*), and the "Etoile" which is a diamond set down in a band.

I try on EVERYTHING. One carat, two carats, one and a half carats, gold bands, platinum bands . . . the truth is, I love them all. In the end, the one I am in love with the most is the traditional "Tiffany setting." I'm a traditional girl, plus it looks just like the engagement ring my grandmother had. I'm also a normal girl, and the bigger the stone, the more I seem to like it. I'm leaning toward 1.5 . . . not too big, not too small, with a platinum band. I look at the price of this ring and lose my breath. Oh my gosh! I never realized engagement rings are so expensive.

Justin has to catch me because my knees get weak and I start to sweat. The previously ultrapolite salesgirl sees my reaction and snatches all the rings off the counter and puts them back into the display.

"Why don't you take some time to think about it," she says coolly.

"Thank you, we will," Justin says without noticing the change in her demeanor.

She walks away and I look up into Justin's eyes, afraid that if I look down at the rings again I might cry.

"Come on," he says, "let's go get some lunch and talk about this."

Even after we walk a few blocks to find a lunch spot that is up to Justin's picky standards, I'm still pretty speechless.

"Why do you think they say it takes three months' salary?" Justin asks.

I guess in my head I had just considered three months of my salary and failed to put together that the ring of my dreams would require three months of a successful investment banker's salary. I can, however, put together what a ridiculous amount of money that is to spend on myself for a fake engagement.

"It's a ridiculous amount of money," I begin. "I mean, if I was in love and really getting married until death do us part, that would be one thing . . . but for what we're doing it's ridiculous, huh?"

Unfortunately, it doesn't even take me going home and poring over my financials to realize that the amount of money I have in my inheritance doesn't come close to covering a sparkling Tiffany diamond.

Justin looks at me and I can tell that his kind eyes feel sorry for me. I've gotten the feeling more than once during this "process" that he pities me. I try to ignore it, because when it gets down to it, I pity myself.

"Eyes on the prize, Molly," I tell myself. "Bridal shower, lacy garter, toasting flutes." I'll get through this.

"I have an idea!" he tells me enthusiastically. "Let's go to Bloomingdale's after lunch and check out the costume jewelry. I bet we can find a cubic zirconium ring that looks the same and nobody will know the difference."

I smile a small, sad smile; he's trying so hard to cheer me up.

"And we can start looking at what you want to register for," he adds.

Okay, I'm cheered up. The ring is not what's important. It's the whole experience, I remind myself . . . and the registry is an important part of that experience.

I smile a real smile, order a turkey burger, and vow not to let these details get me down anymore.

After we stuff ourselves, we make our way down to Bloomingdale's. I have to stop in my favorite candy store, Dylan's, to get some chocolate-covered pretzels (my favorite candy on earth) before we head into Registry Land.

What feels like forty escalators later (thank goodness I have a snack on hand), we finally arrive in housewares and it's almost as much of a religious experience as Tiffany.

I am in awe of the china, the silver, and the crystal. We see an area designated "Bridal Registry" and Justin suggests we start there.

"No, no, no," I tell him, "it's too soon to get official. Let's just look and get some ideas. We'll actually register after we are engaged."

"Okay," he agrees. "Let's start with china."

We spend a good part of the afternoon pretending to eat off different dishes, with different silverware, and sip champagne from different crystal flutes. Justin pretends to make omelets in Le Creuset pans and I wrap myself in Egyptian cotton towels. We are like two little kids playing dress-up. It is so much fun!

We completely exhaust ourselves . . . we're even too beat to look for the fake, fake engagement ring, so we leave Bloomingdale's. Out on the street, I realize how late it is. We really entertained ourselves for a long time.

"Want to come back to my apartment and order a pizza?" I ask Justin.

There is an awkward pause . . . what is it about me that makes people pause, awkwardly?

"Actually, I have a date tonight."

"Oh," I say quickly, "that's great," trying to cover.

"Is it okay? In the beginning you said I could if I was discreet. He asked me out . . . I never would have asked . . . and I'll cancel if you want."

"No," I tell him firmly, and I really do mean it. Justin is above and beyond wonderful to me.

"Are you sure?" he asks.

"Justin, I am positive," I say as I pay him for the date. "Treat your date to dinner."

"Heck, no!" he exclaims, shoving the money into his back pocket. "He asked me out."

He kisses me on the head and we agree to talk in the morning so he can share the details of his evening. I decide to stick with my idea of ordering a pizza and head home to a date with Tiffany.

13

The Linchpin

I wake up the next morning with a good feeling. Despite being involved in the biggest lie I've ever told and losing my best friend, I have an overwhelming sense that all is right in the world. I roll over and look at the clock: 9:27. I smile to myself. Logan's plane landed seven minutes ago. I'm positive it landed safely and on-time because if it had been thirty seconds late my mother would have called, hysterical. She is a complete wreck if any of her children are not on the ground.

I am a complete bundle of nerves, energy, and excitement. I actually can't believe I slept as late as I did . . . I think teachers' bodies know that they have to sleep in throughout the summer to make up for the lack of sleep during the school year.

Tonight's family dinner is really the linchpin of my whirlwind romance with Justin. My parents, Jamie, and Logan really have to love him completely tonight because we will be getting engaged very soon. It's hard to believe how fast time is flying.

I'm not worried about my mom—I had her at "kind soul." And I'm definitely not worried about my sister—

Justin had her at "hello," and we probably could have gotten her blessing to marry right there on the spot when he agreed to teach her prenatal yoga to make the delivery easier. I swear, Jamie is always looking out for herself.

I feel like my dad and Logan will be a bit trickier. My dad is a typical dad . . . overprotective of his firstborn. Plus, he and Justin don't really have that much in common. My dad loves sports and his family. Justin isn't too into sports, and as far as Dad knows, could be doing things to me that he wouldn't approve of. It does give me hope that Dad learned to like Bryan, though . . . they have absolutely nothing in common. Bryan's whole life (besides Jamie and the baby on the way) is computers and Dad is convinced computers will be responsible for the end of human interaction. I don't admit it in front of Bryan, but sometimes I have the same fear. And at least I know that Justin and Bryan can bond over their fear of Dad. Logan is the wildest wild card. I haven't seen him in months and I'm kind of afraid that he'll have animosity toward Justin simply because he doesn't want to share my attention on his homecoming night. I guess there is nothing I can do . . . just hope for the best.

I spend the day trying to distract myself and make the clock move until it's time to head home for the dinner. I do an exercise DVD . . . well, part of it—the fun parts. I clean and collect enough fluffy white cat hair to make Tiffany a mini sidekick a la Mini Me in *Austin Powers*. It's gross. I paint my toenails and wear a face mask. I try to organize my underwear drawer . . . I give up after a while and watch my soap opera.

It's a little embarrassing, but I adore soap operas. I'm not so addicted that during the school year I TiVo them or anything (okay, sometimes I do), but they are definitely one of my summer vacation indulgences. I mean, where else do you see a girl's father get shot to death at her own wedding, then her husband gets killed by his drug-lord mother, and then a year later the girl finds out that the murdered father wasn't her real father when she is an exact rare-blood match to save her true biological father's life? It's pure entertainment and it really helps the day fly by.

Plus I have one student to tutor in the afternoon, so that should help the day move along, too. The school I teach at is highly competitive, which leads parents to go to insane lengths to get their children admitted to the kindergarten. They even hire teachers, like me, to tutor their five-year-olds for the entrance exam . . . which includes things like bouncing a ball, drawing pictures of your family, and tying your shoes. It's crazy, but it is definitely good money.

In the afternoon, Logan calls to tell me he's home, napped, fed (thanks to Mom), and eager to see me. I tell him that I am more excited and we argue over who is the most excited until I hear Mom in the background summoning him for another meal. Our mom loves to feed her offspring. Lucky for her, she got kids with never-ending bellies.

Then I call Jamie to tell her that Logan is home, napped, fed, and eager to see us. Then Jamie and I argue over who is more excited to see Logan. We're a close family and it was hard having an ocean separate us from our baby brother for so long.

The day moves surprisingly fast and before I know it, it's time to get ready. I'd laid my outfit on my bed first thing this morning after I made it. Yes, I'm one of those people who a) makes her bed every day, and b) lays out outfits.

Right on time (he's so awesome), Justin gets to my apartment. He looks great in khaki pants and leather flip-flop sandals with a short-sleeved, button-front shirt. It's so nice to have a boyfriend who isn't totally clueless about what to wear. I'm probably his worst nightmare because I have a clothing crisis practically every time I leave the house.

I am so excited to see Logan that I don't waste time with my usual "Oh my God I have to change three times before we go" routine, and Justin hardly steps foot in the apartment before we step out to pick up Jamie and Bryan. They don't live that far from me, so we walk to their apartment. As I'm hauling ass down the street, I hear Justin flip-flop-flipping and having a hell of a time keeping up with me. We finally get to Jamie and Bryan's, in record time with Justin slightly out of breath, and find them waiting outside.

"Hi, Molly," Bryan says. "What time did you tell Jamie you would be here?"

"Five o'clock, on the dot," I tell him.

"And what time is it now?"

I look at my watch: "4:59."

"That's what I thought."

"So, what's the problem?" I ask.

"I'm just wondering why I needed to stand out here on the street for fifteen minutes."

I shrug and look at Jamie.

"In case she was early!" Jamie explains, "Come on . . . let's go!"

Jamie might actually be more excited than I am. She's late more often than I am, and I don't think I've EVER known her to wait outside somewhere for anyone. If she's meeting you for coffee and you aren't there when she gets there, she'll go to a bookstore and browse long enough to be sure you get to the coffeehouse first.

The four of us hail a cab and pile in. Jamie takes the front since she claims to take up more room now (never mind that Justin is over six feet tall and Bryan isn't short, either, and she is *just* starting to show). It actually looks adorable, and, as I knew she would, she has the cutest maternity clothes.

We get dropped off at Grand Central Station just in time to jump on the train that heads up to our family home. Our parents bought our house when I was five and Jamie was two. It was a wonderful home to grow up in and a perfect place to come back and visit. It's only a short train ride out of the city, but once you get there it feels like it's thousands of miles away. The houses are spread out and there is foliage like you wouldn't believe. As I stare out the window, I watch the view change from city to country and I start to feel homesick. It's a funny thing—when I'm in the city, I never feel homesick for my parents or my childhood home, but when I'm on the train going home, I cannot wait. I am yearning to walk through the big front door and smell my mother's cooking. And having Logan there waiting for me is just icing on the cake.

I steal a glance at Jamie and I can tell by the way she's glued to her window that she feels the same way I do.

When the train finally pulls into the station we are like two little girls. We fly out of the train, leaving the men behind, and run down the platform and into our daddy's arms. Even though it hasn't been that long since we saw him at Brad and Claire's engagement party, there is something different about seeing him on home turf. His arms feel so good and he smells so familiar. Bryan and Justin make their way through the crowd that Jamie and I avoided by pushing to the front to be the first people off the train and they both shake hands, warmly, with Dad. We all pile into Dad's forest green Explorer and head the few miles to our house.

Jamie is, of course, in the front. I swear, she is hardly showing . . . by the time she is nine months she's going to insist on having whole city blocks to herself. I'm in the back, sitting bitch between Justin and Bryan. I'm trying to point out things of interest to Justin as we speed along.

"There's my elementary school," I point right, over him, nearly taking off his nose.

"There's the park where I lost my first tooth," I point left, poking Bryan in the ear.

"Up there is the Dairy Queen I went to on my first date," I point through the two front seats.

We ride along like that until we approach our house.

"And this," I say proudly, "is our house."

We excitedly pour out of the Explorer and I grab Justin's hand and drag him onto the porch. Our house has one of the greatest porches of all time. It spans the entire length of the house and has two big wooden hanging swings.

Jamie reaches the front door first and throws it open, yelling, "We're home!"

As soon as the door opens, the comforting smell of home explodes in our faces and we can't help but be drawn in. The house smells like a mixture of furniture polish, peach cobbler (our mom's summer specialty), homemade barbeque sauce, and our old dog, Skipper.

Skipper, even in her old age, is the first to bound out and greet us. My parents got her my senior year of college, so I never got to live full-time with her, but I can always tell that she loves me best by the way she greets me when I come home. Skipper is a yellow lab, named after Barbie's little sister, but she's starting to look like an old lady now. She's a little heavier than she used to be, and the fur on her face is turning white.

Jamie and I get down on the ground to greet her until Mom walks in, wiping her hands on her apron (I swear, she looks like a picture out of a country-living magazine), and we jump up to hug her. We're thrilled to see our dog, we're thrilled to see our mom, but really . . . they aren't who we are there to see.

"Where is he!?!" I yell.

"He was jet-lagged, so he took a nap, but I woke him a little while ago and he was getting in the shower," my mother explains in her patient-teacher voice.

Jamie and I groan . . . we might be patient with our students, but with our family we immediately revert to our childhood ways.

"Oh well," I moan. "Come on, Justin, I'll show you around the house."

After Justin properly greets my mother and gives a satisfactory amount of attention to Skipper, I take him by the hand and lead him through the living room. I glance over my shoulder and can see my mother take my father's hand and beam at me with Justin. Another pang of guilt hits me . . . I really do hate that they have to be involved in this whole lie.

Justin and I are standing on the back deck. To the unsuspecting person we are whispering sweet nothings to each other; in reality, we're having a run-down of the evening so far. We both agree that things are going really well. I hear someone open the French door behind us and I turn around to find Logan standing there. He is such a sight for sore eyes—honestly, my eyes tear when I see him. He looks amazing; months of backpacking through Europe, lugging all his belongings, have left him tan and buff. Logan, Jamie, and I all look very similar—dark hair and blue eyes, but unlike Jamie and I, who are, let's say vertically challenged, Logan is tall like our dad. Now, with some definition in his muscles, he looks so handsome.

I squeal with delight and run into his open arms. He grabs me and whirls me around in a hug. I cannot believe how strong he has gotten. Once he sets me down, I turn back to Justin.

"Logan," I say, "this is Justin."

Justin smiles warmly. "It's about time I met you, man—your ears must be burning morning, noon, and night."

"I could say the same thing to you," Logan replies.

Oh, yippee! They seem to be hitting it off.

The rest of the evening goes spectacularly well. We sit on the patio in the warm sunset eating tons of my dad's amazing barbeque and corn, and then my mom's amazing peach cobbler with vanilla ice cream and caramel sauce. Logan shows pictures and shares stories from his trip, and Justin fits in like a member of the family. It doesn't even feel like an effort to pretend that he is my boyfriend because in a lot of ways, he is. Actually, in every way but the bedroom way he is. He shares my life, we've become wonderful friends, I can count on him to be there for me, and I feel like it works both ways. It definitely stopped feeling like a business arrangement some time ago.

After we're all stuffed and nearing food comas, Bryan reminds us that some people have to get up and go to work in the morning. Jamie and I groan, but we take the cue to say our good-byes.

First Skipper, who I now see is fat because Mom and Dad have completely lifted the "no people food" rule. As kids, if we fed any animal from the dinner table we were at risk of receiving the death penalty. Now, Skipper sits between Mom and Dad, cleaning up mounds of "accidentally dropped" food. Next we hug Mom and collect our Tupperwares of leftovers to take back to the city. Finally we say good-bye to Logan. I can tell by the way he sends Justin off that he definitely likes him and it makes me so happy. Even though Justin isn't really going to be my husband, he will be around for at least a year and hopefully we'll be able to stay friends after that, so I want my brother to like him. We then pile back in the Explorer and do our journey in reverse . . . including the cab to Jamie and Bryan's, leaving them out front and walking back to my apartment. It has gotten really late and we are both beyond exhausted.

"Why don't you just stay here tonight?" I offer to Justin.

He hesitates for a second, "Is it really okay? It wouldn't be weird?"

I think, quickly, "Not at all—you look too tired to go another step."

Justin looks so relieved. "Thank you."

We drag ourselves up the flights of stairs and into my apartment. The second bedroom (the one that would have been Jamie's) is my guest room/office/library/den. It has a futon that I expertly unfold . . . many a drunk bride has crashed on it post-bachelorette partying. I grab an extra pillow and blanket from the hall closet and toss them on the futon.

We crowd each other in the bathroom getting ready for bed—a gay man's ritual is very similar to a straight girl's— then head into our respective beds for much-needed sleep.

"Molly," Justin says, as I climb into my bed and he heads for the futon, "your family is wonderful."

I smile as I snuggle into my bed and doze off.

14

Dinner With Brad and Claire

The next morning we both sleep really late and don't stir until Tiffany cannot stand the starvation anymore and begins howling at her food dish. I get up and make coffee while Justin gets dressed.

"It was nice having you stay here," I tell him when he comes into the kitchen to get his coffee.

"Yes," he agrees, "it was nice. So, what's on your schedule today?"

"Well," I giggle as I open my mostly empty calendar, "I appear to be open . . . I just have a tutor session at one with the remarkably precocious Taylor Twain. What about you?"

He laughs at my silliness, "I actually have to work a double shift today because of the trade I made to have yesterday off."

"Oh, I'm sorry. That's sucky."

"No, don't be silly, it was well worth it. I'll be home late tonight, but let's meet at our place tomorrow morning."

"Okay, that sounds good. Call me when you wake up."

We hug at the door and Justin kisses the top of my head as he walks out. In my fantasy world I am like a real girlfriend sending her boyfriend off to work and it makes me feel happy.

I decide to spend the morning working on the engagement plan. It is scheduled to take place in just a couple of weeks. It's hard to believe how fast time has flown by. I get out my checklist of "things to do before we get engaged." Yes, I have a checklist titled that . . . and it has SO many checks on it! Mom and Dad—I could have checked it before, but I wanted to wait until I was absolutely certain. After last night, I give it two checks. Jamie and Bryan—check. Logan—check (hooray!). Lauren and Rob—check. Alex and Steve—check, Alex and I aren't extremely close, anyway . . . we're kind of friends through Lauren and I think the amount of bonding we did with them at Brad and Claire's engagement party is sufficient. And then I come to Brad's name on my list. There isn't a check, there aren't any notes . . . it looks so empty and alone sitting on the page . . . and it reminds me of the hole he left in my life. I stare at his name for what feels like the longest time . . . Tiffany even climbs across the desk to see what I am staring at. I realize that I need to maintain my friendship with Brad, I need to be able to put a check next to his name, and therefore, I need to play by Claire's rules.

I dial Brad's work number . . . it worked last time, so I'm keeping my fingers crossed. Ring, ring, ring . . . no luck. Rats. I take a deep breath and dial his cell.

Ring, ring. "Hello?" It's Brad's voice.

"Hi," I say, trying to sound upbeat and normal, "it's Molly." The truth, of course, is that if things were normal I wouldn't have said, *It's Molly*, I would have said, *It's me*.

"Oh, hey there," Brad says in a strange tone . . . he must be with Claire and he doesn't want Claire to know it's me.

"Is it a bad time?"

"Um, no . . . not really. Claire and I are just meeting with a wedding coordinator. Hang on one second."

I can hear him put his hand over the phone as Claire's shrill voice asks who it is. He doesn't answer . . . just says he needs to take it and a few seconds later he's back on the line.

"Hey. It's good to hear your voice," Brad says with a warmth that tells me he means it.

"You could have called back if it's a bad time."

"No, I really want to talk to you."

"Okay." I open my mouth to take a big bite of humble pie. "I miss you, and I want to see you, so . . . why don't the four of us get together this weekend?"

"The four of us?"

"Yeah. I thought the only way for me to be allowed to see you was under Claire's supervision?"

"Well, yes . . . but who's the fourth?"

What?!? "Justin!" I say with a "duh" tone.

"Oh, really? You guys are still together, huh?"

That is such a strange response . . . I'm not even sure what to say. "Yes, of course we are."

"Okay, well, great. I think we're free Sunday. I would love to see you, too, Molly."

"Sunday is perfect." I know Justin has Sundays off.

"Fantastic—I'll call you Sunday morning to set up time and place. 'Bye, Molly."

I set the phone back on the receiver, but I'm kind of weirded out by the conversation. Brad just doesn't seem like himself. It's so strange . . . and so sad. Claire really must be brainwashing him! Sunday should be interesting.

Justin and I really enjoy the weekend. As fall is approaching, the leaves are starting to change color and it's starting to cool down just a little. School starts soon and shortly after that we are supposed to get engaged . . . so there's a lot to do. We spend the days shopping; we look at fake, fake engagement rings . . . it's a little depressing. I get some back-to-school clothes (yes, teachers get them, too), Justin gets some "straight boy" clothes, as he calls them, for the post-engagement events we'll be doing, and we play with all the knickknacks at Williams-Sonoma in preparation for our registry. Justin even packs a weekend bag and spends Saturday night at my apartment. It's like having a slumber party . . . we make mai tais, put on face masks, and stay up half the night talking and giggling. As much fun as I'm having, our Sunday night plans with Brad and Claire leave an uncomfortable knot in my stomach. It's similar to the feeling of dread I get when I have an impending dentist appointment. And just like the time leading up to a dentist appointment, it flies by and before I know it, it's Sunday night.

True to his word, Brad calls on Sunday morning to confirm our plans and set up a restaurant in Greenwich Village that "Claire loves." The phone call only makes the knot in my stomach grow because it's SO not Brad to be so responsible. When the old Brad said, *I'll call you Sunday morning to confirm* (if he would even be organized enough to say that), it meant, *Call me Sunday afternoon to remind me.*

Sunday evening, Justin and I get dressed and, thanks to his help, we look damn good. We get to the restaurant ten minutes after the scheduled time . . . we take our time and have the cab drop us off a block from the restaurant and stroll the rest of the way, knowing that this will upset Claire and taking immense, although immature, pleasure in it.

We walk in the restaurant, which is practically empty, but Brad still waves us over like the place is a crowded bar that we could never have found him in. We exchange uncomfortable hellos; Claire doesn't get up, I'm not sure if I'm allowed to hug Brad, so I don't. Justin awkwardly shakes his hand, but Brad is looking at me, not Justin, while they shake. Finally, we all sit down (except Claire, who never got off her bony ass) and I grab the first waiter I see and order a glass of white wine. Then there is silence. Hmmm . . . dumdedum . . . okay . . . this is weird.

An icebreaker, we definitely need an icebreaker. Should I knock something over? Choke on bread? I look helplessly at Justin.

"So," Justin says and clears his throat, "Brad, what's new in the world of extreme sports?"

Oh, hooray! Such a more brilliant icebreaker than me needing the Heimlich maneuver.

"Nothing," Brad replies.

And then there is silence again and we're back where we began. Justin looks back at me with an "I tried" expression.

Okay, I guess it's my turn to try.

"Claire, Brad says you love this place. What do you recommend?"

Justin gives me an approving smile and nod.

"Everything's good," she says.

And back to silence.

"Oh, okay, everything." I pick up my menu and study it.

This is going to be such a long evening.

The rest of the night drags on like the beginning. Justin and I bust our asses to come up with topics of conversation and Brad and Claire rebuff them with monosyllabic answers. It is horribly awkward and uncomfortable. We make it through the main course and even I, the queen of chocolate, am willing to forgo dessert to get out of there. So when the waiter asks if we would like to see a dessert menu, I begin to shake my head no, assuming Brad and Claire are having as horrible a time as we are and are as eager to get out, but Brad says, "Yes, please," before I can shake my head no. I shoot a panicked look at Justin. Why is Brad trying to extend the torture? I mean, he is—or at least was—a fun person . . . and believe me, fun people definitely know that there isn't anything at all fun going on right now.

"Molly never says no to dessert," Brad informs Justin.

"Haha, I know. Where does she put it all?" Justin replies, trying to be nice.

"Seems like you should know the answer to that," Brad answers coolly.

Ouch! What does that even mean? It didn't even make sense, but the way he said it was so harsh. I look at Justin, who looks just as stung as I feel. I take his hand above the table.

"Justin is blind to my potbelly—right, sweetheart?" I say to him stupidly since I don't even have a potbelly . . . I honestly don't even know where I put it all.

"You don't have a potbelly," Justin says, clearly starting to get annoyed with Brad.

"What a good boyfriend." I smile like an even bigger idiot and squeeze his hand, then look across the table at Brad and Claire like a jackass. Brad is looking back at us with a death glare and Claire is looking at her dessert menu as if she was alone at the table.

We finally get our desserts down, Brad has a refill on his coffee, and the check is delivered to our table. There is that weird second when the check is a landmine, and then Justin picks it up and says to Brad, "Want to just split it in half?" Justin is such a classy gentleman.

"Actually, Molly had wine," Claire says . . . it's one of the first things she's said all night.

All three of us snap our heads up and look at her in shock. If I hadn't just sat through this dinner I might have burst out laughing. Any other person in the world would have said it as a joke, but it is clear that Claire is serious.

"Okay," Justin says. "Would it be okay to split it and we'll leave ten dollars more tip on our bill?"

"No," Claire says, "that will make us look cheap to the waiter."

I think at this point my jaw drops open a little. She is unbelievable.

"How would you like to handle it?" Justin asks. It amazes me that he can still be polite to her.

"We'll just have to split it down the middle and you can give us ten dollars in cash."

"Done," Justin says as he slaps the bill in front of her.

I've never seen Justin pushed this far before and I can sense that he is nearing some sort of snapping point.

"Well," I say, "it was wonderful seeing you guys. We really have to do this again."

Justin chokes and gurgles a little.

We all stand up from the table. We exchange good-byes about as awkwardly as the hellos, and Justin and I practically run out of the restaurant and grab a cab. That was so much worse than any dental work I've ever had done . . . and I had my wisdom teeth removed with a local anesthesia!

As the cab pulls away from the curb, Justin and I start screaming.

"That was the most horrific thing I've ever been through!" I yell.

"I think I might need to raise my rates to sit through more dinners like that one!!" Justin adds.

"Oh my God, I am so sorry . . . I would totally understand if you did."

We spend the entire ride home dissecting each awful aspect of the dinner: the rude greeting, the lack of conversation, and the check fiasco.

"And the food wasn't even very good!" I add.

Thankfully, by the time we pull up to Justin's apartment we are able to laugh about it.

"I promise I'll never make you do that again. If the only way to see Brad is to go through that again, I won't see him ever again!"

"I'm sorry, Molly," Justin says.

"I know it's hard for you to understand . . . you never knew him pre-Claire. But, I'm telling you . . . he was so different."

"I wish there was something I could do to make this hurt you less."

"I'm okay," I tell him, and I really am. "That Brad was not the person I loved and definitely not a person I will miss. I just have to get over it."

"It'll take some time, but you will. Sleep well—I'm sorry I can't stay over, but I have an audition early tomorrow."

"Don't worry about it." It's funny how he's started staying at my apartment more and more. "Good luck . . . break legs!" I call out the window as the cab takes off toward my place.

15

The End of Molly and Brad

With the start of school just around the corner, I have to get out of my lazy summer routine and back to getting up at a reasonable hour. So, as draining as the previous night was, I'm still up early and on the phone with Jamie making plans to go to the craft store to get school supplies when my Call Waiting beeps.

"Hello?"

"Molly! Are you on the other line?" It's Brad!!

"Yeah, but hang on one sec."

I flash back over to Jamie and arrange to meet her at Michael's.

"Hi!" I say when I click back over to Brad.

"We had a great time last night."

Huh? Were they at the same dinner we were? Maybe they went out afterwards?

I must have been silent a little too long, because Brad says, "Didn't you?" before I have a chance to think of how to respond.

"Oh, yes, of course. For sure," I stumble and bumble. What do I say?!?

"It was so good to see you. I missed you."

Now what do I say? *It was so good to see the demon that has taken over your body,* doesn't seem appropriate.

"Me, too," I reply lamely.

Then Brad's tone stiffens a little and I'm prepared for him to admit that it was an altogether awful time, but instead he says, "I'm worried about you."

Me? You're worried about me? I'm not the one who's been brainwashed!

"Huh?"

"Molly, there is something about Justin that I can't put my finger on."

For a minute I freeze . . . I'm positive we've been caught. I'm horrified that Brad has seen through the act that Justin and I put on . . . but I'm also relieved that we are still close enough that he can see through me.

"I'm worried about the way he tries to control you," Brad continues.

What?!? People who live in glass houses shouldn't throw rocks.

"What are you talking about?"

"He is always looking at you and touching you."

It's called being in love, dumb-ass! (Or pretending to be in love to fool your family and friends into believing you are engaged, but that's a separate issue.)

"It's because we're in love," I inform Brad, and I'm positive that he's going to see through me because it sounds SO awkward to say it like that.

"Well, what about how he was with the check?" Brad asks.

"What about it?" I say, defensively. "He was trying to make it nice and easy and Claire made a big stink about ten dollars!"

I know that dragging her name into this will escalate the

problem, but I don't care. I'm tired of playing nice. Bring it on!

"She didn't appreciate being swindled by an out-of-work actor."

"At lease he has a line of work to be out of!" Not my best comeback, but what can I say? I'm not great at fighting on my feet.

"There we have it."

"There we have what?" I challenge.

"You are so jealous of Claire."

I am flabbergasted because it's really not true. I will admit that I have been jealous of people in the past. Friends who got engaged before me, my own sister who got pregnant before me, the teacher they selected over me to be third grade dean (yes, Manhattan elementary schools have elementary grade deans). I have NEVER been jealous of Claire Reilly, though!

"Brad!" I yell. "You know me better than that."

"No, Molly, I know you exactly that well. And I know that you are only dragging that stupid Justin character around to try to make me feel guilty for getting married."

"Wh-what?!?" I stammer.

"First you tried to get me to break up with Claire and when it didn't work you took this approach."

Okay, I have to say it . . . he's *forced* me. You see that, don't you?

"Actually, Brad, I tried to get you to break up with Claire because I think she's evil. I see that she has broken your spirit and robbed you of your personality. I see that the sparkle is gone from your eye. My relationship with Justin has *nothing* (okay, this is a tiny lie since it was his engagement that drove me over the edge and forced me to call Justin in the first place, but that's a moot point right now) to do with you or Claire or your miserable marriage."

"Maybe I have changed, Molly, but I've changed for the better. You've changed into a bitter, jealous woman." CLICK.

"SCREW YOU!" I yell before slamming the phone down, then picking up the receiver and slamming it four more times.

16

A Day With Jamie

I am trembling and sobbing and am truly in shock over what just took place. I think Brad and I have argued four times in the past twelve years. The time I spread the news that his roommate slept with one of their fraternity brothers' girlfriend. The time I got super-hammered and hooked up with the same roommate. The time I told my mother he was gay as an excuse for why we weren't a couple. (Ironic that now I am telling my mother a gay man is straight.) And . . . maybe that's it. Maybe we've only argued three times . . . over petty little things.

In all the other instances, we were laughing about it by happy hour the same night. I am positive we won't be laughing about this over Heinekens tonight . . . or ever. I have a very permanent feeling that my friendship with Brad is over. The strange thing is that I don't feel as upset as I would have thought I would be—which is maybe part of why I'm so upset . . . because what I said to Justin the other day comes back to me. The person I just got off the phone with isn't my best friend. He's the brainwashed Claire Reilly version. My Brad has been gone for months.

I take a long, hot shower and pull myself together. I have

to meet Jamie in a little over an hour. When I step out of the steam of my bathroom I realize that a hot shower probably wasn't the smartest thing. The temperature seems to have spiked again and my apartment is now uncomfortably warm. I blast the air conditioner while I get myself ready. I decide to skip blow-drying my hair; it'll dry pretty curly, but blow-drying it in this heat would only lead to a frizz ball, and I could sweat to death under the heat of my blow-dryer.

I'm out the door with just enough time to grab a Caramel Frappuccino before meeting Jamie. Of course, I still get there first and stand outside the craft store getting a sugar-and-caffeine high while I wait for her. When she finally walks up, I do a double take. It's only been a couple weeks since the family dinner and she has practically doubled in size!

"You're huge!" I blurt out.

"I know," she giggles, "I popped."

I stare at her bulging belly for a second and feel a rush of emotion. My baby sister, my beautiful baby sister, looks so much more beautiful with her own baby inside her. It's amazing.

"You look so amazing."

"Ugh, no. Look at my feet."

She sticks a foot that is almost swollen beyond recognition in my face.

"Okay, eew . . . your feet look awful, but the rest of you looks fantastic."

"Thank you. I actually feel pretty good. I've been doing a lot of the yoga that Justin showed me and I think it helps."

We continue chatting about all the pregnancy stuff that Jamie is doing as we walk into the craft store. Once inside, we both pull long lists out of our purses—what do you expect? We're teachers!

After what feels like three trips up and down each aisle and seven bathroom trips for Jamie, we are in line with carts full of construction paper, Elmer's Glue, glitter, paint, markers, stickers . . . you name it, and we're buying it. I must admit that one of my favorite things about being a teacher is putting together my bulletin board before the beginning of the school year.

Usually I start with something fall-themed that can easily be transformed for Halloween and Thanksgiving . . . an orange background is usually the best starting point. Then, in December, I switch to a red background that will take me through Christmas and Valentine's Day. No need to worry about New Year's, because the kids are on winter break. Some teachers steer clear of red because it isn't as Hanukkah-friendly, but I decorate a green tree with all different color dreidels . . . I like the idea of blending the holidays together, especially since that's how I grew up—with a Jewish mother and a Christian father. Technically, we are all Jewish, since our mother is, but she was always very generous about celebrating both sets of holidays. Then, in March, I go to a green background that works for St. Patrick's Day and on through spring. Sometimes I'll move to a yellow background for summer in May, but sometimes I burn out. Depends how trying my class that year is, I guess. It's so much fun for me.

After Jamie and I check out, we lug what feels like most of the store's inventory out onto the street.

"I'm starving," Jamie announces.

Since I can usually eat, I agree that lunch is a good idea. We spot a sidewalk café not too far away, and drag our bags there. As we sit down I admire the place . . . we've never been there and it's really adorable. Small café tables line the patio that is really just the Manhattan sidewalk, but some carefully arranged potted plants have made it feel far away from the hustle and bustle of traffic whirring by. We look at the menus as we try to kick the bags to one side or the other and make foot space under the tiny table.

We make up our minds pretty quickly because we are starving. I order a *panino caprese*, my favorite kind of sandwich . . . it's basically a caprese salad (buffalo mozzarella, tomato, and basil) on yummy Italian bread. Jamie gets the cheese ravioli.

"I crave cheese ravioli all the time—isn't that weird?" she asks me, as if I have any idea what is weird or not for a pregnant woman.

"I dunno."

"It is. People always talk about craving ice cream and pickles . . . but not me. Cheese ravioli . . . which I actually think is more disgusting, because I have eaten it out of the Chef Boyardee can without even heating it up in extreme moments . . . like the middle of the night."

"That *is* disgusting," I agree.

"So," Jamie says, "I have something I need to talk to you about."

"Me, too, actually." I've decided to get Jamie's take on the Brad situation.

"You go first," she instructs.

I go way back to the first Brad-Claire problems . . . my being unable to reach Brad without Claire thwarting me. Finally reaching him and being told that we can't be alone together. Then I fill her in on the dinner from hell. And I wrap up my tale of woe with the morning's awful phone call.

"You're kidding me," is all she says.

"No, obviously I'm not kidding. He *said* all those things . . . about me and about why I'm with Justin!"

Jamie shakes her head and pulls another list out of her bag. She takes out a pen and furiously scratches something off it.

"What are you doing?"

"I'm uninviting them to my baby shower."

"You're having a baby shower? Why didn't you tell me? When?"

"Actually, that's what I wanted to talk to you about. I want you to throw it," she says as she hands a neatly organized list of names and addresses across the table.

I'm caught off guard only for a tiny second of wondering at how Jamie can so expertly and so innocently take the topic off of my huge problem, get it onto her, and get me to throw her a party in the process. I promise that selfishness only lasts one second, though, because the truth is that nothing would thrill me more than planning her shower.

"Really? You want me to?!?"

"Well, of course. You're going to be the godmother."

"I'm going to be the godmother?!?" My eyes well up and I'm bawling before "mother" is completely out of my mouth.

"Well, of course," she says, bawling as well.

We hug and cry and giggle and then spend the rest of the afternoon talking about the baby shower.

We never get back on the "Brad problem" and that doesn't disappoint me at all.

17

Molly Gets Organized

That evening I sit down at my desk and really prepare to plan. My plate has suddenly become so full that I'm slightly worried that even I won't be able to tackle it. I have to plan my upcoming fake engagement, fake wedding, and the greatest baby shower in the world for Jamie, and, of course, prepare for school—my job. As I'm trying to figure out how I can finish everything in time, the door to my apartment opens and Justin comes in (I gave him a key) carrying Chinese take-out.

"I love you!" I announce while grabbing a box of chow mein (my favorite) and a pair of chopsticks.

"So, what's new and exciting?" he asks as he grabs the container of garlic chicken and the second pair of chopsticks for himself.

I jump into telling him all about my day with Jamie and how I am planning her baby shower and I am going to be the godmother. We talk about that for ages before I remember my awful morning and tell him about that.

"Oh Jeez, Molly...that sucks. Are you sure you're okay?"

I nod my head as I affirm that I really am.

We talk about the Brad situation only a little longer before going back to Jamie and the baby. As the evening grows later we start talking about our childhoods.

"I think I can remember my mother being pregnant with Jamie. I'm not sure, though . . . it might be one of those things you see so many pictures of when you are growing up that you think you remember it actually happening. Know what I mean?"

He does, of course. And we start talking about his childhood in Kansas. And then what it was like realizing he was gay and coming out, and ultimately leaving Kansas.

"I was actually engaged," he tells me. "Then I came home one day and realized how wrong the whole situation was for me."

"Did she hate you?" I ask.

"For a long time she did, but it didn't matter that much because my own mother and father hated me. Not to mention my brother, so it was just one more person."

For the first time, I'm realizing what a painful thing it was for him to come out.

"That's so awful—I'm so sorry."

"Don't be sorry. My family is better than most. They eventually got over it and things are okay between us now. We all went to therapy, together and separately. I even became friendly with Lisa, my ex-fiancée, and helped her plan her wedding to the man she eventually married."

Even though Justin's story has a happy ending, it makes me sad to think of all the people's who don't. "It breaks my heart to think about people whose families let them down when this is something that cannot be helped."

"It is sad," he agrees.

Slowly the topic moves from serious to silly and back again. Before we know it, it's 3 A.M. and we can hardly keep our eyes open. We crawl into our respective beds and I don't know about him, but I'm asleep as soon as my head hits the pillow.

Somehow, although I've only had a fraction of the sleep a person needs to function, I'm awake and alert early the next morning. My body must be realizing that school is nearing and it's getting back on time.

I put on a pot of coffee and sneak into the room where Justin is sleeping to get my schedule off the desk. He looks so peaceful and comfortable. I quietly shut the door and plop myself down on the couch to watch Regis and Kelly on low volume while I figure out what I need to do first.

School stuff is going to need to take priority because it's starting first . . . in a little over a week. Next I'll have to figure out engagement details because that is supposed to happen in two weeks. Jamie's shower, which I'm probably the most excited about at this point, will have to take the back burner for a short time since I think it'll be fun to wait until she's farther along and even bigger.

As far as getting ready for school goes, I'm almost there. I've been doing this long enough that I have my lesson plans pretty perfected as jumping off points. Obviously they get adjusted as the year goes on, depending how the class is moving, but for starting the year off, I stick to what has worked in the past.

I have some new school clothes and all my new school supplies. What I really need to do is get to the school and set up my classroom, my desk, and my bulletin board (yippee). Also, I like to study the previous year's yearbook to try and learn as many names as possible. Sometimes it's really hard because yearbook photos are taken in the fall so by the time I get the kids they are a full year older and many of them look very different. But for the most part it's a helpful way to get started, because I like to learn names quickly. I always hated the teachers who still weren't sure of everyone's names in October, so I vowed never to be one of those.

As for the engagement, the biggest thing I have to do is figure out the ring dilemma. Obviously the Tiffany rings, and really all "real" rings, are outrageously out of budget for a fake engagement (and perhaps for a real one, too), but all the cubic zirconium and costume ones we looked at were so tacky. This is probably the biggest problem with my grand plan, so far. I also need to think up an adorable way for the engagement to happen since I know from hearing countless stories from other people that everyone on earth asks engaged people to retell the story of how it happened. And I definitely want to have one of the ones that brings tears to people's eyes, not obvious disappointment like my poor friend Lily whose husband proposed in line at the supermarket. I want something romantic. Other than figuring out those two things, I don't think there is much else I need to do with the engagement. I don't want to send out announcements to newspapers or anything like that . . . that would just be overkill on the lie.

I move onto the shower planning. As organized as ever, Jamie has given me a typed, alphabetized list of guests. I look at the list, and the black scratch marks through "Bradley Lawson," give me a tiny pang of sadness, but I'm strong and I move on. Jamie basically wants everyone she's ever met (and I think perhaps one or two that she hasn't) invited to this baby shower. Where on earth am I going to hold such a gala? And how on earth am I going to pay for it?

I make good money teaching at a private school and tutoring over breaks, and am comfortable since I don't really have rent since my grandmother had owned this apartment for so long that it was paid off, but Justin's "salary" for the year is going to leave me with less rainy-day money than usual . . . actually, it's leaving me flat broke. Like the shortfall when it came to the engagement ring money, my wedding fund doesn't exactly cover a groom's salary, either. It is taking every spare dime, plus some severe scrimping and saving, to pay Justin to be dutifully by my side for twelve months . . . I've even become my mother's daughter and am a coupon clipper. Ugh . . . I've sunk so low! Obviously, Nana hadn't considered the fact that I might need to pay an actor to pose as my true love when she set the money aside for me. I am thinking about asking my mother to plan the shower with me (aka help me pay for it) when Justin pads into the living room looking very sleepyheaded.

"Good morning, sleeping beauty," I croon at him.

He grunts in my direction. Justin has been around my apartment enough now that I know he is not a morning person.

"Coffee's in the kitchen," I inform him.

He grunts again and heads that way. A few minutes later, the usual Justin emerges from the kitchen with a jumbo mug of joe.

"What are you up to so bright and early?" he asks.

"Planning, organizing, scheduling, and figuring out what I need to do and when I need to do it."

"Ah-ha. And what do you need to do and when do you need to do it by?"

I pick up my papers and go over them.

"I need to set up my classroom and study the old yearbook this week. I need to figure out our engagement stuff and the ring problem this week, too. After that stuff is taken care of, I can start thinking about Jamie's party . . . and how to pay for the biggest baby shower ever thrown."

"Oh, about the engagement. I thought at the Labor Day barbeque at your parents' that I could ask your father for 'permission.' I don't think I'll see him again before it happens, will I?"

I think for a second and realize that we won't see my

family again before we get engaged . . . it's happening so soon!

"No. You're right. Asking for permission is such a great touch. Makes it so legit. You're not scared to do it, are you?"

"No. It's like acting . . . plus, it'll be the only time in my life I'll be able to ask a girl's father for permission to marry his daughter."

He laughs at this thought.

"What about when you got engaged to Lisa?" I ask.

"Oh, Molly, I was not the classy gentleman who stands before you today. I was a confused, often drunk, college student. We were hammered the night I proposed and I was relieved when she passed out so that I wouldn't have to have sex with her," he laughs again.

"I'm sure one day you'll ask a nice boy's father for his son's hand in marriage."

We giggle together at the thought.

"The ring is a real pickle for me," I tell him.

"Yeah, I know. I was thinking: my friend Jake at work got engaged and then, like, three months later the girl broke it off and gave the ring back. Maybe we could borrow it?"

"Really?" I ask, wide-eyed. "That would be so ideal."

"I know, and I remember it being a nice ring. Not exactly like what you picked out of the blue box, but nothing to be ashamed of, either. I think he's working the same shift as I am—I'll ask him tonight."

"How are you going to ask him?"

Justin furrows his brow. "Good question."

We think furiously for a few minutes.

"Tell him it's for a play?" Justin suggests.

"Why wouldn't you use a fake, worthless ring for a play?" I counter.

"Good point."

More thinking.

"I know!" I exclaim. "You could tell him that your sister

had the exact same ring, but lost it and needs to wear one so her husband doesn't realize she lost hers while a replacement is made."

"I don't have a sister," he reminds me.

"Friend?" I offer.

"Yes, something along those lines might work. I'll ask him about it and see how he reacts and feel the situation out from there."

We finish our coffee in silence and watch Regis and Kelly interview Alyssa Milano and then demonstrate how to grill ribs for Labor Day. When the show is over, Justin heads into the second bedroom. He comes out just as the ladies of *The View* are taking their seats.

"Okay, cutie. I'm off."

I stand up to give him a hug.

"See you later, alligator."

"After while, crocodile. Do good on your bulletin board."

"Do *well*," I correct. "I have to get back in teacher mode," I say with a smile.

"I'll call you tonight," he says, returning my smile as he walks out the door.

18

Logan's Surprise

I walk into the kitchen to refill my coffee, and Tiffany's kibble dish, then return to the living room to settle on the couch and listen to Joy Behar complain about a misshapen underwire bra.

Just as Barbara is introducing Harrison Ford, my phone rings.

"Hello?" I answer.

"Good Golly Miss Molly," and then snickering comes through the phone line.

It's Logan.

"Logan. You're a brat."

"I know, but I'm a brat you love."

"Unfortunately true," I admit. "What's going on?"

"Can you have lunch today? I'll come to the city."

"Definitely!" I say, excited to get some one-on-one time with my brother.

"Good, I want to tell you more about my trip."

"Okay," I say, slightly let down. The dinner to celebrate Logan's homecoming was fun, and hearing about all the art museums and ancient architecture that Logan visited was interesting enough . . . once. Doing it again didn't sound super fun.

"I'll come to the apartment when I get in. I'm going to take an 11:30 express train, so I should be to your apartment around one."

"I'll be here waiting for you."

We hang up and I decide that in light of Logan's surprise visit, there is no reason to get my butt in gear right this second as I don't have time to do the stuff I need to do at school and be home in time to meet him. I'll just go there this afternoon.

I settle back and listen to Harrison while wondering why on earth the man is wearing an earring.

"Doesn't he have a mirror in his house?" I ask Tiffany, who looks at me and meows in agreement.

After my soap opera, where a woman is set to get married until she finds out that her betrothed's beloved first wife is not dead as believed and shows up at the wedding with amnesia, I head for the shower.

I take my time, because I know that when school starts I won't have time for luxuriously long showers. When I finally finish my routine, it's time for Logan to show up . . . but he doesn't.

I wait and I wait and I get bored and paint little flowers on my toenails to match the ones on my skirt. Then I wait some more and finally, around 2:30, I hear the buzzer.

I intercom him to come up while I grab my purse and give Tiffany a little more water; when he gets to my door he doesn't look too good.

"What's wrong?" I ask, concerned by the tense look on his face.

"The train wasn't an express. I'm so sorry I'm late."

"Don't worry at all. But I'm starving, so let's go."

My hunger is so overwhelming that as soon as I know he is okay, I push him out the front door without so much as offering a glass of water and lead the way out of my building to a diner down the street that I know has big portions and fast service.

Once we are sitting down with a basket of fries between us, my blood sugar returns to a normal level and I am able to act human again.

"So," I say, bracing myself for more boring museum stories, "tell me more about your trip."

Logan's face flashes a quick look of panic and then he buries it in his menu.

"Let's order first."

"Okay," I agree, torn between the problem of postponing the inevitable and the hope that we'll never get back onto the topic of Italian architecture.

We order two turkey burgers with side salads and onion rings, then make small talk about the train ride, the weather, and Jamie's pregnancy until our food arrives. We both cover our burgers with ketchup and mustard, pull out the onions and dig in. We're halfway through the meal when Logan abruptly puts his burger down and looks straight at me.

"What?" I ask, wiping my face off with my napkin.

He takes a deep breath, "So, my trip," he says.

Ugh . . . I guess I didn't escape. "Yeah, tell me!" I say, forcing myself to be upbeat.

"Okay," he begins slowly as I shovel an entire onion ring into my mouth, "Remember why I went to Italy?" he asks.

"Yes," I nod, speaking with my mouth full, "to find yourself." Whatever that means, I add to myself.

He takes a big bite of his burger. "Well, I did," he says, with his mouth full. Our mother would be mortified at our table manners.

"That's great," I tell him, not really sure where he's going.

He looks at me expectantly, as though I'm missing something obvious.

"What did you find?" I question.

I dip a fry in ketchup and watch him finish the last of his burger, dipping it in ranch dressing. Logan slowly chews and swallows the entire bite, takes a big sip of his Coke and looks up and me. For some reason, I'm frozen. I hold my ketchup-dripping fry halfway between the plate and my mouth and I look at him expectantly.

"I'm gay."

I think my chin drops a tad and I study Logan's face. I'm surprised, but not shocked . . . but I don't know what to do or say. Time is kind of frozen and I don't stop staring at him until I feel the ketchup fall off the fry and go plop on my lap. This breaks my stare and I look down at the red spot on my lap, which thankfully is covered with a napkin. I look back up at my brother, who is still looking straight at me.

"What am I supposed to say?" I ask him gently . . . I truly am not sure what the correct response is. Is he happy about this, should I say "Congratulations?" Is he upset, should I say, "I'm sorry?" Is it "great" or a "bummer?" I have no idea. Finally I say, "I'm happy if you are happy."

He smiles, "That's the perfect thing to say," and it seems like he means it.

"*Are* you happy?" I ask.

"Yes and no," he admits. "I'm happy that I am finally able to realize why I have always felt like I was 'different,' but it's a hard conclusion to come to and I'm nervous about telling everyone. You're the first one I've told."

Flattery will get him everywhere. I am so touched that he chose to confide in his big sister first.

For the record, I never thought of Logan as being "different." I did, however, notice certain little things, like his decision to go to Yale (where they say one in four, maybe more) and the complete absence of any girls in all his college stories, that prevented me from being shocked by this news. I am completely sure, though, that my parents never

considered it for a second, and while they will be supportive, as they always are, I know they will be disappointed, especially my dad, and I know that will make this hard for
Logan.

"When are you going to tell Mom and Dad?" I ask.

"I thought maybe I would tell everyone at the Labor Day
barbeque."

My heart skips a beat and the most selfish part of me
twinges because that was the day that Justin was going to be
asking Dad for permission to marry me so that my fake engagement could take place the next weekend. I swallow the
self-centeredness and nod at Logan.

"Will it be easier for you to tell the whole family together or in little chunks?"

"I've been thinking a lot about it. My original plan, actually, was to tell everyone at my welcome-home dinner, but I
just wasn't ready for it. It felt so good and comfortable and
the same to be home, and I know once I tell Mom and Dad
that nothing will ever be the same again."

A pang of sadness hits my heart like a bullet. I love
Logan so much and it kills me that he has fears like that . . .
and it kills me even more that he could be right.

"They love you, Logan—I have no doubt that will remain the same."

"Thanks, Moll. I hope."

"I'm sure."

"Molly, when I tell everyone, can you pretend like you've
never heard it? The last thing I need is a competition about
who heard it first, on top of everything else."

"Of course, absolutely," I agree with him. Obviously he
is talking about the Jan Brady of the Harrigan family, but
my mother would also have issues about not being the first
to know.

"Have you thought about when and how you are going
to do it?" I ask him.

"I was thinking I'd wait for dessert to be over. High blood sugar and digestion fatigue seem like they will be on my side."

"I think that's probably a good call," I tell him. (Mental—and extremely selfish—Side Note: Justin needs to talk to Dad as soon as we get there.)

"I dunno, I don't want to think about it any more today. Do you want pie?"

"Duh, do I ever not want pie?"

We laugh, order a slice of apple and a slice of peach to share, and for me anyway, things really don't feel all that "different."

Logan and I take our time at the diner, getting three coffee refills, and then stroll around my neighborhood until the last possible second before he needs to head back to the train station.

On the street, outside my building, he hails a cab and I give him a big hug and kiss.

"I love you, Logan. Don't ever doubt it or forget it."

"Me, too," he says as he climbs in the cab and instructs the driver to take him to Grand Central.

I walk upstairs, kiss my cat hello, and pour myself a glass of wine—I need it.

19

Telling Justin

Justin enters the apartment around eight, still in his waiter uniform carrying a bag of food from the restaurant—yippee! He despises the white shirt and black pants he has to wear to work. I'm convinced that most straight men think it's a perfectly acceptable, even fashionable, outfit, but to Justin, it's like punishment.

"I have news," I tell him.

"I have leftover salmon in a citrus reduction with spinach ponzu."

My mouth waters a little as I grab the bag from him and pull the take-out containers from within. I survey what's there and run to the kitchen to get the appropriate utensils.

"So, what's your news?" he asks as I stuff salmon in my mouth.

I take a deep breath. There is something weird about telling this to Justin, but I have to tell somebody and he's the only one I can.

"My brother came out to me today," I tell him and watch for the surprise . . . which never comes.

"Good for him. I wondered if he was out yet," Justin says calmly.

"You knew?!?"

"Of course I knew. Gaydar. Ever heard of it?"

"It really exists?" I ask, wide-eyed like a child hearing about life on other planets.

"Of course."

"Well, if you knew my brother was gay, why didn't you tell me?"

"First of all, it wasn't anywhere near my place to do so. Second, I thought he was pretty obvious. If you couldn't connect the dots it wasn't my problem."

I'm still shocked that Justin is so calm and matter-of-fact about this.

"He told me first. It's still a secret, so don't say anything. He's going to tell the rest of the family at the Labor Day barbeque."

I watch Justin's reaction carefully, not wanting to show my selfishness if he isn't thinking the same thing.

"Uh-oh . . . that's my day to ask good old Dad for your hand in marriage."

Good, he is. Now it's my turn to be calm.

"No, don't worry. I already asked him what his plan is and he said he's going to do it after dessert. So, as long as you ask Dad as soon as we get there, we're good."

"How do you think your parents are going to take it?" he asks.

"Honestly, I'm not sure. My dad always wanted a son and he was always trying to share the 'guy things' he loves with Logan. I think this will shake him."

Justin gets a slightly hurt look and I am immediately aware of the weirdness of the conversation.

"How did you take it?" he asks.

"I just love my brother—his happiness is all that matters to me."

Justin's face softens a bit.

"He's lucky to have you. He obviously knows that—that's why he told you first."

"I guess," I say, beaming on the inside that Logan feels as close to me as I do to him.

"Poor kid," Justin says. "He's got a rough road ahead of him."

"He does?" I ask. "What else besides telling the family?"

"Telling the world," Justin answers with a small snort. "It's not an easy life, Molly. Manhattan is easier than a lot of places, but not everyone is as forward-thinking as you and I."

I take another shot of pity for my baby brother.

"Maybe he could talk to you? Maybe you could share your experiences with him?"

"Molly. Think about it. How can I talk to Logan about being gay when I'm supposed to be in love and getting engaged to you . . . and presumably heterosexual."

I think for a second. The lie seems so incredibly pathetic and ridiculous in light of this real situation going on.

"I'll tell him the truth. He'll keep our secret."

Justin looks at me, but he doesn't look totally convinced.

"It'll be helpful to have a third person in on it," I add, "and to be honest, it doesn't matter. If being able to help Logan means screwing up our story, it doesn't matter. It's not a time to be selfish."

Justin's face completely softens and he moves from his usual spot on the chair to sit beside me and hug me. I cuddle into his hard chest and we stay snuggled like that for the rest of the evening while we watch TV and eventually doze off.

20

Justin Asks for Molly's Hand

The next week flies by. I get my stuff done at school; my bulletin board is truly a work of art this year—one of the best I've ever seen. My desk is set, and my faces are memorized. I'm ready to go, but still in a certain amount of shock that school starts the day after tomorrow.

As I sit at my dressing table plucking at my forever-uneven eyebrows, I am a bundle of nerves. In a few hours we will be at my parents' house and Justin will be blatantly lying to my father's face as he asks for permission to propose to me. And soon after that, my brother will be rocking their world with the announcement of his homosexuality. Those of us in the know are nervous wrecks.

I think I have spoken to Logan eighty-nine times a day for the last week. And Justin, Mr. Confident Actor, isn't doing much better. Justin did end up agreeing with me that we could let Logan in on our little secret, but thought we should do it after the engagement/coming out. I am fine to wait . . . it gives me more time to think of a way to explain it to Logan without him having me committed on the spot.

As I study my face, I hear Justin clunking around in the bathroom. He has basically moved into the second bedroom. He admits that my place is nicer than his. He lives in Brooklyn with a self-proclaimed "slutty" roommate. Plus, my apartment is also closer to his work. I like the company, so I'm happy to have him around. As he clunks and I pluck, the tension in the apartment is thick; it's shattered like a glass by the ringing of the phone.

"Hello?" I grab it on the second ring.

"Molly, I'm just not ready," Logan tells me. I can tell by his voice that our nerves have nothing on his.

"Yes, you are," I tell my brother, and I am surprised by the confidence in my voice. "You can do it," I encourage.

"Okay," he says.

"We'll be there soon. I love you."

"I love you, too." CLICK.

I know he's ready because most of the eighty-nine calls per day have sounded exactly like that one. During one of the earlier calls I also questioned his readiness, but he assured me that now was the time—he just needed me to reassure him whenever he asked, which is often.

I walk back into my bedroom and look at the sweater set and skirt I have laid out on my bed. It's the third outfit I've laid out today and I'm still not positive it's right. I put the items back in my closet and take out a knee-length denim skirt and a white top. I lay them on the bed, study the look for a minute, and then put it on. I slide my feet into red sandals and tie a red scarf around my brunette ponytail. I'm ready to do it.

I walk out of the bedroom and stick my head in Justin's room . . . funny that I think of that room as his now. He's wearing knee-length khaki shorts, a short-sleeved, button-front shirt, and brown leather sandals. It kind of surprises me that nobody has questioned me about his sexuality because he would undoubtedly be the best-dressed straight man in Manhattan.

"You ready?" he asks me.

"Whenever you are."

He nods his head and walks out of the room, toward me. Hand in hand, we exit my apartment and head for the country.

We do the usual meeting with Jamie and Bryan to take the train together, but it's hard to act like nothing is going on in front of them when such major stuff is happening.

Luckily the train is not crowded today and all four of us get seats, with Jamie and me by the windows and our significant others beside us. I try to let Jamie distract me with her tales of the problems of finding fashionable maternity clothes and her fear that she will pee her pants at school. Apparently she read somewhere that pregnant women lose bladder control and Jamie, being Jamie, is not afraid of the labor and delivery of something the size of a watermelon through something the size of a peanut, but is terrified that she will pee on herself. I must admit, she does do a pretty good job of getting my mind off what is to come that evening; before I know it, the train is in Connecticut and a few stops later we are getting off.

As always, my dad is waiting for us on the platform with his warm smile and open arms, and as always, Jamie and I run into his embrace like we are seven and ten . . . not twenty-seven and thirty. When we finally let go of him, he turns to the boys and gives each of them a hug. I sneak a smile at Justin and he is grinning back at me because this is the first time that Dad has hugged him hello. So far, things are going well for us. I just hope they are going as well for Logan.

As we drive the short distance to our house, I can't help but be in awe of all the beautiful leaves changing to their fall colors. Fall has always been my favorite time of year . . . especially in the country. It always feels like a fresh start—that must be a teacher thing because the new school year starts—

and I love all the beautiful colors and changes that happen in nature. We pull down our long driveway and pile out. I can feel that the air is starting to get crisper than it was just a few weeks ago when we were last out here.

As always, the house greets us with the wonderful smells of the feast to come. Mom comes out of the kitchen and pecks us each quickly on the cheek before rushing back to tend to a timer going off.

"Where's Logan?" I call after her.

"He's in the back with Brad. They're playing with Skipper," she yells from the other room.

Brad is here!! I stiffen and tensely look from Justin to Jamie . . . they both know about the recent conflicts, but apparently I'd failed to fill Mom in so she included him, as she always does, for holiday things.

Dad hangs up his keys on the key peg I helped him make (more like supervised) when I was eight and offers drinks.

"I'll have a glass of white wine, please," I say.

"Gosh . . . I miss wine," Jamie complains.

If wine was so important you shouldn't have gotten pregnant, I cattily say to myself . . . don't worry, I swear it was to myself. I'm trying to get past my awful jealousy and so far I've been doing pretty well.

"Can I have apple juice in a wineglass?" she asks like a little kid.

Dad just smiles at her and then looks at the boys.

"Why don't I help you get the drinks, Mr. Harrigan, and the others can head outside to see Logan. I know how the girls are always dying to see him."

"Justin. For the umpteenth time, call me Larry. And that's a lovely gesture. You all get yourselves comfy on the deck and we'll be out with the drinks soon."

I sneak a peek and a nervous smile at Justin. My stomach now feels like I swallowed a hive of bumblebees . . . I'm about to burst . . . I'm practically tingling all over. Thankfully, neither Jamie nor Bryan protests and the three of us head outside, leaving Justin with Dad.

We walk onto the deck and holler hellos down to Logan and Skipper (and Brad), who are playing fetch in the yard. As soon as Skipper sees us, she comes flying up the steps and exhausts herself completely trying to greet three people at one time. Logan and Brad follow her trail pretty closely. Logan greets me warmly and I give him a big, hard hug and an extra shoulder squeeze as we pull away. He then turns to Jamie and gives her a hug as well.

"Look at me!" Jamie exclaims, thrusting her protruding belly forward.

"Jeez, James . . . that thing seems to be growing—have you consulted a physician?"

Everyone giggles at Logan's joke. Then I turn to Brad.

"Hey there," I say. Being face-to-face with Brad forces me to deal with the sadness I've been suppressing.

"Hi, Molly," he replies and I think I sense the same longing in his voice. "Where's Justin?" he asks gently.

"He's inside getting drinks for everyone, with Dad," I answer, and I can visibly see him stiffen when he learns that Justin is not only still in the picture, but also on the property.

"Where's Claire?" Jamie pipes up from behind me.

"She's in Paris for the weekend trying on wedding dresses."

I can hear Jamie holding down a gag. I turn around to face her, with my back to Brad, and roll my eyes. We then make ourselves comfortable on the deck—the opposite side from Brad, who is chatting with Bryan (who apparently hasn't been kept up to date on the recent events, either), but I notice that Brad is definitely keeping one eye on me. This night is huge in a lot of ways and I'm not going to let him mess it up.

A short time passes and still no Dad or Justin. I would give my right eye to be listening to their conversation. The anticipation is literally killing me. I can only imagine how Logan must be feeling.

"Maybe I should go in and see about those drinks?" Brad offers.

"NO!" I shout, uncontrollably. Everyone looks at me a little strangely. "I'm sure they're fine," I add, trying to regain my composure.

"What if they need help carrying stuff?" he asks.

"Mom has about a million trays," I hiss at him. I swear, it's like he has a sense of what is going on and wants to ruin it! "Jamie," I say, turning to her, "tell Logan about those funny maternity outfits you were talking about on the train." I figure they distracted me, maybe they'll help him, too.

"Logan doesn't care about those," she says, which is probably true.

"Of course he does," I answer for him, since he is so brutally honest that he would probably confess that he didn't give a crap about her maternity clothes woes.

Jamie is retelling an anecdote about a conversation she had with another pregnant woman at the Pea in the Pod dressing room about turquoise maternity pants when Dad and Justin walk onto the deck with a tray (told you so) of wine and beer and apple juice in a wineglass. They are both beaming ear to ear—I catch Justin's eye and my own lips can't help but spread toward my ears as well.

"All right, gang," Dad says as he spreads around the drink orders, "here you go."

Everyone thanks him and we sit back on the comfortable deck furniture and watch the sun begin to set. Jamie, of course, picks up right where she left off.

"I mean, can you believe it? Turquoise pants wouldn't be flattering on the skinniest woman, and they want pregnant women to wear them?"

Nobody really responds to her question and she gives up, sitting back with her juice. Bryan strokes her head. It's so sweet the way he adores her . . . and doesn't want to murder her when she goes on and on about ridiculous things. He's amazing at appreciating who she is. Justin joins me on my lounge chair and secretly gives me a thumbs-up. I smile at him, but feel like I'm being watched. I look across the deck and see Brad staring icily at us. I give him a quick scowl before turning back to Justin.

A little while later, Mom hollers for help setting the table and I jump up, followed by Justin . . . and Brad.

"That's okay, man, I got it," Justin says nicely to Brad. Brad just scowls again and sits back down.

As we head into the house to help Mom, I take a second to ask Justin how it went.

"Incredibly perfect," he says. "You're going to die when you see what your dad gave me."

"What?!?" I ask, unable to take the suspense.

Justin puts his hand in his pocket and holds out the exact engagement ring I had fallen in love with at Tiffany's. I can hardly breathe . . . I'm shocked and excited, but most of all, confused.

"Where did that come from?" I ask.

"It was your grandmother's," he answers.

My eyes fill with tears as I finger the perfect solitaire diamond. Justin quickly snatches it back.

"Not yet, Miss Molly. Your dad actually hoped that I would propose tonight in front of the whole family, which would have been a great idea and a great story. But I couldn't do that to Logan . . . so I just said I already had something really special planned for how to ask you."

I squeal with delight and give Justin a quick hug before heading into the kitchen where Mom is waiting. He grabs my arm and pulls me back for a bigger hug.

"I really do adore you, Molly."

"Me, too."

Of course neither of us means it in *that way* . . . we've just grown to be the closest of friends and we both realize that friendship can often be even better than a romantic relationship. Things couldn't be better . . . right about now, my plan feels downright brilliant.

21

Logan Comes Out

Dinner is lovely, but strange. I'm a combustible combination of excited beyond belief about Justin's conversation with Dad and the ring and a complete nervous wreck for Logan's revelation . . . the blend has me acting completely goofy. Justin is a milder version of me. Jamie, as always, is doing anything and everything possible to keep the attention for herself, including yelling, "Oh my God! Did I just pee a little?!?" as Mom serves the salad.

Bryan is, as always, happily sitting by, never threatening Jamie's spotlight for even an instant. Logan is uncharacteristically silent . . . although nobody seems to notice but me, so I wonder if I'm just imagining things. Dad is extra jolly and so is Mom, so I assume he told her about his conversation with Justin. Brad is silent and still staring at me. It's starting to creep me out.

We mow through the salad, ribs, corn, garlic bread, and baked beans until there isn't a drop left. Then Jamie (much to her dismay, "I'm pregnant!" and my insistence, "Pregnant, not handicapped") and I clear the table and bring out the dessert. Suddenly everyone has found just a little extra room for Mom's peach cobbler. Mom always complains that we never let her make anything else, but we insist that once you have found perfection, there is no need to fool with it.

We dish up the cobbler and ice cream and pour coffee for those who want it and milk for the rest and we are about halfway through when Logan clears his throat.

"I have something I need to tell you all," he says with a prepubescent crackle.

"What's that?" Dad asks warmly.

Justin takes a deep breath and looks at me. A wave of nausea washes over me and I want to stop him. I want to send him to the other room and break the news for him so he doesn't have to see any looks of disappointment or anger or who knows what . . . I want to save him from any second of pain, but I can't.

"As you all know," he begins slowly, "I had a wonderful time in Italy, but the purpose of the trip was to find myself. And I did."

"You're going to go to graduate school, aren't you?" Jamie yells out, "I should have gone to graduate school."

Let me tell you, if looks could kill, Jamie would be dead now. She catches my glare and shuts up.

"No, James, I'm not going to grad school," Logan says kindly. "I'm gay."

Silence.

More silence.

I look around the table and see my mother's eyes filling with tears. My father is biting his bottom lip and staring at his cobbler. Jamie looks confused, and Bryan (of course) looks concerned about Jamie. Brad continues to look at me, but I think his stare has slightly changed.

"I'm happy if you're happy!" I say loudly, repeating what Logan had told me was the right thing to say at our lunch last week.

He looks up at me with the most grateful eyes I've ever seen. "Thank you, Molly."

"I'm sorry, sweetheart," my mother says, and I'm not sure if she's saying it to Logan or to Dad. They both nod.

I am about to burst into tears looking at Logan hang his head in shame for being honest about who he is.

"Daddy," I command, "say something to him."

My father looks up at me, still avoiding Logan's eye. "What am I supposed to say?"

"Tell him you love him," I command.

My father's face lightens with the relief of knowing what to do. "Of course I love you, son. Nothing could change that."

Logan looks up and his eyes fill with tears. "Thanks, Dad."

"Of course, of course," my mother adds.

"Obviously us, too," Jamie says for herself and Bryan. Bryan does nod his head in agreement.

Suddenly, everyone is talking at once, offering words of encouragement and support for Logan, and his face is lighting back up to its normal hundred-watt sparkle. Everyone except Dad, that is. Dad pushes back from his chair and stands up.

"Son, I will always love you the same, but I need some time to deal with this."

Then he slowly walks out of the room and my mother goes flying after him. Logan's face goes crashing down once again.

"Hey, Loge, it's okay. He's gonna deal with it," I say.

"Seriously, man," Justin adds, "it took you twenty-three years and a trip to Italy. You gotta give him some time."

I'm impressed with Justin's wisdom, but then again, duh . . . he's been through this, and everyone agrees with what he says. Mom comes back into the room and walks up behind Logan. She puts her arms around his neck and gives him a tight hug.

"We're disappointed, Loge. Not in you, just with the situation. But we really do love you as much as ever and we're gonna work through this."

She kisses his cheek and heads back to Dad.

Brad takes this as his cue to exit.

"I'd better escort you off the property," I say, our running (although lame) joke, and get to my feet before remembering that things aren't like this with Brad and me anymore.

Once I'm standing, though, I have no choice but to walk him to the door. In silence, I lead as we walk through the dining room, living room, and foyer. We finally arrive at the front door and are standing face-to-face.

"Molly, you're a wonderful sister," he says kindly, putting his hand on my cheek. It feels so normal for him to be doing this that the weirdness between us is temporarily erased.

"He deserves the best," I say as I take his hand off my cheek and kiss it. "Don't you need a ride to the train station?"

"No, that's okay . . . I drove Claire's car up here."

I come screeching back to reality and drop his hand . . . for a few seconds there, I'd been able to forget that Claire Reilly existed.

"Okay, then. Drive safely," I say as I open the front door and then close it behind him.

I walk directly back to the dining room. Everyone is exactly where I left them, so I ask my brother, "Wanna spend the night in the city?" hoping that getting him out of the house will do everyone some good.

"Yes, I do," he says gratefully.

The four of us accompany Logan to his room to pack a bag and I leave for just a second to tell Mom and Dad that he's coming with me . . . and we're taking their car. They are grateful . . . I'm not sure if they are grateful that I'm getting him out of their house or that I am taking care of his needs . . . maybe both. When I get back to his room, his bag is packed and the five of us head out. We pile into the green Explorer, with Justin behind the wheel, and drive back to Manhattan. The car is quiet as the Manhattan skyline approaches, but there is a closeness among the people in the car.

22

Time to Get Engaged

The night that Logan was to stay at my apartment turned into a week . . . so far. As happy as I was to have him there and be able to help him (and Mom and Dad), the week coincides with my first week of school, which makes it exceptionally hectic. Between twenty-seven third graders and one recently out of the closet twenty-three-year-old, I feel like I am caring for people twenty-four hours a day, which I suppose I am. Things are so hectic that I actually forget about the engagement, which is supposed to take place on Saturday. I talk to Justin almost every night, but with Logan always sitting a few feet away, we can never discuss plans.

On Saturday morning, I wake up early . . . once I'm in early-rising school mode, I don't stop for weekends. I quietly pad into the living room and pick up a stack of school papers that need correcting. It is a generic "What I did over the summer" essay, which I know isn't the most creative assignment, but it's so much fun to read how the most privileged children in Manhattan spent their break, and it's a really good way to assess everyone's writing skills.

I'm in the middle of reading about Carter's trip to Nepal when my stomach begins to rumble. I take a short break from the part about the flight on the family jet where the flight attendant spilled orange juice on Carter's nanny (poor girl) to get some OJ and a bowl of Cheerios for myself. I happily munch away as Carter describes the car from the airport, the train he rode on, and a bike he saw in the town. It's well written for an eight-year-old, but I have to roll my eyes at the fact that his parents took him around the world and the things that really stuck out in his mind were the things he sees in the city every day: planes, trains, automobiles, and bikes.

"Do you wish you spent your summer in Nepal?" I foolishly ask my cat, who meows a scolding at me for being so silly.

I am on to Gabriella's essay about the month she spent at Dragonfly Camp in Cape Cod and have to admit I'm shocked that parents would send an eight-year-old away for a whole month, but I can tell from her writing that she loved it, so I guess it works for them. She's describing a large bug she saw on a nature walk when the phone rings. I grab it at the speed of light to catch it before a second ring that would definitely wake Logan up.

"Hello?" I whisper.

"Molly? Did I wake you up?" Justin asks.

"No," I reply hoarsely.

"Are you sick?"

"No," I whisper again. "Logan is sleeping."

"Gotcha. Throw on your cute sweats and meet me at our place."

I look at the stack on the coffee table and decide a break from being jealous of little children's summers is probably not a bad idea.

"Okay," I agree. "I'll be there in twenty minutes." CLICK.

I silently pad to the bathroom and close the door. Meeting Justin this morning will be the perfect private time to finalize our now-delayed engagement plan. I go through my morning routine: face washing, tooth brushing, moisturizer application, etc., as noiselessly as possible, but as always seems to be the case when I am trying to be quiet, I bump into things and knock things over. I finally emerge from the bathroom and am shocked that I can still hear Logan's soft snore from the other room. I scribble a quick note to Logan and tape it to the TV screen where I know he will see it; he's spent most of the week at my apartment sleeping and watching TV. I pour a little more kibble in Tiffany's dish and head out the door, scooping my hair into a sloppy ponytail as I go.

When I get to Starbucks, Justin is already waiting at our favorite table (by the window—it's best for people-watching) with my favorite breakfast (a nonfat latte and a pumpkin scone) in hand.

"Good morning, Sunshine!" he greets me with a kiss on the head. "How's our boy doing?" he asks, regarding Logan.

"Same," I admit. Part of the reason I never got around to talking to Justin about the engagement plan is that any second I did have alone on the phone with him I was telling him about Logan's behavior and trying to gain insight.

"That's okay, this is new . . . it's gonna take time," Justin reassures me for the umpteenth time this week.

"Thank you for this," I say as I pick up the coffee. I take a big drink . . . so yummy. "So, what's going on with you?"

"Not much," Justin says.

We chat, as only we can do, about Justin's week at the restaurant, an audition he went on and a callback he got, my week at school, and Logan's situation, for over an hour. Finally, Justin looks down at my scone, still in the Starbucks bag.

"Aren't you going to eat your scone?"

"I'm going to save it for later. I had a bowl of Cheerios this morning."

"Since when does a bowl of Cheerios fill you up?"

I think about that for a second . . . that's true, it never has. And then I notice that my stomach *is* feeling a little on the empty side. Whenever I stop and pay attention to my stomach, I notice that it is a little on the empty side.

"Yes, you're right," I say as I pull the scone out of the bag. As I set the scone on a napkin, there it is. Nana's stunning ring is sticking out of the icing.

"Oh my God!" I squeal.

"This is it, Molly," Justin tells me with a big, warm smile.

"This is it," I parrot.

I carefully take the ring from the scone, using both thumbs and both index fingers, and hold it up. My eyes fill with tears—it's such a beautiful ring, and I can still see it on Nana's perfectly manicured finger.

"How's this for a story?" Justin asks me quietly.

"It's perfect," I say and look up at him with my tearful but grateful eyes.

"You want to put it on?" he asks.

"Yes!" I almost shout.

He slips the ring on my finger and the entire Starbucks bursts into applause. (They must have thought that I was saying yes in response to "Will you marry me?" not, "Do you want to put the ring on?") I jump, unaware that anyone had noticed what we were doing. People start calling out congratulations and the Barista brings us two little cups of sparkling apple cider to toast with. My cheeks are blazing, but I love it. Justin and I toast the little paper cups and then stand up and he grabs me in a tight embrace. The crowd cheers once again and I pull back a little and look into his deep brown eyes.

"Here we go," I say.

23

Molly Is Finally Engaged

"**O**h my God, oh my God, oh my God," I say as I stare at my hand. It's so hard to believe that it has actually happened. Wearing the ring on *the* finger has become a complete distraction, and I cannot seem to do anything but look at my hand and say, "Oh my God."

I've been fake-engaged for two hours and I am still in a complete state of shock. I'd been planning and waiting for thirty years for the moment I got engaged; then, after it happened, I realized I have no clue what to do the next instant. Am I supposed to call friends and relatives? Or just skip the phone company middleman and yell if from the rooftops? Who do I call first? What do I do first? Despite all my preparation, I hadn't made a plan past the ring being put on my finger! So far, all I've been able to do is smile ear-to-ear and look at my hand.

When Justin and I left the Starbucks, we went for a walk in the park to try to figure out the next step, but we were both so distracted by our excitement. Who could have predicted that the entire coffee shop would have gotten in on the action? They cheered for us, they offered their congratulations, and the employees showered us with complimentary baked goods and sparkling cider. It's a story that rivals many of the most impressive and romantic stories I've heard.

Two hours later, I'm still admiring my left hand, but realize that it's time we figure some stuff out.

"Who should we tell first?" Justin asks.

I think about it . . . my head is a swimming pool filled with names of my nearest and dearest. Do I tell my mother? My sister? My father? My brother? That's it . . . I stop at Logan because he is the one I need to tell first. After all, he's not only staying at my apartment and will see the ring on my hand when I walk through the door, but he told me first when he came out. The tricky thing about telling Logan, though, is that I intend to tell him the truth . . . the whole truth.

Justin and I head back to the apartment and find Logan, as expected, sitting on the couch watching TV.

"Logan," I say. "We need to talk to you."

Logan looks up from the TV and immediately spots the ring on my finger.

"Oh my gosh, you guys," he says, clearly trying hard to feign enthusiasm.

"Yes . . . no . . . but it's not what you think," I stop him. "You need to sit down."

I start all the way back at the very beginning . . . my birthday, my breakdown, and Justin's ad. Justin and I explain about our business arrangement and the three-part plan: whirlwind romance, engagement, and wedding.

"But Logan," I say, "you are the only one besides the two of us who knows the truth and we're trusting you with it."

Logan looks at us like we are both completely insane . . . which we may very well be.

"Why are you doing this?" he asks us.

"It's me," I explain. "It was my decision. I'm tired of always being a bridesmaid and never being a bride . . . and having to hear about it. All my friends have gotten to be brides and be celebrated and I want to experience that."

"But you guys are the perfect couple . . . you really seem like you love each other."

"We do love each other!" Justin jumps in. "We have become wonderful friends—we love each other as friends."

I feel slightly like a parent having to explain a divorce to a small child . . . except that we're not married or breaking up and Logan's not a small child. He does stare at us blankly like a child, though, and I know none of this makes any sense to him.

"Oh!" I jump in, realizing he needs to understand one more important element to kind of get this, "Justin is gay."

"You're gay?" Logan asks Justin.

Apparently in the short time he has been out, he has not had a chance to hone his own gaydar skills yet.

"Yes. That's why Molly felt really strongly that you should know the truth . . . so that you could talk to me and I could help you with what you're going through . . . since I've been through it myself."

"Does it make sense now?" I ask him.

"Not really," he admits. "Molly, why do you think you have to do this?"

"I don't have to. I want to. It's my decision."

"And how did you find Justin, again?"

"An ad in the *Village Voice*," I say, somewhat sheepishly.

"But isn't that Nana's engagement ring?" he says, pointing at my finger.

"Yes. Justin asked Dad for permission to propose and Dad gave it to him."

"But why did you ask our dad for permission to marry Molly when you're gay?" he says in Justin's direction.

"Because Molly has hired me to spend the entire year pretending to be her boyfriend and fiancé. You are the only person who will ever know the truth besides us," Justin patiently explains.

"So you're doing it for the wedding?" Logan asks, and I can't tell if he is starting to get it in a supportive way or in an I'm-going-to-call-for-a-straightjacket way.

"Well, yes . . ." I admit. "I'm using the wedding money that Nana left me. She wanted me to have my dream wedding, you know."

Logan nods vaguely. Listening to the whole situation explained makes my stomach sick. It makes me realize how pathetic and disgusting I am. I am on the verge of just calling the entire thing off when Logan says, "Okay, I think I can get it . . . kind of. I'm happy if you're happy," he says to me and smiles kindly.

"Thank you," I tell him with my words and my eyes.

"So, you're gay, too?" Logan says, turning to Justin.

"Yes."

Justin and Logan spend the rest of the evening talking and I decide to take a bubble bath, relax, and not think about the "plan" for the rest of the night. I think I am still comfortable with my decision, although explaining it was a shameful experience. Dressed in my most comfortable pajamas, I stick my head into the living room just before I climb into bed. The boys are still talking.

"You guys doing okay?" I ask.

"Definitely," they both agree.

"Loge," I say, "you're gonna keep our secret, right?"

"Of course," he answers. "You guys are here for me and I'm gonna return the favor—even though I think you're both insane."

I smile and nod . . . that's all I can ask for.

24

Shouting It from the Rooftops

I wake up the next morning and am surprised how well I slept. I thought I would be too nervous or too excited, but I guess after such an exhausting week nothing was holding me back. I creep into the living room, half believing that Logan and Justin will still be where I left them and still be talking. They aren't, though. Logan is gone, presumably in his bed, and Justin is stretched out—as best he can—and hanging over the couch.

I cross the room and sneak into the kitchen to get the coffee going. Once I have a full mug in my hand, I tiptoe up to Justin and gently shake him awake. His eyes open, partially, and I hold up the coffee cup so he can see it.

"Coffee," I whisper.

He makes a small grunt, pushes himself up to a sitting position, and stretches. His bones make some disturbing cracking noises as he takes the mug from me.

"You know this couch pulls out to a bed, don't you?"

"No, I wasn't aware," a grumpy Justin answers.

Normally in the mornings I wait for Justin's coffee to kick in before I speak to him, but today I cannot wait.

"How did last night go? How's Logan?"

Justin takes a big, slow gulp of the coffee before fully opening his eyes and looking at me.

"I think he's doing as well, or better, than anyone else in his situation. You made the right decision to tell him the truth—it was very unselfish of you. I feel like talking to me helped him a lot. He said it did, anyway."

I am overwhelmed with relief. I had been worrying about Logan from the second he told me his news. Now that I feel like Logan is definitely going to be okay and I know I have Justin on his side, I turn my attention to spreading the fake word about the fake engagement. I start with my mother because I realize she'll never forgive me if she isn't first— plus, I'm sure Dad told her about his conversation with Justin, which means for a week she's been waiting by the phone for my call.

I give Justin a hug good-bye at the door (he's going home to try to catch a few hours' sleep in a normal bed before he does a lunch shift) and then pick up the cordless and dial my mother. She answers on the first ring, so I guess I wasn't that far off when I said she'd been sitting by the phone, waiting for my call.

"Mommy . . . " I taunt her.

"Yes?" she plays the game back.

"Guess what happened yesterday?"

"I have no idea. Why don't you tell me?"

"Come on," I urge, "guess."

"I can't. You tell me."

Finally I end her suspense. "I'm engaged!"

"I know you are!" she cheers.

It's both thrilling and dismaying how excited my mom is. In the week she's known it was coming, she's already started wedding planning. She has location suggestions for me to look at, florists for me to talk to, dress styles for me to con- sider. All that is the thrilling part . . . what is the dismaying part is the little angel on my right shoulder constantly re-

minding me that I am a liar, liar, pants on fire. I allow the
devil on my left shoulder to shush the angel and I resolve to
enjoy my moment.

My mom really has been working on this project already,
so I spend a good half an hour on the phone with her, hearing about everything that she has researched. *And*, she's
made an appointment for us to look at the banquet room at
The Plaza hotel next Saturday at three, since when I was a
little girl I always said I wanted to get married there. The
fact that she remembers this brings a tear to my eye, the fact
that it might actually happen brings the tear rolling down
my cheek. We chat, excitedly, a little longer until I convince
her that I have to get off so that I can tell other people,
namely Jamie.

When Jamie answers, I immediately say, "I'm engaged,"
and she immediately squeals and screams and then reassures
Bryan that she is totally fine.

"Oh my God, I can't believe it. I'm so happy for you!"
she gushes.

"Thank you," I say, beaming through the phone line.

"Uh-oh, when will the wedding be?" she asks.

Why "uh-oh," I think to myself. "The end of June, June
30th," I say, cautiously.

"Oh, thank goodness . . . the baby will be born! I was
afraid it was going to be when I was really huge and there
would be a risk I would pee during the ceremony."

Jeez, again with the pee fear.

"No, don't worry," I say patronizingly. "You'll be back to
normal, and I want you to be my maid of honor."

"Matron of honor," she corrects me before agreeing to
it.

"Do you know how many bridesmaids you're going to
have?" Jamie asks.

"I've been thinking just you," I tell her.

The truth is that a) I'm not a big fan of big wedding parties . . . sometimes it can start looking a little crowded up there, and b) I would feel too guilty making a ton of my friends buy dresses for a fake wedding . . . even though nobody but me, Justin, and Logan will ever know it's fake. Plus, c) I've been in so many people's weddings that to select a small group from all those girls would be sure to hurt feelings, whereas just having my sister avoids it. And, d) it turns out that my sister is *extremely* touched by this.

"Just me? Molly, I'm so honored. I promise you that I will be the best Matron of Honor ever."

"Thank you, Jamie . . . I know you will be."

And the truth is that I really do believe that she will be. It is the ideal job for her. She loves weddings and anything to do with them. She's creative and generous, plus her love of the spotlight will work perfectly because she'll like the attention of throwing showers and planning bachelorette parties. She loves to be in charge. And it's an added bonus that I know she has good taste, since her own wedding was stunning.

Jamie and Bryan got married at Bryan's family's country club on Long Island. It was a fantastic location, made worlds better by Jamie's meticulous flower selections, insistence on far more votive candles than anyone on earth thought necessary, and one of the best wedding bands I've ever heard. She looked more beautiful than I'd ever seen her in a white chiffon, strapless, gown, which was perfect for her petite frame. It was floor-length and flowed perfectly when she walked and danced. She even chose the only bridesmaid's dress I have ever worn and not only not hated, but wore again (to my friend Sabrina's wedding later that summer)! It was also chiffon and strapless, but hit just below the knee in a stunning grass green color. I actually still have it—not in the dress graveyard, but hanging in my closet!

"Have you started thinking about your dress?" she asks as I am remembering hers.

"Honestly, no," and I can't help but giggle, because I have thought about my wedding dress practically every day of my life, except the one and a half I've been engaged. "I mean, I have an idea of what I want just from seeing dresses on other people and walking through Barney's bridal department every time I am near the store, but I haven't given it serious thought yet."

"How about me? What should I wear?"

"Gosh, I hadn't thought about it yet. What do you want to wear?"

I'd never been able to nail down a bridesmaid's dress style, color, etc., that I wanted. I know it wouldn't be big, or ugly . . . but then did any of these brides who had tortured me realize they were doing it?

"Maybe something similar to what I wore in yours?" I offer, tentatively . . . Jamie's always sensitive about people "copying" her.

"Mine were stunning, weren't they?" she replies confidently.

Her modesty amuses me.

"You should pick your dress first, though," she explains expertly, "so that my neckline will compliment yours . . . it'll look better in pictures."

I nod . . . that makes sense. I can tell that while Jamie will be annoying at times, no doubt about it, she will also be a wealth of information. She gives me a list of book titles I need to pick up, and another list of things that I need to accomplish immediately, and makes me promise to call and check in with biweekly updates before she will hang up. As I set the phone back on its cradle, I'm smiling ear to ear.

I flip through my phone book and call all the important friends and relatives (the ones Mom hasn't already gotten to, anyway) and share the exciting news. I graciously accept their "Congratulations" and "Best wishes," and answer questions about Justin and any plans made so far. All in all, it's a pretty fun way to spend the morning. There is only one downer . . . I keep flipping past Brad's name and I'm not quite sure what to do about it.

Should I call him? Are we on speaking terms? Will we ever be on speaking terms again? I haven't heard from him (and, obviously he hasn't heard from me) since the awkward night of Logan's outing, but I decide to, once again, be the bigger, better person and I dial his cell (I said bigger and better . . . not braver), hoping that on a Sunday he'd be busy at some sporting event and I could leave a generic message. No such luck.

"Hello?" he answers.

"Hi, Brad . . . it's Molly," I say, awkwardly.

"Oh, Molly. Hi," he replies stiffly. "I meant to call you, to see how Logan is doing . . . but . . ."

"Right," I cut in. "He's doing okay. Thanks for asking."

"Sure."

"That's actually not why I called you."

"Oh, what's up?" he asks cautiously.

"I'm engaged."

After a long beat of silence, he says, "Really?"

That's right . . . not "Congratulations," not "Best wishes," not even, "Wow." "Really?" A question.

"Really," I confirm.

"I guess that makes you happy."

"Yes, really happy," I reply defensively. "We're getting married June 30."

He snorts, "You've gotta be kidding me."

"No. We've set our date."

"And you've set it for one week before my wedding. Nice, Molly."

Oops . . . totally an oversight. I hadn't thought at all about when Claire and Brad were tying the knot when Justin and I agreed that the last weekend in June seemed like the perfect time.

"I guess so. Is that a problem?"

"I guess not. Well, congratulations. I have to go now."

"Thanks," I say, but before it's completely out of my mouth I hear CLICK.

I shake my head a little . . . that was weird. Could have been better, could have been worse . . . couldn't have been weirder.

I decide that I've done enough spreading of the good news for one day and snuggle into my big couch with the remainder of the summer vacation essays.

25

Brunch With the Girls

The next week flies by. Logan has remained a permanent fixture on my couch and I'm pretty convinced that he has decided to move in, permanently, without informing anyone. Every evening he and Justin talk, endlessly, and I whisper on the phone to my mother the updates of how I think he is doing. I think he's talked to Mom a few times, and maybe to Dad once. Mom has not asked me when he's coming home, though, and he hasn't mentioned going back there. Justin has either slept on the pull-out sofa, or taken a cab back to Brooklyn after midnight when they are finally talked out.

Outside of the apartment, things have been hectic as well. Going to school on Monday and sharing my exciting news with all my co-workers was as much fun as I always thought it would be. Everyone oohed and aahed as I held my hand out for them to admire my ring. And my little students were all very excited that their teacher was going to be a bride, especially the little girls who are at an age when Barbie Bride is hot and weddings are already starting to be on the mind. I must admit that I felt a specific type of awful, lying to a room of eight-year-olds, but obviously they will never be scarred by what I'm doing, so it's okay. I just try to keep out of my head that I am technically supposed to be a role model for them.

So far, it seems like I have a great group of students this year. They have moved at top speed through my lesson plans, which is a good thing, but it also means that my evenings are spent adding to the next day's teaching and devising new ways of keeping them interested and involved. Between trying to keep an eye on Logan, dealing with my mother, and doing *my* homework, I've hardly had time to think about anything else.

On Saturday, I awake early and jump into the shower before either of the boys stirs. Today is my monthly "girls' morning out." I meet Alex, Lauren, and Maggie at a coffee shop where we used to go to for hangover breakfasts in college. I am especially excited for this month's breakfast because for the first time ever, I won't be the lone single girl! I am certain that Lauren will be bouncing off the walls since her wedding is now a few weeks away, but now that I am also engaged, I don't feel the jealous pangs I used to. I'm excited to hear all of her details because I need to start planning some of my own. Plus, Maggie was just married a couple of months ago, so she should also be a wealth of information.

I'm out the door before the boys even stir and am the first one to arrive at the café, so I put our name in. It's become a popular and trendy breakfast spot over the years, which we credit ourselves with, but since we've been coming for so long, people know us and our wait is generally much less than the average two hours that so many New Yorkers are willing to wait for a cup of coffee and an omelet.

By the time the other three girls arrive, our table is being set and we are led in, followed by grumbles of "We got here before them," and "I thought this place didn't take reservations." I love the VIP feeling as we sit down and four mugs of coffee are immediately set in front of us. The reaching and grabbing for whole milk, cream, half-and-half, nonfat milk, sugar, raw sugar, and Sweet 'n Low—not Equal—begins and ends before Alex finally cries out, "Let us see your ring!"

I flash a beaming smile as I hold my hand over the table and try to look modest. I can tell by their reactions that they really do love the ring. This isn't a crowd to sugarcoat things. If they didn't like it, I would know.

"It's stunning," Alex declares authoritatively.

"Thank you," I gush as I replace my hand in my lap.

"So," Maggie pipes in, "how do you like being engaged so far?"

"So far it's been wonderful . . . it's only been a week."

"I thought being engaged was the greatest thing ever," Alex admits.

"Me, too," Maggie agrees.

"Same here," Lauren adds. "I'm starting to feel disappointed that it's almost over."

The girls laugh and giggle about all the wonders and romance of being engaged. They talk about the princesslike experiences of their showers and dress fittings and champagne tasting; I listen carefully to every detail, and my excitement grows that I will finally be experiencing all this wonder.

"And engaged sex is the best sex!" Alex bursts out.

I'm a little shocked, but the other three girls immediately jump in with their agreement.

"I've only had sex nine times since I got married," Maggie confesses, "and five of those were on the honeymoon."

"Ugh," Alex agrees, "and when you do have sex it's like, 'Quick, hon . . . SportsCenter's on a commercial.'"

"But when you're engaged," Lauren gushes with a glow

about her, "it's all about romance and being together. It's even better now than it was in the very beginning!"

"Don't you think, Molly?" Maggie asks me.

"Oh, absolutely." I try to gush like Lauren had, terrified that they are seeing right through me.

"Yours must be amazing," Lauren adds, "because you got engaged so quickly. So it's new sex *and* engaged sex in one. And obviously Justin is romantic to fall so head over heels and get engaged so quickly."

"Definitely," I agree lamely, "Justin is so romantic, it's just wonderful, every day of the week."

"EVERY DAY?!?" they all gasp in unison, jaws hanging open.

"Sometimes twice a day!" I lay it on thick.

They respond with shocked-and jealous-sounding gurgles and chokes.

"Well, it's like you said . . . new sex and engaged sex."

While I realize I may have taken things a little far with the details of my fake sex life, part of me is rather pleased . . . my fake sex life is better than their real ones! *Ha*, I think to myself, and I feel pretty smug about the situation. Having sex with a hot guy twice a day might be a fantasy for me, but that's what my whole fake wedding is about—living out my fantasy . . . I might as well live it up.

After a while, the girls move on to other engagement topics. Lauren tells us about the last-minute fires she's putting out. Stuff like welcome bags for out-of-town guests, pedicure polish color decisions, and seating chart assignments. I take a million mental notes on everything the three girls say, but I must admit, I feel a little overwhelmed.

"You okay, little one?" Alex says to me.

"Yes, definitely . . . just trying to take it all in. There's so much."

The three experienced girls giggle.

"Don't worry," Maggie explains. You just need to get a guide book—it lays out for you what needs to happen. You go by that schedule, and you're in good shape."

"A guide book," I say, nodding in understanding. That does make sense.

"Exactly," Lauren joins in. "I'm using Martha Stewart's list, 'cause you know how much I love her, insider trading or not."

"Oh yeah," I agree. "I adore her, too. Where do I get her list?"

"Her book, her Web site, her magazine . . . silly Molly," Maggie laughs at me.

I'm starting to wish I'd brought a notepad to this brunch! By the time we leave we've had way too many cups of coffee, too many eggs, too much toast, and an ungodly amount of potatoes . . . not to mention too many waiting patrons giving us stink-eye for taking our time. We walk out onto the sidewalk and give our hugs and kisses good-bye. Then we each go our separate direction—that's another good thing about this nostalgic breakfast location: it is also pretty central for all of us who live spread across the city now.

My head is kind of spinning from all the information I've gathered in the last two and a half hours. I wander up the street a few blocks and come across a newspaper stand. It is there that I purchase my first wedding magazine, as recommended for the list, *Martha Stewart Wedding*.

26

The Instruction Manual

I run home with the magazine tucked protectively under my arm. I must look like a teenaged boy sneaking his first *Playboy* up to his room. Once safely inside, sitting on my floral quilt with my bedroom door closed, I dare to really look at the cover and I am in awe of the stunning cake surrounded by perfect flowers. A rush of excitement takes over and I open the magazine and dare to enter her world.

The world of Martha Stewart, that is. It quickly becomes apparent that the woman, or at least her staff, is the MacGyver of weddings. All you have are bobby pins, buttons, and dental floss? No problem! You have yourself some lovely and quaint boutonnieres. Have some flowers you picked up at a farmers' market and some wide ribbon? *Voila* . . . corsages! I am entranced at this unsurpassed level of creativity. I've always been a fan of Martha and have stolen many an idea for use around my home, but I now see that weddings are her forte . . . truly her calling.

Finally I come to a serious (yet tasteful) foldout section. I start with the first column of things to do. It includes all the big stuff: setting a date (hooray, check number one for me!), booking the location, and hiring the caterer, florist, deejay, or band, etc. I feel like Martha would be proud that this early on I already have a check mark. Plus, I'm meeting my mom this afternoon to look at The Plaza, so maybe I'll have two checks before the day is over. I read all the other "to-do things," and as they get closer to the wedding date they get longer and more specific. As exciting as it is, it also makes me nervous because I'd never realized how many details and responsibilities there were. I always wondered why my engaged friends would be so tense before their big days—I always thought you just showed up in the amazing white dress. I was wrong!

My head is spinning with wedding "to-dos" by the time I set the magazine down and change into a more Plaza-bride-to-be appropriate outfit.

27

Molly at The Plaza

I arrive five minutes before I'm supposed to meet my mom because I am positive that, unlike all my friends and me, when she says a time she means that time or before. I am only waiting about thirty seconds when she hops out of a cab in front of the hotel.

"You took the train?"

"We're down to one car, remember?"

Oh yes . . . I forgot. Logan still hasn't gone back to Connecticut, and therefore neither has the green Explorer. I do feel bad that my mother had to deal with the train and getting a cab at Grand Central and all that hassle.

"Was it okay?" I ask.

"Of course! I'm not an old lady—I enjoy riding the train once in a while."

Ah, my mother: the queen of making lemonade out of lemons (and P.S.: only an old lady would "enjoy" riding the train).

"Are you excited?" she asks me.

"Beyond."

"Me, too," she admits, and takes my hand as we climb up the front steps of the grand-looking hotel.

With the friendly guidance of The Plaza's extremely attentive staff, we quickly find the office of the hotel's wedding coordinator, Marion Lantz. Marion is exactly how you would picture The Plaza's wedding coordinator to be. She is lovely and classy and perfectly put together. Her St. John suit is the perfect pink to feel bridal and yet professional at the same time, and her hair looks as if she's just stepped out of the hairdresser's chair. She also has a rock on her left finger the size of Gibraltar and equally impressive eternity bands on either side of it. Marion greets us warmly, by name, before we even introduce ourselves.

"Mrs. Harrigan and, of course, our lovely bride, Molly! Welcome to The Plaza. May we get you something to drink? Espresso, Perrier, champagne?"

Mom and I giggle like schoolgirls and decide that some champagne would be lovely. Without so much as a word, Marion's assistant, Ashley (who we are introduced to when she returns with the beverages and a plate of chocolate-dipped strawberries), jumps up from her desk and disappears. Ashley is a younger, slightly hipper version of Marion. I can instinctively tell that Martha would approve of these gals.

Marion invites us to sit at her desk and go over dates before we begin the tour of the ballrooms.

"Now," she begins, "Mrs. Harrigan, you had mentioned over the phone that Molly hoped to be married on June 30 of next year. That is less than ten months away, however, and we normally are booked almost two years in advance," she says and my heart sinks. "Fortunately for you, the bride who was holding the Grand Ballroom for the past eighteen months recently broke her engagement and released the room this morning. It's your lucky day!"

Oh my gosh—it really is my lucky day! My heart soars once more.

"Fantastic!" my mother agrees

"Now," Marion continues (I soon come to find out that Marion says "now" a lot), "this ballroom holds up to 400 guests, but obviously can be adjusted for a smaller wedding. The cost is approximately $250 per person, depending, of course, on the entrees selected and other details like that. Have you started working on your list to figure out your numbers yet?"

I nearly choke on the $250 per person. Not that I know that many people or plan to have a huge wedding, but that means it would be $1250 just for my nuclear family to attend . . . not to mention Bryan, my grandparents, or Justin! I am furiously trying to do quick math in my head to figure out how much of my wedding fund would have to be used to cover the hotel when I hear my mother say something that makes me choke even harder.

"That sounds just fine. Molly's father and I were playing around with a preliminary list and think it will probably end up around 200."

That sounds just fine?!? It will probably end up around 200?!? I cannot breathe.

"Mom?" I choke toward her.

She smiles at me kindly, "We'll work more on the list, sweetie. Of course, however many guests you and Justin want will be fine."

I feel like I've been whacked on the head with a stick or something. My mother, who clips coupons and reuses Ziploc bags isn't even batting an eye at the prospect of $50,000 just for the location, food, and drinks. I can't help but wonder how she would be if I didn't have Nana's money to pay for this wedding.

"Now," Marion stands up, "shall we look at the ball-room?"

"Absolutely," my mother agrees as she gets to her feet and pulls me with her.

We follow Marion, who is closely followed by Ashley

with a clipboard (a fancy one, though), through the hotel as she points out details and throws in historical facts about the hotel. I must admit to you now, my love of The Plaza actually comes from my favorite childhood book, *Eloise*, about a spoiled little girl who lives here with her nanny.

At last we arrive at the Grand Ballroom. Marion informs us that we can only take a quick glance today because it is in the process of being set up for a wedding reception that will take place in a few hours, but that we are lucky to be seeing it in wedding formal. Once again, it is our lucky day. She majestically opens the room's double doors at once and the sight before me reminds me of the religious experience at Tiffany.

The room is stunning. No, it's beyond stunning. There isn't even a word to describe it. Marion is explaining to my mother that this evening's wedding is for 275 guests, that the bride had selected filet mignon for everyone as very few people are vegetarians anymore, and that the gleaming white dance floor set up in the middle of the room is standard at The Plaza, but not at other hotels. I only hear parts of what they are saying because I am in a trance of awe at the room.

"It really is amazing, isn't it?" Ashley whispers to me— the first and only words she's spoken since saying hello.

I nod in agreement and look over at her. Upon closer inspection, Ashley is roughly my age with a conspicuously empty finger. I can only imagine how hard it must be to see Marion's Mount Everest ring every day, and I can see that she looks at the room with the same awe and longing that I am now every time she looks at it.

"So, what do you think?" my mother asks, breaking my trance.

"I love it," I whisper, not wanting Marion or Ashley to know just how much.

"Me, too," she agrees, then turns to Marion. "What do we have to do to secure this room for Molly?"

I turn in time to see Marion's shining grin as she takes the clipboard from Ashley.

"Let's sign a hold contract!" she sings.

We follow her back to her office as she rattles off the details within a hold contract. Basically, we pay a certain, non-refundable amount and they hold the room for us.

At this point, my excitement comes to a screeching halt. I have the money in my Nana-wedding-fund account to cover the hotel—it will be a sizable chunk of the account's balance, but it is there. My personal checking account, however, is a different story. Paying Justin's salary has left my account contents a bit sparser than normal and I don't have enough to cover the deposit on the room.

"Um, do we have to pay today?" I ask, feeling humiliated in front of Marion. "I might need to transfer some funds," I say, getting more miserable by the minute.

Then my mother continues her new habit of shocking the pants off me . . . she joyfully signs her name to the hold contract, writes The Plaza hotel a check, and schedules our next appointment with the lovely Marion.

"Don't worry, we'll figure all the money stuff out," she reassures me quietly while Marion is discussing her schedule with Ashley.

Marion instructs that we should have a completed guest list by the time we meet with her again. It's like she's the wedding teacher giving us homework. She also insists that we call her immediately should any questions or concerns come up. We all shake hands once again and Mom and I set back across the hotel lobby and don't say a word to each other until we are back out front on the sidewalk.

Once we are safely away from the properness of the hotel we start squealing, and crying, and hugging, and even jumping up and down a little bit. Finally Mom pulls back and looks me in the eye.

"We love you so much, Molly. You deserve all this."

I feel a twinge of guilt, but it passes quickly because she embraces me again and we dance around the Manhattan sidewalk a little more.

Eyes on the prize, I tell myself. *You're going to have a wedding at The Plaza!*

28

Molly Makes a List

I kiss my mother good-bye as she gets into a cab on Fifth Avenue and promise that Justin and I will begin work on our list immediately. I decided to walk home through Central Park since it is still pretty warm and won't be dark for a couple more hours. On my walk, I start thinking about the list and who will be on it.

Obviously all the usual suspects: my college friends, the few high-school friends I keep in touch with, and the even fewer grade-school friends I still talk to. Plus all my family and the people I work with. Needless to say, I would like to invite everyone I've ever met to share in the joy of it finally being my day, but since a small but persistent voice in the back of my head likes to remind me that this marriage isn't real, I try to keep my list in check.

Then I start thinking about Justin and his side of the ceremony. Who is going to sit there? Obviously he isn't going to invite his friends and family . . . they would know right away it was a sham. That is an enormous problem I hadn't given any thought to yet. I walk and I think, and I walk and I think, and before I know it, I am standing outside my building and I still don't have an idea.

When I walk in the door I smell something amazing. It smells how I imagine something cooking in my kitchen would smell, but since I don't cook, I'm not positive. I peek around the corner and see Justin and Logan, squished together in my tiny kitchen, cooking dinner.

"Hey, Molly!" Logan greets me with a happiness in his voice I haven't heard in a while.

"Hey, Loge, whatcha cookin?"

"Haha . . . it's a surprise."

"Hey there, sweetie," Justin adds, leaning across the kitchen to kiss the top of my head (yes, that's how small the kitchen is—a person can simply lean and reach all the way across it). "How was The Plaza?"

"Amazing. Mom put a deposit on it!"

They both cheer that this enormous detail is set. Justin pours me a glass of wine from a bottle that looks like he and Logan have already had several drinks out of, and I sit on a stool at the edge of the kitchen telling them about Marion, and Ashley, and the Grand Ballroom. It's all starting to feel so real and so exciting.

All through dinner (a delicious feast of amazing home-made paella) we keep the wine flowing and talk about who should be on the list and I ask the boys about the problem of Justin's empty list.

"I could sit on his side," Logan offers with a slight slur.

"You can't! Besides, you're in the wedding," I remind him.

We have definitely had too much wine to be discussing something this serious, but we forge ahead amid a lot of giggles and a few hiccups. The decision we finally come to is that Justin can fill his side to a certain extent by inviting people to a *Tony and Tina's Wedding*-style play. *Tony and*

Tina's Wedding was a mid-nineties phenomenon that was an audience-interactive play. So the "actors" stayed in character the entire time and the "audience" stayed in character as guests. It might be the wine talking, but it actually seems like a brilliant solution by 1:15 A.M.

29

She Checks It Twice

The next day, Justin and I head to Starbucks, which is a little embarrassing now because we are kind of celebrities there and they always applaud when we come in and give me a free pumpkin scone, which, don't get me wrong, is awesome and it's my favorite . . . but once in a while I like something different. We sit down at our favorite table with my laptop between us and type out our "official" list.

Martha suggests that along with the date and the venue that the guest list be one of the first things completed. Since Marion seems to concur, we figure we'd better get started. I have my old-fashioned Filofax phone book with me and Justin has his spiffy, high-tech Palm Pilot.

I start with all my friends. I include everyone who has invited me to their wedding, which pretty much is all my friends since they're all married already. I pause briefly at Brad's name, not because he wouldn't be invited, regardless of how things are now—he's a special friend and an honorary member of the family—but because I'm hoping there is a way to invite him without Claire. Justin insists there is not, so I give up and add two more. After my friends, I add family members. I'm sure my mom's list will be a more complete list of the Harrigans and Nelsons (her side of the family), so there will be plenty of cross-referencing to make sure we have everyone, but this is a start. Finally I decide on the people from work who should be included: the principal of my school, my fellow third-grade teachers, and a couple other staffers. That's it for me. I count them all up and it comes to eighty-four. Not bad.

Then Justin flicks on his little device and starts going over the names of his friends (and family?) who would go to this "play." He starts with his friends from work, since he explains that is a more gay/straight mixed group than his college friends. Next he adds a select group of college friends who would be good at playing along with the play and not make jokes about "the gay groom" the whole night. Finally, he thinks about his family. Definitely his brother and sister-in-law would come . . . he thinks. His parents are another issue. Since they aren't completely comfortable with his sexuality to begin with, he's not sure how they would handle watching him "play straight." Also, would they come all the way from Kansas anyway to see a play? I'm nervous about putting them on the list, and I'm nervous about not putting them on the list, because it would be awkward to explain to my family why Justin's family isn't invited. We decide to leave their name on the list and make the decision about whether or not to actually mail the invitation to them when the time is closer. His list is 32, bringing our total to a whopping 116.

While 116 guests means $29,000 at The Plaza, which makes me nauseous, it doesn't make me nearly as nauseous as the 200-person total my mother was predicting. This will be a sizable chunk of Nana's money, but it does leave enough to cover other essentials, like my dress. We look over our list once more, confirming that all of the important people are included as we finish our fourth and fifth lattes, and then we leave the Starbucks, surprised that we have been inside for almost four hours.

Justin needs to get back to his apartment and get changed for work, so we say our good-byes on the sidewalk out front. I open my purse and hand him money for today's "date," but he puts his hand up.

"No, not today," he says.

"But—"

"No, I don't charge my friends and we're friends now."

"You're a really good friend," I tell him as I give him a big hug.

30

Wedding Central

On Monday morning, as instructed by my mother, I get to school early to use the fax machine in the administration office to fax her the list. I have everything organized neatly and orderly and I must admit, I'm pretty proud of my list. I've checked over it twice more since Justin and I left Starbucks yesterday afternoon, and I had Logan look over it to make sure there wasn't anybody painfully obvious that we missed.

At lunchtime, I call my mom at home since she has cut down to a part-time teaching schedule this year.

"Wedding Central!" she answers.

"Mom! Is that really how you are answering the phone?" I giggle.

"Absolutely. I got your list. But, actually, Mol, it would be easier if you could e-mail it to me so that I could merge it into my list and get it a little more organized."

Huh? E-mail? Merge? *More* organized? Who is this woman and why didn't she think my perfectly organized list was organized enough?!?

"Um, sure," I reply lamely.

"It looks great, though," she encourages. "You did a good

job with your friends and co-workers. I'm just going to delete your family list since mine is more complete. Now, is that Justin's complete list or will he be getting more names to me?"

Did my mother just say, "now?" Is she turning into Marion?

"Um, that's all his names. Most of his family is in Kansas and he doesn't really keep in close contact with them."

"Uh-huh, well, why don't you give me his mother's phone number so that I can give her a call and arrange to get her list?"

"No!" I yell a little too fast and a little too loud.

"What?"

"Oh, no, sorry, not you, Mom. One of the kids was about to eat sand on the playground. Um, about Justin's mom: she's just not that into the wedding stuff and they aren't really that close. The list he wrote is his final list. Don't worry about it."

"Well, okay," Mom says, sounding slightly confused and disappointed. "I just thought she might want to be involved."

"I know, that's so sweet of you. She's just not like that."

Ugh . . . more lies. It's like Shakespeare says, *Oh what a tangled web we weave when first we—something—to deceive.* I can't remember the exact quote, but I totally get the sentiment.

Mom and I agree (well, Mom says and I say OK) that she will finish the list this week and meet the following weekend in the city to shop for invitations and dresses. This all feels like it's happening so fast, but Mom insists there is no point to waiting, so I go along.

After we hang up, I'm feeling quite overwhelmed, and I know Jamie is also on lunch break, so I call her cell.

"Have you called Mom recently?" I ask after we say our hellos.

Jamie laughs, "Is she back on the 'wedding central' thing?"

"Yes! Did she do that when you were getting married?"

"I can't believe you don't remember. She alternated between 'wedding central' and 'mother of the bride speaking.'"

We laugh at our mother. We both realize how lucky we are to have her and how wonderful it is that she is excited and involved . . . but we also both share the sentiment of wanting to beat her with something sharp.

"We're going dress shopping this weekend. Wanna come?"

"I would love to, but Bryan's sister is going to be in town."

"Oh," I say, disappointed not to have a Mom filter, but trying to hide it so Jamie doesn't feel guilty. "Amanda or Marisa?"

"Marisa . . . and her boyfriend du jour."

"Well, it'll be good to see her. Give her my best. So," I continue, in need of a change of topic, "how's Bumper?"

"We have our doctor's appointment this afternoon to find out if it's a boy Bumper or a girl Bumper!"

"Oh my God! That's so exciting."

"I know, it's moving so fast . . . it's getting so big. It's cra—"

I hear a loud whistle in the background. Lunch must be over at Jamie's school. I check the clock—I've got five more minutes. We say our good-byes and she promises to call me as soon as she knows if I'm getting a niece or a nephew.

Then the bell rings outside my class and the kids come piling back in. They are rambunctious from the time outside, and I take a deep breath and prepare for a trying afternoon.

31

Molly's Mom Goes Crazy

Later in the week, I arrive home to find Logan hidden behind a huge stack of what looks like extremely thick magazines.

"Logan?" I call out to him.

"I'm back here, Molly. Mom sent over these wedding magazines for you."

There must be twenty-five magazines stacked all over my poor little coffee table. The shipping alone had to have been more than all the publications, and Mom has helpfully attached a short note to the front of a particularly thick *Modern Bride*.

The note says,

> *Molly,*
>   *Go through these magazines to get ideas of bridal gown styles you would like us to consider.*

I look up and down the pile of magazines and peer over the top to find Logan on the couch reading another one.

"This style looks nice," he says, holding up a picture of a long, straight dress that would look amazing on Cindy Crawford and few others . . . seriously, you would have to be six feet tall and the width of a pencil.

I don't have time to respond before the phone rings. It's Mom calling to ensure that her package arrived and I understand my "assignment."

"There were supposed to be packages of colored paper clips," she explains.

I look around the table, and sure enough there are: one yellow, one green, and one pink.

"Use those to clip pages with dresses you like. Pink for your favorites, yellow for the maybes, and green for the not-sures."

"Okay," I nod, actually taking this all in.

Thankfully the Call Waiting beeps and I'm able to get off with Mom after just a few more instructions about disregarding length and color of dresses in ads as they might be available differently.

On the other line is Jamie.

"Thank goodness! I was on with Mom."

"Haha," she laughs. "Did the magazines come today?"

"You knew that was going to happen?!?"

"Of course. It's all part of the fun of planning a wedding. And you always thought you were missing out."

I really always did think I was missing out . . . but so far, all it's been is work! If Jamie knew what I was really doing to have this wedding, she'd think I was completely insane, which I probably am.

"So?" I ask, "in the spirit of all wedding all the time, is it a flower girl or a ring bearer?"

"It's a flower girl!" Jamie screams into the phone and I scream back.

Then I scream across the room, "Logan! You're getting a niece!"

Jamie stops screaming. "Logan's there? You told him?"

"Yes, he's right here."

"I wanted to tell him," she pouts.

Ugh . . . I forgot who I was dealing with.

"Hang on, I'll put him on," and I hand the phone to an eager Logan, who is now standing beside me.

I am grinning ear to ear at the thought of my niece on the way. I can't wait for her to arrive! As Logan chats with Jamie in the background I pick up the magazine on the top of the tall pile and start flipping through. The thing is about 80% ads. I'm trying to remember Mom's color-coded system as I see pictures of stunning dresses and hideous dresses and everything in between . . . quite frankly, I'm starting to doze off. I hear Logan say "Hang on" to Jamie in the background and answer the Call Waiting.

"Hey, Molly," he calls over to me, "Mom also says that you need to select a date for your engagement party and get her a list for that by the end of the week."

Then he clicks back over to Jamie and keeps chatting.

Engagement party? Now *that's* what I'm talking about. All this wedding planning has been a lot of work—it's about time something fun got planned for me. This news gives me a second wind of energy and I pick up the next magazine on my stack and get to work.

32

A Crazy Thing Happens

Smack-dab in the middle of all the wedding insanity, a crazy thing happens. Do you remember Kevin? The handsome groomsman whose fault it was I had to ride the subway home the morning after Maggie's wedding in the lavender curse? Well, I didn't, either . . . but he remembered me and recognized me in the check-out line at D'Agostino!

Turns out his name is Evan, not Kevin, but he *is* as handsome as I thought he was the night I created a Jack Daniel's drought in Manhattan. Thankfully I was just picking up some apples, bread, and paper towels (I would have died if it was tampons and Ben & Jerry's, which it regularly is) when he warmly called my name and waved from across the market like we were long-lost best friends.

We ended up talking for an hour in the frozen food aisle, and he never noticed the engagement ring on my left hand. Perhaps this could be because I carefully kept it tucked into the pocket of my jacket, but I think it was probably just luck . . . or maybe fate . . . because he asked me out for Friday night! Wouldn't that be crazy if the "he's the one" sensors that were going off back at Maggie's wedding had been onto something? Wouldn't that be an adorable story to share with the grandkids?

The tricky, and somewhat disappointing, thing about dating when you're "engaged" is that you have to keep it a secret from everyone else. So, like a high-school junior, I have responsibly told Justin and Logan that I will be at Lauren's all evening, but not to call because we are having a wedding movie marathon. I've told Lauren, and all my other girlfriends, that I'm having a romantic night out with Justin. Bases are covered and I'm only slightly horrified, but mostly impressed, at how good I've become at lying.

At eight o'clock I am looking fabulous in black leather pants, my favorite cashmere sweater, and pointy black boots. I specifically leave my engagement ring in the top drawer of my jewelry box—I'm ready to meet Evan. I feared that the outfit could arouse suspicions in Justin and Logan, but thankfully I was able to slip out the door without seeing them. Instead of being planted in front of the television like I'd feared, they were in Logan's room with the door closed. I lucked out!

When I arrive at the bar Evan suggested, I am completely relieved that it is fairly dark, and not too crowded . . . I definitely don't want to run into anyone I know tonight. He is waiting for me and I feel a flicker of excitement because he is even better-looking tonight than he was standing in front of the Lean Cuisines the other day. I join him for a pre-dinner drink, but remind myself not to get as drunk as the first time we met. I sip a glass of white wine while he drinks two imported beers and we chat about everything under the sun.

He is comfortable and easy to talk to, plus he's funny and interesting, too. Before I know it, we've hardly touched dinner and are on to hardly touching dessert. I know, it's rare for me to pass up food, but I am too excited to eat! He pays the bill, even though I genuinely offer to treat, and we quickly walk out of the restaurant and then stop, somewhat awkwardly, on the sidewalk out front. The sexual chemistry between us is too much to hold back any longer, and I am greatly relieved when he grabs me and pulls me into the alley at the side of the restaurant and starts kissing me. We make out for a few minutes before the lust is curbed enough to realize the shame of going at it in a public alley.

"Let's go to your place," I say in my best sexy voice. I think we all know that nothing about me is sexy, but maybe I can fool him for just a little longer. I know what you're thinking, and yes, you are right . . . I am being a total slut . . . but do you understand how long it's been? Sure, my fantasy sex life is amazing, but I am human and I could use a little nookie.

"We can't, I have a roommate—let's go to your place," he disappoints me.

Crap. "I have roommates, too," I moan. No need to explain that my roommates are my fake, gay fiancé and my younger brother.

And then do you know what he says? "Let's get a hotel."

And do you know what slutty Molly says? "Okay."

I only suffer a minute of shame as we check in at eleven o'clock at night without a single bag, because before I know it, Evan throws me onto the bed and we start tearing each other's clothes off. It's not the best sex I've ever had . . . but it's not the worst, and when someone has been in the desert for as long as I have, they aren't demanding Fiji water when Arrowhead (or maybe even tap) is being offered. Know what I mean?

When we finish, I feel like a total guy lying there calculating how long I need to stay. I mean, he did pay for a hotel room . . . but I think me being gone all night would arouse too many suspicions to deal with. I am greatly relieved

when, less than thirty minutes later, Evan gets up and starts
to put his clothes back on.

"I wish I could stay all night, Molly, but I have a dog," he
explains.

Phew! "I have a cat!" I exclaim to reassure him that I,
too, need to be getting home.

Hand in hand, we exit the hotel, sneaking past the con-
cierge since now that our brains are working more regularly, we know to be embarrassed and stop out in front of
the hotel.

"Molly, you're amazing. I have to see you again," Evan
says, and he looks so sexy with his messed-up hair that I
have half a mind to pull him back up to the hotel room.

But instead I am a lady, and just say, "I would love to."

"Are you free on Sunday?"

For a second I wonder to myself why he skipped Saturday,
the official "date night," but seriously, what do I care? He
asked me out . . . it's not like he said, *Call ya.*

"I am," I inform him.

"Great, let's have lunch."

Lunch? Ugh . . . beggars can't be choosers.

"Lunch sounds great."

33

A White Dress, At Last

I've been a good girl . . . I've gone through every magazine that Mom sent my way. It wasn't easy . . . the first half-dozen were fun; after that it became exhausting. Pretty much any minute that I wasn't at school or doing work for school I was looking through bridal magazines. To the untrained eye (aka Logan and Justin) it didn't look like work, but trust me, it was. I hardly had the time to whip up my engagement party list and select a date in early December.

I suppose it was all worth it, because when Mom arrives at my apartment early Saturday morning I do have a very definite idea of the bridal gown I want . . . never mind the fact that it's the same style I was pretty certain I wanted before I looked through every bridal magazine published this year (and maybe last year, too). Mom looks over my magazines to see the things I've marked and I'm pleased that I get approving nods from her.

"Okay, good work. Now, are you ready to go?"

I swear, Mom talks to Marion too often, and if you think the "now" thing is annoying coming from Marion, it's nothing compared to when it comes from my mother. But just wait, it gets better—she pulls out a laundry list of bridal salons in Manhattan that we have *appointments* at today. Since when do you need an appointment to go shopping? I ask Mom this and she informs me that, according to Marion, the only places really worth looking at require them. Ugh—Marion is starting to annoy me.

Mom and I stop for a quick cup of coffee, and even though I'm starving, she won't let me eat before we try on dresses. My hunger pains attack me as I look over her long list and realize that I won't be allowed to eat a single thing all day! I'm hoping and praying that some of these bridal salons will offer snacks, the way Marion did at our Plaza meeting, when we stop in front of the first store on our list, the Bridal Suite.

We ring a little doorbell to get buzzed in . . . I swear, the place has more security than a jewelry store, and a girl named Emily, dressed to the nines, greets us politely only after she has confirmed that we do, in fact, have an appointment. Emily looks me over, head to toe, and for the first time in my life I'm feeling uncomfortable to be in Gap, not Gucci.

"Well," she says icily, "did you have any particular styles in mind?"

I'm about to explain what I want when my mother jumps in to answer for me.

"I'd like to see her in something strapless, don't you think?"

Emily nods in a way that clearly shows she could care less if I'm in strapless or not. She expertly walks over to her racks of dresses and starts pulling out choices.

"You're a four," she says, not asks, over her shoulder.

"Or a six," I add . . . I really don't want to feel like a stuffed sausage.

She carries the pile of dresses toward what I assume is a fitting room and instructs my mother to sit in a plush chair next to a small, stagelike thing and tells me to come with her. Once in the dressing room, she stands there, waiting expectantly for me to strip right in front of her. When it becomes clear that she isn't going to leave, I take off my clothes, feeling sorry that I didn't wear nicer underwear . . . who knew?

"Bra, too," she orders me.

So far, dress shopping is not fun. I take off my bra, as instructed by this strange girl watching me like a hawk, and before I can think of a way to try to cover myself, she's literally strapping me in this strapless bra/corset combination thing.

"You have to wear the proper foundations with a bridal gown," she informs me.

Then she gives me quick instructions on how to dive into the first, enormous dress and buttons up the back.

"What size shoe do you wear?"

"A seven."

Emily places a pair of white satin, but very used-looking, heels in front of me and I slip my bare feet into them as I assume I'm supposed to.

"Lovely," she says without any warmth in her voice.

I walk out to where my mother is and climb onto the little stage thing, which sits behind a three-way mirror. My mother's eyes fill with tears when she sees me in the dress. I turn and look at myself, since I'm not even sure what it looks like, and uncontrollably, my eyes also fill with tears. Then, for a split second, I wonder if Evan would like the way I look in the dress . . . is that weird?

This is it, this is the dress. It's stunning. It's exactly what I dreamed it would be. It's shiny white satin, with a plain top and a princess waistline. It's full to the floor with a modest

train. It could not be more perfect. Mom is crying, I'm crying, and Emily is looking at us critically.

"That's the wrong backline for you," she declares authoritatively like a needle being ripped across a record.

We both stop crying and look at her.

"Because you are small-chested, you need a backline that
goes straight across, not scooped."

I whirl around, trying to catch a glimpse of my back, but
I can't really see it. I guess I'll just have to take nasty Emily's
word for it. Mom sniffles once more, then says, "She's right.
Take it off."

I head back to the dressing room to strip down naked in
front of the lovely Emily again. It's the first dress at the first
store and I'm already exhausted.

By the end of the day, I have learned that Emily is actually one of the kinder women working in bridal couture, as
they like to describe it. I have been called too skinny, too
flabby, and one woman actually suggested I get breast im-
plants for the big day! Another woman didn't even greet
me before proclaiming, "You can't wear white," even
though my dream dress is undoubtedly white, and another
woman actually said that I could wear strapless but I'd be
sorry. Not to mention the *two* places that sent us away immediately because nine months before the wedding did
not give them enough time! These people are cruel and
insane.

Halfway through the day, Mom relented and let me have
a small salad. I literally thought I was going to die, and
while a salad usually doesn't fill me up, in my highly starved
state it did enough to give me a small amount of energy, but
mostly what kept me going was the drive to get it over with
and get Mom back on her way to Connecticut. We finally
arrive at Barney's, our last stop of the day.

I've always been a big fan of Barney's—not so much for

the shopping, since I can't afford much of what they sell, but for the fact that they have a restaurant right there in the store, and a good one at that. We make our way up the escalators to the bridal salon and are greeted by a friendly lady, about my mother's age. She introduces herself as Helen and offers us coffee and madeleines. I love madeleines, I love coffee, and now I love Helen!

I make a mental note to definitely add her to the wedding list—heck, maybe I'll give her Jamie's matron-of-honor spot—as Helen leads me back to the lovely bridal fitting room. She politely waits outside the room until I am undressed, and although I've become accustomed to being treated like bridal cattle today, I am greatly relieved to be treated like a human once again. Then things get even better . . . I find *the* dress . . . *MY* dress. It is beyond stunning, beyond beautiful, and above and beyond anything we have seen today. The top is plain, simple and elegant. Around my waist is a wide sash that ties in a knot at the back. The fabric for the sash knot is so long that the excess hangs all the way down to the ground, creating a small train. It's just the right amount of A-line, so it looks full without looking antebellum and the backline is straight across (since our appointment with Emily I've become extremely back-conscious). This is the dress, I absolutely know it, and I know my mom knows it, too, when I look at her.

"This is the one," we say to each other at the exact same time.

"This is the one," we turn and say to Helen in unison.

"I thought it might be," Helen says wisely.

Mom stands up and hugs me, we cry again, then I change back into my regular clothes and we both hug Helen and cry before leaving the store. In the end, wedding-dress shopping wasn't exactly how I'd imagined it in all my bridal fantasies, but I'm determined not to let tiny hardships like being insulted by half the bridal salons in Manhattan take away from my happiness. I can't wait to get home and tell Justin all about it . . . I wonder if it's bad luck to tell your fake, gay groom what your wedding dress looks like . . .

34

Date Number Two

As exciting as yesterday was . . . finding my dream wedding dress and all . . . part of my mind was not there. Part of my mind couldn't stop thinking about Evan and the excitement of our second date. I won't lie and tell you that I wasn't a little disappointed and surprised when he suggested lunch, but it is a school night, so I suppose it's for the best.

I spend Sunday morning going back and forth between worrying about what to wear to a lunch date and worrying about what I will tell Justin. In the end I decide to wear a moderately low V-neck, camel-colored sweater with some ultralow-rise jeans and a conspicuously empty ring finger, and to tell Justin that I am going to the 99 Cents store. I had to come up with an errand that he wouldn't want any part of. With a straight guy you can name any store and they will do anything to get out of it . . . with a gay guy, most likely they'll want to tag along. The 99 Cents store is the exception—no self-respecting gay man would be caught dead there.

When I head out of my room to make a beeline for the front door, I bump smack-dab into Justin and Logan, who seem to be doing the same thing. Justin is uncomfortably carrying a kite, which thankfully distracts him long enough for me to jam my left hand into the undersized pocket of my jeans. I look awkward, but at least my finger is hidden.

"Where are you off to?" he asks me.

"Oh, I just have some errands to run," I explain. "To the 99 Cents store!" I quickly add to ensure his disinterest.

"Nice outfit for the 99 Cents store," Logan butts in.

"This? Thanks . . . I just threw it on." That seems like a good answer, but just to get the focus off me, I add, "Where are you guys going?"

"We're going to fly a kite," Logan tells me and Justin nods somewhat sheepishly.

"Sounds like fun," I say as I open the door and hold it as Logan, Justin, and their kite exit. Once on the street, I hail a cab.

As I'm climbing in, Justin asks me why I'm taking a cab to the 99 Cents store, and I quickly blurt out that my boots aren't that comfortable before slamming the door of the cab. As we drive off, I turn back and watch the boys fiddling with their kite . . . if I didn't know better, I would think they were a couple.

When the cab pulls up outside the restaurant, Evan is outside waiting for me—what a gentleman. He greets me with a warm hug and a kiss on the cheek. I swear . . . every time I see the guy he looks more handsome. Today, he has his straight black hair tucked under a worn green Dartmouth hat, which brings out his eyes, and a white polo shirt with jeans that show off his muscular body.

"Hi," I say, trying to use my nonexistent sexy voice.

"Hey there," he says . . . he has his down pat.

"Ready for lunch?" I ask as I start toward the restaurant.

He grabs my arm and pulls me back toward him. "I had another idea," he says as he holds up a key and points to the hotel across the street.

My first instinct is yes. God, yes! My second instinct is

no. I'm not that kind of girl. In the end, instinct number one wins over. Obviously this isn't a one-night stand . . . clearly this is heading toward a relationship, so there is no reason not to be romantic—plus, we can go get lunch afterwards.

We end up not going to get lunch . . . we end up not getting out of bed for most of the afternoon. Room service brings us some food, but we don't even bother to get dressed. It feels like something out of a movie . . . it's hard to believe that I am actually here in this hotel room with an incredibly handsome guy who is crazy about me and wants me so badly.

When the sun finally starts to go down, we realize it's time to go back to our real lives. On the street, Evan gives me one last kiss before hailing a cab for me. As I'm climbing in, he says, "I'll call you."

"Okay, " I agree.

Obviously he will call me; I mean . . . we're practically in a relationship now. Okay, stop . . . I know what you're thinking—I'm engaged. Well, I might be engaged, but I'm still a single girl and this could really be "the one!"

35

The Much Anticipated Engagement Party

The next three months fly by quickly. Mom has turned into a little bit of a wedding Nazi, so anytime I'm not at work or making a concerted effort to avoid her calls (thank you Caller ID), she's got me thinking about or doing wedding stuff. It has been a lot of work, though much of it enjoyable, and tonight will truly be the first payoff: the first time that I finally get the bridal experience I was longing for . . . our engagement party.

Justin and I talked it over and decided a smaller engagement party would be better so it would explain why he didn't have many (any) guests of his own there. We chose the first week of December for the party and at the time it felt worlds away, but here we are . . . tonight is the night.

Much to my surprise and disappointment, Evan didn't call me after our afternoon in the hotel . . . undaunted, I called him . . . but then he didn't return my call for a whole week. When he did call back, it was Friday afternoon . . . when he should have realized I'd be at school. And then I left another message for him and didn't hear back . . . for a week, which turned into a month, and then two, and then . . .

you get the picture. He never called again. For the first month I was stricken with panic that he had been hit by a train or murdered on the street . . . but after many extensive Internet searches, I finally became convinced that he was alive and well . . . and just not interested in me. Obviously I was crushed . . . but since I couldn't share the reason for my despair with anyone, I got over it and only think about him once or twice a week now.

Logan has permanently moved in with me and Justin has become such a regular fixture on the sofa bed that most days we don't bother to put it back together. Although there are moments when I miss the privacy and peace that Tiffany and I shared six long months ago, in general I am happy having "my boys" (as I've started calling them) around. Except tonight, that is, when I really need the bathroom in order to get ready for the party, but they are being total hogs.

Laid out on my bed is my stunning engagement-party outfit. I decided it was one of those times when I could go all-out, so Justin and I spent three Saturdays in a row scouring New York City for the perfect dress, and we finally found it at a trendy boutique in Soho. The dress is a strapless, knee-length cream satin A-line, with black satin bands around the top and bottom and a black satin sash around the waist. It looks fantastic with my black satin stiletto sandals. Justin and I had decided that something whitish would be bridal and therefore appropriate, but not too whitish that it could take away from my actual wedding dress. The only catch is that it's freezing out and my only coat that is warm enough is my regular black wool one. What I needed is a floor-length black velvet coat, but with what I spent on the dress, I'm going to be eating Top Ramen for the rest of the month, so a coat was out—Nana's wedding fund just can't cover every wedding desire. Justin and I plan to get to the party early so that I can check the coat before any guests arrive and see me in it.

Logan finally saunters out of the bathroom, looking pretty much the same as he did before he went in, and I dart in behind him like lightning. I hope he enjoyed his long shower . . . 'cause now I'm going to need to speed-clean in order to be ready on time. Luckily all the excitement has me overflowing with adrenaline, so I have no problem washing and conditioning my hair, shaving my legs, bikini (who knows why), and armpits, and all the other shower necessities in record time.

I hop out of the shower and wrap my head in a superabsorbent towel before wrapping myself in my warmest robe and heading to my bedroom. I close my door, put on my "Wedding Sounds" CD, a hand-me-down gift from Maggie, and settle on my bed to paint my toenails a bright, iridescent red. They look really fantastic, and I spend just a few minutes of relaxation lying on my bed, singing along to Bette Midler belting, "We're going to the chapel and we're gonna get ma-a-arried, going to the chapel and we're gonna get ma-a-arried . . ."

Of course, my relaxation is cut short by a tap on my bedroom door.

"Molly," Logan calls through, "Mom's on the phone."

"Okay, thanks," I say as I roll over and pick up the old-fashioned corded phone next to my bed.

I must admit that there is something so familiar about living with my brother again that I absolutely adore. Of course, there is also the familiar lack of privacy and other sibling-related annoyances, but in general it makes me feel good to have him around.

"Hey, Mom."

"Good Golly Miss Molly! Are you ready for your night?"

"Just about," I lie.

"We're almost to the city—I just wanted to check in on you."

"Thanks, Mom. We're all great here. Tell Daddy to drive safely and we'll see you soon."

"We love you, sweetheart." CLICK.

I roll onto my back again and smile as Bette sings on in the background . . . right about now, being engaged is every bit as wonderful as I ever imagined it would be—as long as I ignore the little voice in the back of my head that keeps asking me what the hell I'm doing.

Somehow Logan, Justin, and I manage to get out of the house at the designated time and we arrive at the restaurant where my parents have rented a private room five minutes before the actual start-time of the party to give me a chance to hide my coat. I know my parents are already inside because Mom has called me three more times from her cell phone since I got out of the shower. She is perfecting the last details in the room with the restaurant manager and Dad is sitting in the bar watching the football game. The man is amazing . . . it is remarkable that he never shows up anywhere where there isn't a TV playing sports.

Would you like to guess who arrives at the same time we do and is standing on the sidewalk as we climb out of our cab? You guessed it—Claire Reilly (and Brad). Of all the people I didn't want to see me in my informal, non-matching wool coat, Claire is number one. To make matters worse, would you like to guess what she's wearing? A floor-length velvet coat! I swear, I cannot catch a break when it comes to that girl. I greet her as warmly as I can muster and give Brad an awkward hug before darting through the restaurant door to ditch the coat and show off my dress, which is as fabulous as the coat is unfabulous.

Brad and Claire saunter in behind me, and the bitch actually whines that she's cold and needs to keep her coat on. God, I hate her . . . maybe I can get a bartender to spit in her drink. Before I can plot any further, my mother comes flying out of the room and grabs me in a huge embrace.

"Good Golly Miss Molly!" she exclaims as she holds my arms out and admires my dress.

I smile, smugly, in Claire's direction. I decide that she must be keeping her stupid coat on because her dress is really ugly.

Justin comes up behind me and reaches over to give my mom a hug hello, and then she awkwardly looks to Logan, who is standing slightly behind Justin and greets him. Things are definitely not 100% normal between Logan and the parents, but I know everyone is trying their best.

"Hi, Baby Boy," she gently says her nickname for him.

"Hi, Mom," he says gratefully as he leans forward to hug her.

Justin and I look at each other and smile. When Mom lets go of Logan, which feels like it takes a while to happen, she gives a quick greeting hug to Claire and Brad (I still haven't told her all that's gone on with him—I know it would upset her). Then she directs everyone into the party room.

The room is stunning. The restaurant is beautiful to begin with, but they have transformed the room to look like a starry night. It's so pretty and romantic and honestly takes my breath away. I'm still gawking at the room when Jamie walks in. She is three weeks from her due date and is the size of a house. Even dressed in all black, she looks so enormous that I am shocked—at this point, I think her pee fear is pretty realistic.

"Kate got huge," she announces, motioning to her belly and my niece inside, who will be named Kate Anne Harrigan-Hope.

"Thank God . . . I just thought you got majorly fat," Logan pipes up and everybody can't help but laugh.

One by one, all the guests arrive and the party is in full swing before I know it. This night is making all the work and insanity of wedding planning worth it. I am having the best time. It's wonderful being at a party when you know and like everyone there (except one person), and everyone is being so nice to me and to Justin. I wish every day was like this. Plus, the table overflowing with presents in the corner isn't exactly ruining my good time.

The food is fantastic, the drink is free-flowing, and the music is great. I dance most of the night, not just with Justin but with all of my girlfriends and their husbands/fiancés. For the first time all evening, I finally break away from the dance floor and grab a seat at the bar, where I suck down a club soda to try and quench my thirst, when there is a tap on my shoulder. I turn around and find Brad.

I assume he's there to say good-bye, but he's not. He asks me to dance and out of shock I can't think of anything else to say except, "Okay."

He leads me to the dance floor just as the song, "Just the Way You Look Tonight" comes on . . . go figure. I search around the room for Justin and we give each other "oh well" shrugs as I begin to dance with Brad. To be honest, I'd forgotten what a good dancer Brad is and it feels good to be back in his arms. I snuggle a little, almost surprised at how easily I fit and how comfortable he is. I haven't let myself admit or think about how much I really do miss him. I'm still hurt and mad at him.

"Are you sure Claire would approve of this?" I ask, trying to hide the smugness in my voice.

"She went home. She was tired."

Interesting . . . she went home and left him behind. That

could not have been her choice and definitely couldn't have made her happy. This information softens me a little.

"I've missed you," I admit out loud.

"I've missed you so much, Molly."

We pull apart for a split second and look into each other's eyes. It's so good to look into such familiar eyes. It's the same feeling as coming home.

"What's been going on?" I ask lamely.

"Shhh . . . I love this song," he says.

I'm taken back four months to his engagement party when we danced to the exact same song and he said the exact same thing. It's hard to believe how much is completely different since then. We silently dance until the end of the song. When the music starts to fade out, part of me is sorry it's over.

"I'm realizing some of the things you said about Claire are true," Brad says before he lets go of me and without looking me in the eye. I'm stunned and can't say a word in response. "I love her, though, and we're working through them," he adds stiffly, as if that part were rehearsed.

"I'm glad," I muster lamely.

"I've gotta go," and with that, Brad gives me a kiss on the head and turns toward the door, stopping to kiss my mother and sister, give Logan a hug, and Justin a cool handshake. I'm still standing on the dance floor, slightly shocked. The front of my body suddenly feels cold where his had been keeping it warm as we danced.

By the cab ride home, many hours later, I'm still at a complete loss regarding my conversation—if you could even call it that—with Brad. I retell the story three times for Justin and Logan to try to get a handle on it, but they don't have much luck, either.

Besides that, though, the evening was straight out of a fairy tale. Everything was perfect and wonderful. It's hard to imagine that the night just six short months away is going to be one hundred times more magical. Actually, maybe the months won't be that short after all and the night won't be that magical, I try to remind myself . . . unfortunately, myself isn't listening too well lately.

36

The Real Cheater

I'm really riding high now. I am finally into the fun parts of wedding planning, Brad and I have found a place where we can be friends in spite of Claire's restrictions, Justin is nicely filling in as the everyday best friend, and I no longer think about the way Evan dumped me.

Justin has even "officially" moved into the apartment. Obviously he isn't giving up his own place since he can't stay with me after the wedding, but we decided that him moving in was another key element to avoiding suspicion. So, we added his name to the answering machine and the mailbox . . . and he went to Pottery Barn and picked up some "straight-guy knickknacks" to add to the apartment. I didn't have the heart to tell him that a) straight guys neither know what knickknacks are nor own them, and b) if they *did* own them, the ones he purchased wouldn't be them.

The Saturday after our engagement party, Justin and I are at D'Agostino together getting ingredients to make a special birthday dinner for Logan. Logan is spending the day relaxing at a spa, compliments of us, and I am following Justin around the store like a hired servant while he tries to figure out how to make lasagna (Logan's favorite) fat-free.

As he examines the fat content of different noodles, he orders me to get thirty ounces of fat-free ricotta cheese and report back to him immediately.

"Aye-aye, Captain," I salute him before heading to the dairy section.

It takes me a while to figure out what I need because, of course, none of the brands make a thirty-ounce size, so I need to figure out if it's more cost-effective to get smaller ones that add up to thirty or a bigger one and not use all of it. I finally figure it out, add the items to my basket, and turn on my heel to head back to the noodle aisle . . . but it doesn't happen quite like that.

I quite literally run headfirst into Evan. Of course, because of my size I run headfirst into his hard chest and don't realize who it is until I look up, up, and straight into his green eyes. We both look like deer caught in headlights. While one part of me is angry and hurt that he never called, the other part holds a shimmer of hope that this reunion is just what we needed to rekindle the spark.

"Um, Molly, hi," he mumbles at the exact same time that I mumble, "Gee, Evan, hello." Then we both laugh awkwardly and stare at each other.

"So, um, how are you?" he asks.

"Oh, me—I'm great. You?"

"Great, too."

The exchange is followed by some awkward nodding. I'm trying to figure out what to say next, but before I do, a third person joins our exchange.

"Honey, did you find my strawberry yogurt?" a voice calls from behind Evan.

His expression of fear increases greatly as he whirls around.

"Got it right here, hon!" he screeches in a frightened tone.

As he says this, the eater of the strawberry yogurt comes

up and joins us. She looks at Evan, then at me, and then smiles warmly.

"Hi, I'm Jenny," she says as she extends a friendly hand toward me.

At this moment, Evan jumps in as if his life depends on it, taking only a split second to regain his composure. "Jenny, this is Molly. Molly is a friend of Maggie, Pete's wife, and we met at their wedding."

"Oh, that's awesome," Jenny nods enthusiastically. "I was so sorry to miss their big day."

Wait . . . now I'm confused . . . who is this girl? I must be staring at her with some sort of strange expression because she asks me if I'm okay.

"Who are you?" I ask, without trying to sound too accusatory.

She giggles for a second. "I'm Jenny, Evan's fiancée."

I giggle, too . . . then I realize what she said. Evan's fiancée? My giggle abruptly ends and I stare at Jenny and Evan with my mouth hanging slightly open. Jenny is stunning . . . she has a curvy, knockout figure, tan skin, and cascades of dark, curly hair. Next to her, I feel completely mousy. And her voice really is sexy . . . not trying and failing to sound sexy. She probably couldn't stop sounding sexy if she wanted to. Just as I realize that I've been staring too long without saying anything, I hear Justin hollering my name—a little too gaily, I might add—from somewhere inside the market.

I close my eyes for a split second and pray that he doesn't find me . . . he does, of course. He comes up behind me and slips his arm around my waist, flawlessly transitioning from gay best friend mode and into fiancé mode.

"Hi," he says to Evan and Jenny, "I'm Justin, Molly's fiancé."

I look sheepishly at their faces . . . Evan's does an exact

replica of what mine had done seconds earlier, but he catches himself faster than I did.

"Nice to meet you—I'm Evan. This is my fiancée, Jenny."

"How do you all know each other?" Justin asks cheerfully.

"Evan is a friend of Maggie's husband, Pete," I answer quickly.

"Oh, fantastic. Were you both at their wedding?" he asks them.

"Evan was a groomsman," Jenny explains. "Unfortunately, I was stuck in California that weekend."

"You were stuck in California that weekend?" I parrot. That means that since the very first time I met Evan he had a fiancée? What a creep!

"Yes . . . my job sends me away a lot."

"That's cool," Justin continues. "What do you do?" He has no clue.

"Well, I was a sales rep, but with our big day right around the corner, I'm on leave," Jenny continues chatting with Justin as if they are old friends. "How long have you two been engaged and when's the big day?"

"We've been engaged . . . oh, let's see . . . since September and we're getting married in June."

"You're been engaged since *September*?" Evan asks, looking directly at me.

"That's right . . . how long have *you* been engaged?"

"*October*," he emphasizes, clearly trying to make the point that I was engaged before him.

"Well, congratulations," I say coolly. "Nice meeting you, Jenny. You've got a swell guy here." I turn and start walking away, feeling like I might throw up, while Justin says his good-byes and nice-to-meet-yous.

Can you believe that? He had a girlfriend all the time?!? That poor thing was probably away on business in California while he was screwing my brains out in a New York hotel room. Sure, I might have been cheating on my fake, gay fiancé . . . but that is totally different from what he did.

I pause for a second so that Justin can catch up with me, and when he does I give his arm a grateful squeeze. I'm so lucky that I have him and don't have to deal with creeps like Evan.

37

Wedding Planning, Shower Planning

According to Martha (and Marion), six months before the wedding date we should have: finalized the wedding date, reserved ceremony and reception locations, completed the guest list and organized the addresses, chosen attendants, and ordered my dress. I am proud to say that I get checks for all of them!

Unfortunately, she also says that I should have: ordered the wedding cake, booked the caterer, booked the music for the ceremony and reception, booked the photographer and videographer, arranged for wedding-day transportation, ordered invitations and thank-you notes, booked the calligrapher, reserved groom's attire, chosen attendants' attire, purchased lingerie, chosen favors, chosen gifts for the wedding party, reserved accommodations for out-of-town guests, and hired a florist.

She doesn't offer many hints on how to accomplish all this . . . especially when you are planning a baby shower at the same time and trying to complete your Christmas shopping. Jamie's shower is less than a week away and I am running around like a chicken with its head cut off.

Somehow, with the help of my mother and Justin, I managed to reserve a private room at one of Jamie's favorite restaurants, Isabella's, and send out invitations to her specific list of forty-two guests. I have neatly recorded the thirty-nine "yes" RSVPs, and that is about all that I have accomplished. In the next seventy-two hours, I need to figure out favors, menu selections, centerpieces, and order a cake. Perhaps I can order the wedding cake and the baby shower cake at the same time and kill two birds with one stone?

On Wednesday, I am on the phone with my mother during lunch, trying to figure out a few of these details. We are going back and forth over which two salads should be offered. I am sticking firmly to Chinese chicken salad and Classic Cobb (Jamie's favorite and mine). Mom is obsessed with providing a vegetarian selection and a pasta choice. I swear, I included her to make things easier for me (and cheaper), but she's made every step of the way more complicated. She *has* made it cost me a lot less, though, so I am forced to deal with her insanity. Finally, after a three-way call to the restaurant (whoever gave mothers access to technology should be shot), we settle on three choices: the Chinese chicken, the Cobb, and a pasta *alla checca* (pasta *and* vegetarian, thank you to Nathan at Isabella's). We are about to do battle over party favors when I am rescued by my lunch bell.

I try not to pull my hair out for the next three hours of book reports, current events, and division with students who are only interested in Santa Claus, menorahs, and ski trips. Finally the last nanny has picked up the only remaining student and I have until 8 A.M. tomorrow to think 100% about Jamie's shower, breaking only to think about my long and incomplete Christmas list.

I bundle myself up to prepare for my short walk home and think about shower favors as I head back to my apartment. Baby-shower favors are trickier than you might think. We all know that Jamie is fussy, and, in typical Jan

Brady fashion, she's been very sensitive about getting her fair share of attention since she is pregnant and I'm "just engaged." I know that if I go with any of the traditional shower-type gifts that she will be disappointed with my lack of creativeness . . . but I have severe time and money constraints that could prevent what I know would be her dream favors. Who knew that planning a baby shower would be so stressful?!? Not to mention the fact that my sneaky brain keeps thinking about wedding favors instead of baby-shower favors.

I enter the apartment to find Logan sitting on the couch, reading a book . . . which I guess is an improvement over watching TV. While he doesn't seem as down all the time as he did a few months ago, he still hasn't gotten motivated enough to do much besides move the remainder of his belongings from his childhood room at home to the second bedroom of my apartment . . . oops, *our* apartment—I've been corrected many times.

"Mom left four messages for you," he informs me.

That's our mom . . . she knows exactly what time school lets out, which is exactly why I turned my phone off for my walk home so that I could think. Poor Logan.

"Thanks, I'll call her back. Any fun ideas for Jamie's baby-shower favors?" I ask him as I head toward my bedroom, peeling off the numerous layers needed to keep from freezing outside.

"Nope."

Just as I'd expected.

I collapse on my bed and try to quickly think of some good favor suggestions before calling my mom back. Unfortunately, I not only can't think of anything good for Jamie, I can't think of anything good for the wedding, either. Before I have a chance to dial the phone, it rings again and I know it's her.

"Where have you been?" she asks.

"Sorry, walking home from school," I answer truthfully.

"Your phone wasn't on."

"The battery died," I lie seamlessly . . . it's truly awful how good at lying I've become in the past four months.

"Do you have the list of things you need to do before Saturday?"

"Yes," I answer miserably, knowing how hard they will be to accomplish.

"Good, I'm trusting you with the favors, centerpieces, and cake."

What?!? She's trusting me with all that stuff? My mother, of all people, should know how untrustworthy I am!

"Do you have any favor ideas?"

"Honestly, Molly, I haven't had much time to think about it. I'm trying to plan a wedding, you know. I've gotta run, sweetie . . . I was supposed to call Marion fifteen minutes ago, but I was waiting for your call." CLICK.

Okay, I think we have some obvious problems here. 1) I am the bride . . . why does she seem to think that she is the one planning the wedding? And 2) What am I going to do about the stuff for Jamie's shower?!? In a panic, I do what any girl would—I call my fake, gay fiancé.

As always, he is there for me. Well, not here for me this exact second as he is at work, but he promises to come "home" (Justin calls my apartment home now, too . . . it's like I run a boardinghouse!) as soon as his shift finishes and to bring restaurant food and favor ideas with him . . . salvation is on the way. I look down at my list. The next thing is the centerpieces.

Thankfully, Marion gave me a list of "Plaza Approved" vendors, which includes florists in Manhattan that they believe work to The Plaza's high standards. I flip through the information she gave me and see that one of the florists is only a few blocks from my apartment. My Secret Garden— that's the one for me! I check the clock and think there is a good chance they could still be open, so I put all my out-door gear back on and head out to take care of the flowers while I'm waiting for Justin to come and save the favor day.

I'm on such a roll ordering flowers for Jamie's shower that I don't even realize how much time has passed until my cell phone rings. It's Justin.

"I'm here with food and you're not," he says jokingly.

"Oh no! I'm on my way. Keep it warm!"

I explain to the florist that my fiancé is waiting for me . . . I get a giddy schoolgirl feeling whenever I use the word "fi-ancé" in everyday life. I pay her the deposit for the shower flowers and arrange to pick them up and a time to come back to make the final flower selections for the wedding.

"Bring your fiancé," she instructs me.

"Great idea!" I agree, knowing that Justin's taste in flow-ers is bound to be as flawless as his taste in everything else is.

I make it home faster than I got there and join the boys, who didn't wait for me, over the seared ahi rolls and Saporos.

"Good news!" I exclaim. "Favors are taken care of (Iris brilliantly suggested making the centerpieces potted roses that guests can keep) . . . tonight we can actually relax!"

They cheer as we all dig in.

38

Cake Tasting

When I wake up the next morning there is only one thought running through my head: TGIF. Thank Goodness It's Friday. Although my weekend is going to be anything but restful, I'm still glad that this insane week is coming to an end. Plus, Fridays are half-days at my school, which means that by 1:00 P.M. I will be able to completely focus on finding the cake for Jamie's shower (and, I hope, my wedding).

I shuffle through the living room, still in a sleepy haze, toward the kitchen to make coffee. It's so hard to get out of bed on these cold, dark mornings. At least I have the lure of a two-week winter break from school in just one week to keep me going. While my little students look forward to Canadian ski trips and tropical cruises for the holidays, I just look forward to a little more free time and my own little Christmas tree . . . although this year it will be tricky since space is sparse here nowadays.

Justin stirs as I move past him, and by the time I shuffle back through the living room, a little more bright-eyed and bushy-tailed thanks to a huge mug of coffee, he's sitting up.

"Good morning," I say quietly.

"Morning," he grumbles.

I swear, he is the worst morning person I have ever met.

"Coffee in the kitchen."

"Good."

I head into the bathroom to start my morning routine. I do the same things every morning. First stop: coffee. Second stop: shower. When I get out of the shower, I put my hair in a towel and go back to my room to make my bed and lay out my outfit. Then I return to the bathroom for the teeth brushing, moisturizer application, deodorant application, and blow-drying . . . plus a little makeup so I don't frighten the children. Then I go back to my room, get dressed, and head to work, grabbing some sort of food from the kitchen on my way out . . . how elaborate the food is depends on how quickly I've completed the morning's routine.

Today I've moved pretty quickly, so I have time to fully toast a low-fat Pop Tart before heading into the cold. Justin comes into the kitchen to fill what is probably his third cup of coffee.

"I'm going cake shopping for Jamie's shower cake and hopefully the wedding cake this afternoon. Want to join?"

"No way, Molly! I'm off carbs this week. I can't cake taste."

"Right, I forgot . . . no carbs. Do you have any wedding cake requests?"

Not that he's going to get to eat it, but I'm being nice.

"Something low-carb if they have it."

"Right," I say as I think, *no way*.

I head out the door, bundled in as much wool as I own. It is really cold this year . . . or maybe it's the same. Every winter I think, *this is the coldest ever*, and every summer I think, *this is the hottest ever*. Who knows? As I walk, my mind is a whirlpool of thoughts. I've got wedding thoughts, baby-shower thoughts, Mom thoughts, Jamie thoughts, Justin thoughts, and the one that my brain keeps stopping on the most: Brad thoughts.

I haven't spoken to him since we danced at the engagement party and things seemed like they could possibly return to a quasi-normal state. I was hoping he would call me in the past week, but he hasn't. *What the heck?* I think as I pull out my cell phone and dial his. I'll be the bigger and better person . . . plus I'm not expecting to actually get him.

"Hello?" he answers. Why is it that whenever I am expecting a machine I get a person?

"Hey, it's Molly."

"What's up?" he says warmly, but not as warmly as he used to . . . or am I being as overly sensitive about this as I am about the weather thing?

"Not too much . . . wedding planning, baby-shower planning, finishing school. What's up with you?"

"About the same . . . but without the baby shower and the finishing school . . . and really, just doing what a snotty coordinator who goes by the name Bliss tells me to do for wedding planning."

"Haha . . . what are your 'jobs?'"

"Well, I've had to get myself measured for a tux . . . twice because Claire and Bliss didn't think the measurements looked right, even though they were. And I have to select the cake since Claire doesn't eat refined sugar, and I have to pick the band. I think that's all they've trusted me with."

"Hey, your list doesn't sound totally different than mine, except my snotty wedding planner goes by the name Mom."

We laugh together and it feels slightly like old times.

"So you're on cake patrol, too? Gee . . . what a surprise."

"Well, I am a bit of a connoisseur." I pause for a second,

hoping that I don't get hurt by Brad again. "Actually, I'm going cake tasting this afternoon—want to join me?"

He pauses for a second and I'm sorry I asked, but then he says, "I'd love to!"

"Fantastic. School lets out at 12:15. I'll call you then."

"Great. See you in a few." CLICK.

Wow. I can't believe he said yes. What a pleasant, happy, wonderful surprise. This is how wedding planning should be . . . not with an overly controlling mother or a fake, gay fiancé . . . with a best friend. I'm completely excited to pick my wedding cake with Brad . . . and the shower cake . . . ugh . . . I've got to remember the shower cake!

Thankfully, the day flies by, and before I know it the kids are gone for the weekend and I'm packing up my stuff. I jump when I hear a knock at my classroom door and stiffen with nerves about who could be on the other side and how long they will detain me from the afternoon I'm looking forward to.

"Come in."

You won't believe who it is. Brad. Standing at the door of my classroom with his big, twinkling grin.

"What are you doing here?!?"

"I thought I'd surprise you."

"Well, you definitely have. A very pleasant surprise," I admit as I cross the room and give him a big, warm hug.

Brad waits while I pack up the rest of my stuff, which recently has been more wedding-related than school-related, and then we head off to Cakery Bakery on the Upper West Side. Marion had recommended it (it's "Plaza Approved") and Bliss had also given it her stamp, so we figure we will be in good hands. I called this morning during recess and although they didn't seem thrilled by the last-minuteness, they gave me an appointment for this afternoon. Phew.

Brad and I take the bus through the park and have only a

short walk between the bus stop and the adorable storefront that is Cakery Bakery. We walk inside and quickly find that this bakery is as charming as its name. Every surface from the floor to the ceiling seems to be painted a different color . . . some solid, some patterned. There is SO much going on, but it works. There is a hip yet motherly woman behind the counter who I assume must be the same woman I spoke to on the phone this morning.

"Hi," I say, "I'm Molly. We have an appointment to do a wedding-cake tasting."

"Oh! Fantastic," she says, as if my presence is a complete, but happy, surprise to her. "I'm Annabelle. Why don't you guys take a seat and I'll bring out the samples."

Annabelle walks into the back room, hollering, "Look through the picture books," over her shoulder as she exits.

Brad and I each pick up one of the "books," which look more like overstuffed family albums, and start looking. They are, in fact, family albums of sorts. There are hundreds and hundreds of pictures of happy couples cutting cakes presumably made by Annabelle and the staff here at Cakery Bakery. In typical Brad and Molly form, we spend more time making fun of the pictured brides and grooms than actually looking at the cakes.

We are practically in tears with laughter over one groom with a particularly atrocious mullet when Annabelle returns. She carries with her dozens of little squares of cakes and dozens of little take-out sauce containers, which she explains contain filling choices. Each little cake square is a different cake choice that they offer. She recommends some popular combinations, such as banana cake with chocolate-fudge filling or carrot cake with cream-cheese filling, but says that the sky is really the limit and to just tell her if we need any more cakes or fillings.

"Wow!" I exclaim with glee as I plop a whole piece of what I discover too late is pistachio cake in my mouth.

"Molly! You're supposed to taste the cake, not just eat it. Here, try this," Brad says, handing me a square of chocolate cake with raspberry-mousse filling.

"Oh my God. That's amazing. Try," and I plop the other half of my bite into his mouth.

We ooh and aah and spoil our mouths with all the amazing combinations. Honestly, we haven't made one that didn't work yet. We thought lemon and chocolate wouldn't . . . but it actually tasted really good.

"We're never going to be able to decide!" I exclaim.

"Don't forget," Annabelle calls over to us, "each layer of your cake can be different."

"That's brilliant," Brad declares.

After a while we aren't any closer to making the decision, but we are so hopped up on the sugar that we are literally bouncing out of our seats. That is when one of us, and I'm not sure who—okay, it was me—decides that we should practice the cake-face smoosh.

"I don't think Claire will ever go for this," Brad admits as I smash chocolate cake with strawberry filling on him.

"Haha . . . neither will Justin," I say with a pang deep down from the knowledge that my wedding will never come this far. Sure, people will stay at the reception and eat the cake . . . that's my plan, but I won't be cutting it with Justin, or smearing it across his mouth. A feeling of sadness washes over me, but doesn't last long because Brad shoves pumpkin cake with cinnamon filling up my nose while laughing hysterically.

By the time Annabelle comes back over, we are covered with cake, filling, and shame. She just laughs.

"Honestly," she says, speaking loudly over our giggles, "you two are the cutest couple I've seen in a long time."

We stop dead in our tracks.

"We're not a couple!" Brad spits out.

"We're friends!" I add.

Annabelle stares at us for a second . . . she's confused and we're uncomfortable. "Really? Um, oh . . . I'm sorry. Well . . . has either of you made any choices?"

"Gee, you know," I stammer, eager to get out of there now and avoiding Brad's eyes, "I think I'll just order the cake for my sister's shower today and come back later to order my wedding cake."

"Me, too," Brad says, "but not the shower cake. My sister's not having a shower. Actually, I don't have a sister. I just have to go."

"Okay," Annabelle says, even more confused by us.

I arrange to pick up a lemon cake with raspberry-mousse filling decorated in all pink and saying, "We Can't Wait for Kate," first thing in the morning, and pay Annabelle as quickly as I can. Then Brad and I leave the Cakery Bakery and walk down the street. Finally we stop and look at each other, making a mutual, unspoken decision to just be cool about what happened.

"That was so weird that she thought we were a couple," I say, trying to act normal but being uncomfortably aware that Claire will bust a gut if she hears about what happened today.

"Seriously," Brad agrees. "So, anyway, I gotta go."

"Me, too!"

And with a quick, awkward hug, we take off in opposite directions down the street . . . unfortunately, the wrong direction for each of us, so a few paces later we are forced to turn around and cross each other again with another awkward, "'Bye."

I can't help but feel disappointed as I ride the bus back home. It felt so good to have Brad back in my life, but the incident with the mistaken engagement has left me concerned that he will shy away from rebuilding our friendship and I will be without him again. I guess it's a good thing that tonight I'll be wrapped up in writing people's names on little metal cans for the florist to pot the centerpiece/party favors in. It's going to be a long night.

39

In Need of a Long, Hot Baby Shower

When my alarm goes off the next morning it is so cold and so dark. I pound it with my fist while cursing myself for forgetting to turn it off for the weekend. I roll over to snuggle under my down comforter before remembering with a start that today is Jamie's shower! I almost break my neck as I jump out of bed and trip over the thirty-nine personalized, metal cans that kept me up until the crack of dawn.

I turn on my bedside lamp, and after the initial blindness wears off, I pick up the one under my foot and examine it. I really do think it was worth the work because they are adorable. I sleepily collect the cans, which need to be delivered to My Secret Garden by 6 A.M. so that they can pot the mini roses and have them all ready in time for the party, as I reach under my bed for a shopping bag large enough to fit them all. I stack them in neat columns to make them fit into a large Restoration Hardware bag left over from the wedding-shower gift I bought for my friend Elizabeth. It was just a pillow, one of the few items on her Restoration Hardware registry that I could afford, but it came in a big box, which I liked. I try to silently get myself and thirty-nine tin pails out of the apartment without waking Justin . . . not an easy feat, but thankfully he is a heavy sleeper.

I get down the dark flights of stairs and am surprised to find the sun on its way up once I am out on the street. I consider hailing a (hopefully) heated cab to go the two and a half blocks to My Secret Garden, but decide against it in hopes that the frigid air will wake me up since getting back between my flannel sheets isn't on today's agenda.

I arrive at the floral shop at 6 A.M. on the dot, unaware of another time I've been up and active so early except for perhaps catching a flight somewhere . . . or more likely a flight from the night before landing. The florist, Iris (yes, I found a florist named after a flower), on the other hand, is as bright and chipper as if it were ten, not six, in the morning.

"Hello, sweetie!" she practically sings as I drag myself and my pails through the door.

"Hi, Iris. Here are the pails."

I hand her the bag and she pulls one out to see my work. I hope she likes them because, quite frankly, I worked my ass off. I wrote each person's name in cute, pink writing with little dots at the end of the letters, then painted little pink, lavender, and yellow roses around each name.

"Oh my gosh, aren't you the most adorable thing ever?" Iris asks as she admires my work.

She doesn't realize it, but she just made my day. Now I truly have the energy to take on all that needs to be accomplished in the next few hours.

"Thank you! So you'll have your delivery person drop them at the restaurant at 11 A.M.?"

"Absolutely—I have all the information right here, and your cell phone number . . . just in case."

Iris quickly became familiar with my somewhat paranoid ways, but she seems okay about working with my insanity. Good thing, since I'm coming back to order wedding flowers next week and I've already mentally changed my mind four times since I met with her two days ago.

"Thank you, Iris. I'll see you next week, okay?"

"Yes. Have a wonderful shower."

I start to head out. "And you said you have my cell phone number, right?"

"Yes, Molly, I have it. Go," she says with a laugh.

I turn and walk out the door. Now I have to get across town to pick up the cake from Cakery Bakery and drop it off at the restaurant. Then it's home to get ready. I decide that for the ride all the way across town, a heated cab is a reasonable splurge.

I duck into a Dean & DeLuca to grab a latte—I know, my fans at Starbucks would be crushed, but I am just not up to being a celebrity right now—before hailing a cab. The warm, caffeinated beverage does wonders for me and I'm practically among the living by the time I get out of the cab in front of Cakery Bakery.

I can tell right off that Annabelle is less like Iris in the morning and more like me. She looks grumpy and holds a venti Starbucks cup in her left hand as she flips through the order slips with her right.

"Ah, here it is," she says as she pulls the slip out. "Jose!" she screeches into the back room. "Bring out the baby-shower cake for Molly Harrigan."

He hollers forward some sort of response that makes sense to her and she tells me that it'll be a few minutes and that I should take a seat. I'm all for sitting down. As I wait, I flip through the cake album again. Without Brad there it's easier to pay attention to the cakes and think seriously about what I might want to order for my wedding.

The sculptures they create with flour, sugar, and water are unbelievable. There are the traditional tiered cakes with fresh flowers and sugared flowers. Even some with fresh and sugared fruit, and one that I particularly like with an amazing silhouette design made from chocolate. But that's just the beginning. There is one that looks like a pile of presents, and another one that looks like a pile of presents from Tiffany in blue boxes with white ribbon! And yet another one that is made up of little cupcakes . . . not to mention the one that looks like a boat; the people seem to have had some sort of a wedding cruise.

These are not the blah white towers I am used to seeing. Some are white, but those are elegant white-on-white with scrollwork or pulled-sugar ribbons. There are also chocolate cakes, pink cakes, blue cakes . . . you name it, they make it. And they are all different shapes, too! Round, square, rectangle, and combinations. Who knew there were so many options? I know from yesterday's cake tasting that these cakes taste good . . . it's hard to believe that they are also so stunning. I'm drooling over a particularly amazing four-tier chocolate cake with sugared raspberries and pink roses when Annabelle breaks my trance.

"Okay, Molly, here's your cake."

I walk up to the counter where she is holding a large pink box open for me. This cake is my favorite of all the cakes in the book! It's a big, bright pink circle with light pink roses painted on . . . they almost look stenciled, and the words, *We Can't Wait for Kate* in turquoise script across it. My sister is going to love it, which makes me love it even more.

"It's amazing, Annabelle. Thank you."

"Of course, sweetie. We'll see you in a few weeks to order yours. You know you can do the same stencil flowers on it, if you like."

"Really? Maybe?" Oh Jeez . . . another option for me!

I carry the cake, which is not only bigger but much heavier than I'd expected, out of the bakery and somehow manage to hail a cab by kicking my leg in the air . . . without falling over and dropping the cake in the street. The cab speeds down the nearly empty streets a few miles to the restaurant, where he lets me out without so much as an offer to open the door. I kick it shut with my foot and he speeds away again. Then I try to follow the restaurant manager's instructions to find the service door where someone will be there to take the cake and put it in their refrigerator. For the life of me, I can't find the door. I walk back and forth three times, carrying the world's heaviest cake, and I'm not having any luck. Finally, on my fourth time past, I remember that he said you have to walk up a little stairway at the side of the main door. Ugh . . . I need to start taking gingko biloba or something . . . my memory is shot. I think I might pass out by the time I reach the top of the stairs. I kick the door gently, since I don't have a free hand to knock, and stand there sweating under my layers of wool and the weight of the cake until Nathan, the restaurant manager, finally opens the door.

"Ah, Molly with the cake," he says.

I gratefully hand it over to him and go over the schedule for the lunch once again, still trying to catch my breath. He seems calm and organized about everything, so I leave to go home and change so I can be back in a few hours. I check my watch when I get onto the street . . . hard to believe it's only 8:00 A.M. I feel like I've already had a full day. I have three hours to get home and get changed. Plenty of time . . . maybe I can even sneak in a little nap? I yawn at the thought of my bed and decide that a nap is definitely in order. I jump in a cab and before I know it, I'm home. The apartment looks exactly how I left it . . . both boys are asleep—it's clear they never even knew I was gone. Sleepily, I pad to my room, remove the wool, and climb back into bed.

The day is going even better than I'd planned. The morning errands went so quickly and smoothly that I actually have time to sleep for one hour! It won't completely make up for the total lack of sleep the night before, but it will definitely help. There is only one problem . . . as I drift off, thinking about what I will wear to Jamie's shower, I don't think one drop about setting my alarm.

I awake from a dream, where I am actually dancing with one of the cakes I saw pictured at Cakery Bakery to "Just the Way You Look Tonight," to Justin shaking me and yelling.

"Molly! You overslept!! You were supposed to get the pails to the florist and pick up the cake. Oh my God!! Logan! She's still sleeping!"

I manage to open my eyelids and focus on Justin, almost surprised that he isn't a life-sized cake man, and take a second to process what he is saying.

"Wait, no, it's okay. I got up and did it all this morning. What time is it now?"

"It's ten!" Justin says, panic still in his voice.

I bolt straight up.

"Did you say ten?!?"

"Yeah!"

"Oh my God! I did oversleep. I gotta get ready. The shower starts in an hour, across town."

Justin gets out of my way just in time to avoid being flattened by Hurricane Molly as I speed around my room trying to collect God-knows-what before flying into the bathroom and jumping into the shower.

I wash at the speed of light and even decide in the interest of time that I will forgo washing my hair, which is a little gross, but I'm hoping if I wear it up the grossness won't be obvious. Not getting my hair wet will save me a good twenty minutes, and I need the time. I go through the normal points of my getting-ready routine, but today they are at warp speed. I slow down momentarily to put on some makeup because I once had a bad experience putting on makeup in a hurry and I ended up frightening a child who was afraid of clowns.

I fly into my bedroom and run to my closet door frantically because I still don't know what to wear. Have you ever noticed that it is the days that you are running late that are the hardest to pick an outfit? If I have nowhere to be, I pull out the cutest thing on the first try. If I need to be somewhere fast, I inevitably pull out hot-pink leggings and a green tank top. I look at my clothes and groan.

"Molly!" Justin calls from the other room. "Outfit's on your bed."

I turn around, and laid out on my bed, just like I would have done it, but cuter, is the perfect outfit for Jamie's shower. A winter-white cashmere turtleneck sweater . . . more of a funnel neck, really, and a gift last Christmas from Mom, so it's a double win because it's adorable and seeing me wear it will make her happy. He's paired it with a knee-length, camel-and-winter-white-plaid skirt, but the plaid is very faint, and my brown knee-high boots. Let me tell you, this is why I am fake-marrying the guy.

"I love you!" I call out to him.

"I know," he answers.

I throw the outfit on and am so happy that I don't need to do the frantic rip-on-and-off, what-do-I-wear? dance that is usually an inevitability when I'm running late, and head for the door. Before I can reach it, the phone rings. I grab it in a hurry.

"Hello?"

"Molly, it's Mom. There was a traffic accident on the highway and I'm running late."

"That's okay," I tell her, "the shower doesn't start until 11:30—we just said we'd meet at 11:00 to give ourselves time to set up."

That half-hour bumper is the only reason that I didn't go completely ballistic and go to the shower in my sweats.

"But I forgot my card at home, so I need to stop and buy one," Mom whines.

"Mom, just give her the card another time."

"Now tell me, Molly, how will she know which gift is mine if it doesn't have a card?"

There are two problems with this question: 1) the "now"—damn Marion . . . it's such a little thing, but it really irks me and 2) the gift. We were supposed to get her a gift?!? The shower wasn't enough? We need a tangible, wrapped present? The panic wells up in my chest again.

"Mom! I've gotta go—just get there when you can." CLICK.

I hear Mom starting to say something else as I hang up the phone, but all I can think is "gift." I yell to the guys that I'll see them there (because of her extreme hipness, Jamie is having a co-ed baby shower), grab my coat and purse, and pull them on as I run down the steps and to the curb where I hail the first cab I see.

"Pottery Barn Kids on Broadway at Sixty-seventh!" I yell at the driver, who I think I frighten because he puts the pedal to the metal and off we fly.

I jump out of the cab, throwing a generous tip through the little window, more because I don't want to wait for change than to thank him for his excellent service. I run inside the store and look around, at a complete loss. In typical Pottery Barn style, a friendly employee quickly greets me.

"Help!" I yell at the poor girl, who is probably just working there while she is on winter break from college. "I need a shower gift for my sister!"

"Is she registered here?" the girl asks, trying to keep her calm but obviously frightened by me.

"I don't know?!?"

"Let's check," she says as she scurries over to a terminal that looks identical to the hundreds I have stood before to select engagement presents, bridal-shower presents, and wedding presents. "What's your sister's name?"

"Jamie Harrigan-Hope," I say and start to spell it, but

before I get to the second R the Pottery Barn Savior says she has found her and prints out a list.

Who knew you could register for baby gifts?!? This probably is not good information for me to have. I scan the list over . . . I wish I had time to adore all the cute things Jamie has selected for baby Kate.

"Ah-ha! Bumpers. I'll take the bumpers," I inform the girl.

"Don't you want to see them first?"

"Yes . . . but I'm in a huge rush."

"Okay," she says, going back into fear mode. "They are right over here," she says, leading me to a display and taking down some adorable pink-gingham, quilty-looking crib bumpers.

"Perfect, adorable—can you wrap them?"

"We have a courtesy wrap that is—"

Before she can describe it, I say, "I'll take it!" and whip out my credit card.

As I'm waiting for the trembling girl to wrap the package, I fill out the courtesy wrap card, *Bumpers for Bumper. Love, Auntie M.* Perfect. I grab the package, slip my card through the ribbon, and am back in a cab headed for the restaurant in record time.

I arrive at 11:10, thank God, exactly three minutes before my mother. The restaurant has done everything perfectly, with white tablecloths and pink napkins. Iris has set up the centerpieces and party favors/seat assignments perfectly. Everything is perfect. And all the running around and panicking and insanity is worth it when Jamie walks through the door, incandescent with pregnancy glow, and gets teary at all the perfection.

Jamie is in her element. Her adoration of the spotlight helps her to shine even more and the party goes off perfectly. Everyone goes crazy for the cake. And Jamie receives the thirty-nine cutest gifts I've ever seen. I think she likes mine the best, though, because it's the only one she cries a little for. It's a wonderful afternoon. Phew. Now I can get back to wedding planning . . . oh yeah, and Christmas shopping.

40

Tiptoeing Through the Tulips (and Calla Lilies and Hydrangeas)

It's Friday morning, the last day of school before the winter break, and I think I am more anxious for vacation to start than my students . . . but I like to think I contain myself better than they do. I have a room full of eight-year-olds literally bouncing off the walls. If I thought last week all they could think about was Santa, this week is off the charts. Luckily, nobody is expected to actually learn anything today.

Because of the start of the break, today is an ever-more-abbreviated Friday than usual. I do have a quick (and easy— I didn't want to be a Grinch) spelling test to give, as I do every Friday, but after that it's a holiday party and then everyone is home free. I decide to take it ridiculously easy on the kids and test them on twenty words that are all holiday-related. What can I say? I'm in the spirit, too.

Although they make a fuss when I announce it's time to take out a piece of paper and a pencil, they eventually calm down and take the test. Then I let them color holiday cards while I grade the tests. Some of the students, even at eight years old, are very intense and would be stressed about the test results over the two-week vacation. I don't want anybody stressing on vacation! Overall, the scores aren't as high as I'd expected, considering how easy I thought the words were, but I look up and see them giddy with anticipation and understand what they are going through. I give it a 50/50 chance that I would misspell the word "presents" today, too.

The wedding is fast approaching and baby Kate is approaching even faster. Even though she's not due for over a week, Jamie's doctor said she has already dilated three centimeters and the baby could come any day now. I am so impressed with Jamie that she decided to work up until the break . . . she must be more terrified than ever about the peeing thing, though.

I pass out the test results, and though there are moans and groans, I can tell that nobody really cares. They want the party, and you know what? I do, too! By 10:00, the kids are stuffing their faces with cupcakes and Christmas cookies and Hanukkah gelt. I pity the nannies who are going to have to spend the afternoon dealing with these kids on extreme sugar highs.

By 11:30, all the hyper ones have been picked up and I am pretty excited about the pile of presents that a few parents (but mostly nannies) have dropped on my desk upon picking up their charges. One of the most insane (read: awesome) things about working at the private school that I do is that the families are extremely generous with their kids' teachers at the holidays. From where I'm sitting I can already see three *blue* boxes!

I load as many as I can into my bag and hide the rest under my desk to pick up later, then take off to meet Justin for lunch. I feel like I've hardly had time for him lately . . . I suppose he doesn't really care, but I do, and I want to include him in the wedding planning, so we're having lunch to go over stuff.

I meet him at a California Pizza Kitchen . . . don't ask me

why, but I am crazy about that place. Brad always used to make fun of me for it, and it took quite a bit of convincing to get Justin to agree to go there, but for some reason, although I am a New York girl at heart and loyal to NY pizza, every once in a while I crave a barbeque chicken pizza. I said don't ask me why! Of course, I get there first and secure a table for us and am chowing down my third slice of bread when Justin shows up.

"Good Golly Miss Molly," he jokes with me, "when are you planning the move to the suburbs?"

"Huh?" I ask with my mouth full of bread.

"They love chain restaurants out there . . . you'll fit right in."

"Shut up," I instruct him as I take another bite of bread.

I continue to take shit for my love of the CPK as Justin complains about the menu, but finally finds a salad (ugh, healthy people can be so annoying) that will be acceptable. We order and I pull out my wedding binder. Yes, I have become one of those brides with a binder. Actually, according to both Maggie *and* Alex, you have to have one . . . it's, like, a law or something.

"So, flowers . . . we're meeting with Iris after lunch."

"I love that you found a florist named Iris."

"I know—me, too. So, I was thinking roses."

"Bor-ring. Everyone thinks roses. Let's think calla lilies."

"Calla lilies," I echo.

"And lily of the valley for your bouquet so it will smell good. We should also think about hydrangeas and tulips."

"See, this is why I needed you with me."

Justin and I finish our lunch, and although he complains about how awful the food is, he eats every last speck of his salad. We then head out to meet with Iris. Our plan is to order the flowers and then go Christmas shopping. We step onto the cold street and I can't help but feel warm. I adore Manhattan at Christmastime more than any other time of the year. There really is a hustle and bustle that I know drives a lot of people crazy, but I adore it.

We arrive at My Secret Garden and Iris is cheerfully waiting for us. She warmly introduces herself to Justin and we get down to work. It's like she and Justin are sharing a brain and I'm not even there. Iris had already decided that roses were "too ordinary" for us and was also thinking hydrangeas. Luckily, I love hydrangeas . . . although nobody asks. Then we—actually, *they*—move on to the bouquets.

"What color is your dress, Molly?" Iris asks me before taking it back, realizing I cannot discuss it in front of Justin.

"Oh no, that's okay, it's white," Justin tells her, and on they go.

They decide that my bouquet will be pure white hydrangeas. Iris shows Justin a sample of how the flowers will look, and although nobody is asking for my opinion, I do think it will be stunning. I always thought down-home garden weddings were charming (in fact, it's what I always thought I would have), and the feel that Iris and Justin are creating will re-create that in The Plaza! Next, they move on to the maid of honor's bouquet.

"What color is Jamie going to be wearing?" Justin asks me.

"I dunno—I was going to let her pick whatever she wants."

"NO!" Iris and Justin yell at the same time.

Okay, apparently it is very important that Jamie wear a dress that follows the "feel" of the day. Justin decides it would be stunning if her dress was white, like mine, with a blue sash. Then Logan can wear a tie the same blue as the sash. I'd never thought about a white bridesmaid's dress, but in all honesty, it does sound stunning. The flower aficionados pair a blue hydrangea bouquet with Jamie's dress and coordinate boutonnières for the men. They quickly and easily select the rest of the flowers while I sit there like a little kid. I'm okay with it, though; impeccable taste in flowers is just another advantage to having a fake, gay fiancé. After we have finished and are getting up to leave, Iris pulls me aside and informs me that Justin is the most involved groom she has ever dealt with and is therefore quite a catch. I have no choice but to laugh to myself . . . quite a catch, he is. Sure, part of me wishes that he was like most fiancés and got out of my way . . . I mean, I am paying him good money to let *me* have *my* dream wedding; but on the other hand, it's easier to deal with my enormous (and possibly atrocious) lie if I just sit back and let someone else do all the talking.

41

Christmas Shopping

Later that afternoon, as I follow Justin around a crowded Bloomingdale's while he suggests perfect gifts for all my friends and loved ones, I share Iris's comment with him. To say it tickles him pink is an understatement. Honestly, it gives him a new burst of energy, and minutes later he selects the most stunning cashmere gloves and scarf for my mother.

Some people on my list are easy, like my mom, and some are really hard . . . like Logan. I'm trying really hard to find the perfect gift for him. Giving perfect gifts is a compulsion, even an obsession, of mine. It is important to find the gift for each person that just clicks. For Mom it was the gloves, since the week before at Jamie's shower she stuck her thumbnail through the tip of her old, wool glove. I knew she would simply stitch it up when she got home, but these brand-new gloves are the perfect way to be practical, which she insists on, but also spoil her, which I insist on.

I comb the housewares department, looking for something for Logan to put in the apartment that will help make it feel like his, too, but nothing is calling to me. I take that back. Nothing is calling to me that would be right for Logan . . .

tons of things are calling to me that would be perfect to register for. I cannot wait to have my home filled with all these nice things. Eight years out of college, and I am still using the cheap, crappy stuff I could afford as a student. All of my friends have replaced this stuff with their registry gifts, so you eat at their homes on matching Villeroy & Boch plates and Target specials at mine. It probably doesn't bother anyone but me . . . but still.

I'm still searching around the housewares . . . Justin has actually gotten bored and wandered off to the men's department. You know you've been shopping too long when you tire out a gay man. I'm close to giving up for the day when my cell phone rings.

"Good Golly Miss Molly!" my mother practically screams with delight into the phone. "Your sister is in labor!"

My heart skips a beat . . . maybe four or five . . . and lands up somewhere in my throat.

"Jamie's in labor?!?" I confirm.

"Yes, we're already in the city. Meet us at the hospital. Maternity is on the fifth floor."

"The fifth floor," I repeat like a robot. "We're on our way."

I race out of housewares and fly down countless flights of stairs, since I am too impatient to wait for the elevators. I finally locate Justin in the dressing room of the men's section, trying on leather pants. (Don't ask . . . but I do make a mental note that the pants are a possible Christmas gift for him.)

"Jamie's in labor!" I yell.

"Oh my God!" he replies as he starts thrashing around the room like a fish out of water, trying to get the leather pants off and his regular (designer) jeans back on. Finally he does, and we fly out of Bloomingdale's like the place is on fire. We hail the first cab we can (a week before Christmas, cabs are few and far between) and for a moment I curse the hustle and bustle I normally adore.

What feels like hours, but is only minutes later, we arrive at the hospital and run in like we are the ones about to give birth. We locate my family in a pleasant, but mostly bare, waiting room on the fifth floor.

"Where is she? We didn't miss it, did we?" I breathlessly ask my mother as we hurry toward her. My father and Logan, who must have come from our apartment, which is closer to the hospital than Bloomingdale's, sit tensely on the little mauve waiting room chairs.

"Not yet . . . but she's been in labor all day, so it could be soon!"

"Why didn't anyone call us sooner?"

"I guess she'd been having a lot of Braxton Hicks contractions this past week and she didn't realize until her water broke about an hour ago that this was the real thing. Of course, when her water broke she actually thought she'd peed herself, but thankfully Bryan figured it out."

I can't help but laugh at my sister as Justin and I sit down with my family to wait for the newest Harrigan (Harrigan-Hope) to arrive. We sit and wait for a week . . . okay, not really a week, but it feels like it. In the meantime, Bryan's parents have arrived and all seven of us are beyond restless when, four hours later, an exhausted-looking Bryan comes out to inform us that Kate has arrived.

"She's amazing!" He glows with warmth and personality rarely displayed by Bryan Hope. "She's so beautiful—she looks just like Jamie. She is big and healthy—eight pounds, one ounce. You can see her in the nursery."

We all jump up and try to walk, but really we run and scramble over each other to get to the nursery window first. She's hard to miss because she really does look like Jamie. I've always thought it was crap when parents said a baby looked like one parent or the other the day it was born because in my experience all babies tend to look the same, but Kate is different. She looks like an old soul. She has Jamie's upturned nose and full lips, plus, unlike all the other babies who are lying there sleeping, Kate is looking around making sure nobody is getting anything she's not . . . just like her mom would be. She could not look more amazing, wrapped in a pink blanket and wearing a tiny pink hat. They have her in a little plastic crib thing with a pink paper taped to the front that says, "Harrigan-Hope, Kate Anne." Her handwritten name sign makes her so official. My niece has arrived. My mother has a granddaughter, Logan is an uncle . . . so we do what we Harrigans always do: we burst into tears while my father gently shakes his head at us . . . except today there are tears in his eyes, too.

42

Too Many Distractions

Needless to say, the two-week holiday break that I thought would be devoted entirely to wedding planning hasn't exactly turned out that way. It's just impossible to think about wedding bands and photographers with Kate in the world. I have spent almost my entire vacation at Jamie's house staring at the baby sleep, staring at the baby eat, staring at the baby stare at me. She is beyond amazing.

I've also been amazed staring at Jamie. I never quite realized just what a born mother she is. She is so natural with Kate. There is only one thing she needs constant, and I repeat *constant*, reassurance about. Her fear of peeing in public has been irrationally replaced with the fear that Kate is an ugly baby and she can't see it. She is convinced, as is probably true, that all mothers think their infants are stunning, no matter how monkeylike they actually look. Fortunately, in her case, Kate really is an exceptionally beautiful baby, but we still have to reassure Jamie at least twenty-five times a day.

So . . . here it is, New Year's Eve, my vacation is more than 75% over, and I *need* to get some wedding planning done. I've forbidden myself from going to Jamie's; in fact,

I've forbidden myself from leaving the apartment before Alex and Steve's New Year's Eve party tonight. Right now, I am sitting in front of the television, looking at tapes of wedding bands . . . for the most part, they are making me want to shoot myself. Marion explained to me the importance of finding a band that had experience emceeing events, because more important than the music, they would be leading the entire evening. She gave me a stack of tapes of "Plaza Approved" bands, but so far, every single one of them has at least one member with a mullet and boasts their renditions of "Part Time Lover" and "Still the One." They are so dorky that they make Adam Sandler in *The Wedding Singer* look studly.

"Ugh," I grunt miserably.

Lately, anything and everything to do with the wedding has been causing a hard and uncomfortable knot in my stomach. I'm quickly realizing that wedding planning isn't all fun . . . it isn't even half fun, and without the balance of actually being in love, it is often a big disappointment. There are some times, usually at moments like this, when I start to think that my decision might not have been a good one.

"Pull it together," I command myself. "Eyes on the prize . . ."

I think hard about why I am doing this—I need to think of something positive right now!

"Kate in a flower-girl dress," is what I finally come up with.

I take a deep breath and decide that her sweet baby smell is exactly what I need to pull me out of this funk, so I put the rest of the wedding planning aside and head off to see my niece.

Of course, I spend too long with her, so I am rushing like a maniac to get ready for Alex and Steve's party on time. It is definitely worth having to hurry, though . . . the infant was able to cheer me out of my wedding-planning depression with a single, *Ah-goo*. I already have my outfit for the evening selected . . . actually, specifically purchased with the help of my gay fashion team, Justin and Logan. It's a black satin slip dress with sequins sewn in loops around my body. All the hems of the dress are sewn in magenta and I've even splurged and purchased a pair of magenta satin shoes to complete the look. They are extremely high, pointy, and strappy, and I can't walk too well, but I look amazing hobbling around in them. There is a very real possibility that I could freeze to death in my mad dashes between homes and cabs, but the floor-length velvet coat that Justin gave me for Christmas greatly reduces this risk.

What is taking so long in this getting-ready process is that Justin and Logan also decided that I needed to wear my hair curly tonight. This is trickier than it sounds because although my hair will dry wavy when left to air-dry, I cannot go out with it damp tonight because it will freeze . . . and frizzing is also a huge risk. I have every product I own on it, and I'm using a combination of every hair-styling tool . . . I think eventually it will be cute—either that or completely fall out—keep your fingers crossed.

Justin is dressed in the black leather pants I gave him for Christmas. I secretly think he looks a little too gay in them, but aside from looking gay, he definitely looks fantastic and I know he loves them, which makes me happy. He's paired them with a dark-red, button-front shirt and black Prada loafers, and even though I know he has no interest in me or anyone of my gender, it's hard not to think he looks incredibly sexy.

Logan, our "third wheel" for the night, also looks fantastic. I guess Justin is helping him to hone his gay fashion instinct because I have never seen him so well dressed. He has on gray flannel slacks and a black cashmere crew-neck sweater that nicely shows off that he has added working out to his busy schedule of sitting on the couch watching TV and sitting on the couch reading. He is also wearing the identical Prada loafers that Justin has on. I swear, they have become the Gay Bobbsey Twins.

As we walk into the party, which is already in a pretty full swing, I swear that heads turn and look at me, flanked by the two best-dressed guys in the room. It's a good feeling. We break from our entry formation so that Justin and Logan can go get drinks, and I cruise the room, looking for my friends. Before I can find anyone, a server comes around with a tray of icy-cold vodka shots and I take two . . . what the heck? It's New Year's Eve. The first familiar face I see is Brad. I take a deep breath and hope he's here alone as I approach him.

"Hey, stranger!" I greet him warmly.

He turns around and stares at me blankly before finally muttering, "Molly, wow," under his breath and then, "Hey there," at a normal volume. I can't help but smile.

For the third time in our friendship . . . the first was the day we met and the second was that infamous night junior year . . . I notice how handsome Brad is. He is wearing a blue shirt that brings out his sparkling eyes and I feel a little twinge. It must be that I see him so infrequently now that I forget what he looks like. When we were hanging out all the time, it was easier to ignore, or not notice, his looks.

"You look great," I tell him.

"No, *you* look great." I smile and feel another little twinge. Damn those vodka shots. "So, where's Mr. Molly?" he asks.

I feel slightly let down for a second at the reminder that we are both there with significant others, mine being exceptionally significant because of his fakeness.

"At the bar with Logan. What about Claire?" I ask, and hold my breath.

"She actually went to Aspen, Colorado, to ski with her family for the holidays."

Hallelujah. The party will be fun!

"Why didn't you go?" I ask, hoping that the reason is that he has freed himself from her evil clutches since I know he does in fact love to ski.

"Work," he answers blandly.

We chat idly for a few more minutes before Alex comes up to greet me. She looks stunning, as always, with her pale, freckly white skin and shockingly natural black hair. Alex has clearly had plenty of vodka shots and she is cracking us up.

I love seeing all my friends dressed up and all together for the holiday. I must admit, we clean up nicely. The vodka, and later champagne, flows freely and everyone is having a fantastic time. It feels like we've only been there a couple of hours when Steve clinks some glasses together and informs us that it's time to turn our attention to their big-screen TV because the ball is about to drop in Times Square.

In a vodka-happy blur, I turn toward the TV as Justin comes up behind me and whispers in my ear.

"Molly, we're gonna have to kiss at New Year's."

My heart jumps . . . I hadn't thought about this important detail, but he is right. Obviously, all couples kiss at New Year's, engaged ones with presumably more passion than most, and since I'd shot my mouth off and informed everyone we do it every day, they are probably counting on us to provide the celebration fireworks. I nod in agreement and everyone starts counting backward from ten. It'll be okay, I tell myself . . . it'll be nice to have someone to kiss.

"3-2-1-Happy New Year!"

And as "Auld Lang Syne" begins to play in the background, Justin takes me in his arms and we share our first kiss. He is an undeniably good kisser, but it is one of the grossest experiences of my life. It's a lot like being forced to French kiss my brother. We pull apart and I see that we have matching looks of disgust on our faces, which we quickly erase as I turn to kiss my brother (on the cheek, of course) and he shakes hands with Brad and then we switch and he hugs Logan, warmly, and Brad and I kiss (on the cheek, of course). I then grab another glass of champagne from a passing server and take a large, celebratory swig.

43

Registering

A month and a half later, it's hard to believe it's already Valentine's Day and the wedding is four and a half months away. The pride I'd had at completing all the items on the six-months-ahead list has vanished because I have hardly made a dent in the "four-to-six-months-ahead" list. Considering it will be time to hit the "two-to-four-months-ahead" list in two weeks, I am frantic about getting stuff done.

I need to: arrange for wedding-day transportation (I'm not quite sure what that entails, but Martha says to do it), order the invitations and book the calligrapher to address them, register for gifts (hooray!), find the attire for Jamie and Logan that Justin specifically selected so long ago, choose the favors, and reserve accommodations for out-of-town guests.

Although Justin has been swamped lately, he has promised to take me back to Bloomingdale's to officially register as our Valentine's Day date. I have been warned it can't go too late, though, because he has also promised to take Logan to his first "Gay Valentine's" at a gay bar. As the older sister, I have asked to specifically be left out of any details regarding this adventure.

I'm trying to stay "up" and excited about my Valentine's Day, but a little part of me feels completely miserable—364 days a year, having a fake, gay fiancé is fantastic. On Valentine's Day it completely sucks . . . it really rubs my nose in the fact that I am alone. I'm trying to stay focused on the wedding and not think about this, though.

"Eyes on the prize," I tell myself as I lay out clothes. "Bridal registry, bridal shower, being the bride." This is getting harder every time.

Thinking about the wedding brightens my spirits a little. Hey, I might be alone, but at least I'm a bride. I finish dressing just as Justin rings the buzzer, so I head straight downstairs to meet him. We decide that grabbing a slice of pizza is a good Valentine's dinner for us since restaurants create insanely pricey menus of substandard, heart-shaped ravioli. Then we head off to Bloomingdale's, which is relatively empty at 7:00 P.M. on Valentine's Day, sans the few anxious-looking men purchasing last-minute gifts for wives or girlfriends.

As we make our way upstairs to housewares, I think about Tiffany's . . . I had wanted to register there, but for the first time my mother disagreed with Marion and said that it really would be better to register at Bloomingdale's because they have a great variety of prices for people to choose gifts from. As much as I'd had my heart set on filling the apartment with Tiffany crystal, she had a point . . . I remember when my friends Elizabeth and Anthony got married and the cheapest thing on their Tiffany registry was a $250 crystal coaster . . . I was bothered.

So, we make it through the displays of plates and glasses to the Bridal Registry department, where a Bloomingdale's employee, ironically named Tiffany, sets us up on the computer. Once she has our names, wedding date, and shipping address, she gives us a few quick instructions on how to work the scanner gun and then sets us loose in the store. Holding that scanner gun is quite a feeling of power!

We get down to business quickly. Martha is kind enough to include a registry guide in her magazine, so I pull it out of my bag and we follow her instructions to the letter. She recommends starting with china, so we start with china. I have been looking at china for years and years while purchasing gifts for everyone else in the world, so I have a pretty good idea of what I want. Simple, elegant, platinum trim . . . it's an easy decision for me. We're already off and running.

We continue to scan like crazy, adding kitchen utensils for me, kitchen utensils for Justin—we even scan in a couple gifts for Logan. We select two sets of towels: pink Ralph Lauren ones that I will keep and sapphire-blue ones for Justin. My head is practically spinning from all the stuff we've selected and scanned . . . I wonder if that scanner ray is affecting my brain? Then, just as I think maybe I have a second wind coming on, Justin announces that it's time for him to meet Logan, and like that, BAM, my Valentine's Day is over.

We take a cab back to my place, but Justin doesn't even walk me to the door because an excited Logan comes bouncing down the front steps as soon as our cab pulls up and we seamlessly switch seats. The cab speeds away with the boys waving happily out the window, and I head upstairs alone. Inside, I remove my sweater in favor of an old, well-broken-in sweatshirt, and I grab the pint of Ben & Jerry's I'd stashed earlier in the day out of the freezer. Then Tiffany and I settle in for our double date with Ben & Jerry while we watch cheesy, romantic eighties movies. It's much like most of my previous Valentine's Days, but I'm okay . . . I swear.

I honestly don't know why being alone on Valentine's

Day is harder this year than in the past. I mean, this year I'm engaged! I'm months away from my dream wedding!! It seems like this should carry me through this Hallmark holiday, but instead it seems to be making it worse. More than usual, I feel the hard knot in my stomach reminding me that I am living a lie and that what matters is being with someone you love, not just being a bride. I take a deep breath as I take a big, chocolatey bite . . . I probably should have bought two pints of Ben & Jerry's.

44

Mailing the Invitations

I am barely recovered from Valentine's Day when suddenly it's time to mail the wedding invitations. For the past two weeks, I have spent all my free time sitting in my apartment, stuffing the invitations and response cards into beautifully calligraphied "inner envelopes" and then stuffing those into "outer envelopes." It's quite a process . . . believe me, it's harder than it sounds. Now the end is near, and with each lick of an envelope and application of a "love" stamp, the knot in my stomach is growing. In the same way that the handwritten sign on Kate's hospital bassinette made her official, these stunningly letterpressed invitations make my wedding, my *fake* wedding, official.

I have to admit—I'm starting to see that my plan isn't exactly as flawless as it seemed all those months ago when Justin stuck my Nana's engagement ring in a scone. I look down at my left hand with the beautiful engagement ring, and for the first time, I think about how Nana would feel if she knew what I was doing. Well, that's a lie . . . I had thought about it before, and always quickly convinced myself that as the ultimate wedding lover, Nana would be completely happy for me. Now I feel like that probably isn't true . . . Nana loved weddings because she loved romance more than anything else and nothing can be more romantic than a wedding. Of course, that is true—unless the wedding is a total farce . . . like mine. Don't worry . . . I'm not turning back; my dress is to die for, the flowers are going to be amazing, and I've heard rumblings about my bridal shower lately . . . it just feels bigger now, is all.

I finally have them all ready to go, and they sit on the coffee table, lined up in boxes, and they kind of frighten me. My mother and Marion had instructed me to take them to the post office to get them hand canceled, but I'm afraid to go alone. Of course, neither Justin nor Logan is here. Logan got a job as the assistant to the director of art at the Met, and now that he has a little money he and Justin are out on the town nonstop. Justin has convinced me that his hanging out with Logan is the perfect cover story in case they run into anyone who might question things. The truth is that although I feel slightly like my little brother stole my best friend, I am grateful to have a little of the peace and quiet Tiffany and I were once overdosing on way back when . . . except right now, when I could really use some company.

"You don't want to go to the post office with me, do you?" I question the white cat. She meows politely and rolls onto her back for a belly scratch.

I pick up the phone to call Jamie, but realize that it would be selfish to ask her to leave her four-month-old daughter to accompany her thirty-year-old sister to the post office. Then I call Lauren, but I forget she and Rob are away for the weekend. Next I call Alex, but she and Steve are spending the day trying to get pregnant . . . she actually tells me this and it actually makes me quite jealous. Finally, I dial Brad, knowing that if I even reach him he won't be able to go, but I figure I might as well try.

I'm surprised that he answers and even more surprised

that he is willing, even sounds happy, to go to the post office with me. I put the lids on the boxes and stack them neatly in a (hopefully) waterproof bag, just in case, and head out to meet Brad.

Brad and I meet at a Starbucks . . . not THE Starbucks . . . and grab a quick latte before heading downtown to the open post office. Brad had to take his invitations the week before, so fortunately he knows exactly where we are going. We make stupid, idle chitchat about how our respective wedding planning is going, but it is nice not to be doing it alone. With his big day just one week after mine, we are on very similar schedules. I feel like it's kind of weird that we never bring up Claire or Justin, but I don't want to be the one to rock the boat. Even though it feels like there is a giant pink elephant between us, it's good to have Brad back in my life.

We get to the post office and for a moment I am paralyzed in fear before walking up the steps. This really is it . . . this really is the last chance to turn around and end the charade with only a few of the most important people in my life having been viciously lied to for the past eight months. I feel like I might throw up. I move my eyes only because the rest of me is positively stuck and look at Brad. Brad is looking at me with a mixture of concern and confusion.

"You okay?" he asks.

"This makes it feel so official," I manage to get out.

"I know . . . once those babies are out in the world, people start making arrangements," he says, joking because he thinks I'm joking. Only I return his joke with a look of terror and he switches gears. "You don't have to do this."

"Yes, I do . . . they are already being mailed out late."

"No, I mean you don't have to get married . . . to Justin," he says gently.

Suddenly, I am very tense and on edge. What is he trying to do to me? Anger swells through my body. It was one thing for me to try to break up his marriage to Claire right when they first got engaged . . . but for him to be doing this now, just a couple of months before the wedding, at the post office, of all places. It is totally insane. Insanely awful, that is. I am about to explode.

"How dare you?!?" I yell at him.

I can tell from the shocked expression on his face that he didn't expect me to explode like that at him right here on the street, in front of the United States Postal Service building. Then his expression changes to a far more distant, cold one.

"How dare I do what?" he asks rigidly. "How dare I make sure that my friend knows she doesn't have to do anything she doesn't want to do? How dare I only want you to be happy?"

"How dare you try to talk me out of getting married! You're just trying to get even for when I did it to you!"

Brad looks at me disgustedly.

"You know that's not the truth. Forget it, Molly, I'm done here."

And with that he turns around and walks off, leaving me, and my bag of invitations, alone on the steps to the post office. It doesn't exactly register to me how awful I was or that I am completely at fault. I turn on my heel, exactly as he had, but in the opposite direction and march up the steps. I'll show him. I'll mail these invitations right now and I will have this wedding!

I enter the post office and wait in an epic line, but my mind is racing so fast after my fury at Brad that I don't even notice how long it takes. It feels like a few short seconds later that I'm thrusting the envelopes onto the counter and walking out empty-handed. Then I get on the subway and go home . . . it feels like I haven't even blinked yet.

I enter my apartment, still in a rage, and am glad to find Justin and Logan sitting side by side watching TV. I immediately start on a rampage about how awful Brad Lawson is.

I retell the entire incident, and because I am so convinced of my rightness, I stick exactly to the truth and leave out any embellishments. After I have gotten it all out, I feel slightly better from the venting . . . until I look up at their faces, that is. From their expressions I can tell immediately that they aren't going to be on my side.

"Molly, it doesn't sound like he did anything wrong," Logan tells me with a face that pleads, *don't shoot the messenger.*

"But . . . he was trying to talk me out of getting married!" I explain.

"No, he really wasn't," Justin tells me. "He was just telling you that you didn't have to do anything you didn't want to do."

"He was being a good friend," Logan adds.

Crap. There are two things I really hate: 1) being wrong, and 2) admitting when I'm wrong. I look up at Justin and Logan, who are nodding at me like parents encouraging their child to learn a lesson.

"Damn it," I say, and they know I get it because Logan hands me the cordless phone and Justin points at my bedroom. I take the phone and walk to my room, head down, figuring out how I am going to manage to eat this enormous slice of humble pie.

Brad's cell phone rings twice before he answers it by saying, "You realized you're wrong?"

"Yes," I pout.

"And?"

"And I'm sorry."

"I knew you would be."

"I'm sorry I upset you . . . just miscommunication, I guess."

I cannot believe how mature and understanding he is being, but I just decide to take it.

"Claire has been hypersensitive, too. I guess it's just something that happens to brides," he continues.

The mention of Claire's name upsets my stomach, as always, especially the comparison that I am anything like her. I need to figure out a way to stop that response; obviously she's not as evil as she was six months ago, since Brad appears to be allowed to talk to me and see me in public now.

"It must be," I say, grateful that things with Brad are going to be okay. "Thanks for being so understanding," I say humbly. It is a relief to me that he is acting like his good old self. "How's your planning going?" I ask, in an attempt to be selfless.

It takes all my energy to act happy for Brad as he cheerfully chats about his wedding plans. The truth is, that besides the pain that comes from knowing what a horrible person he is marrying, there is also the pain of knowing that even though what he has may be bad, at least it's *real*. It's more than a little hard for me to deal with the "realism" of Brad's wedding in contrast to the "fakeness" of my own, but somehow I manage to hold it together.

45

A "Date" With Justin

It has been easy to lose sight of why I originally got into this wedding nonsense . . . in fact, it feels easier all the time. With all of the "unfun" requirements and demands of wedding planning, it has been an effort for me to keep my "eyes on the prize" and remember that this is my chance to experience being a bride and truly relish it. That is, up until this week when things have become much more fun and I am constantly reminded of why it is worth it to lie to everyone I hold near and dear. Most days it feels worth it again.

Now, with two months until the big day, the lists from Martha are getting shorter and the items on them are more enjoyable—they are the kind of tasks that made me long to be a bride. Instead of long lists of tedious and stressful decisions like selecting florists, caterers, and photographers, my mind is now occupied with much more pleasant subjects like hairstyles, makeup, and shoes.

Today, Justin and I are at Capella Salon on the Upper West Side to have my hair and makeup run-through. The girl who will be doing my hair and makeup for the big day admits that we are the first couple to come in together . . . obviously what she doesn't know is that we are also the first couple where the "future husband" is paid to act as such. That's okay, though. The truth is that I really need Justin's advice on these important decisions.

I am really glad that he has come along, and he definitely seems to be enjoying it, but Eden, the hairstylist, probably wants to kill us both. Every time she picks up a section of my hair, Justin says, "Eh, eh, eh," and tells her a different way to do it. He might have been annoying to her, but in the end I LOVE the hairdo they have created. Plus, I think it will look stunning with my dress . . . poor Eden almost lost it when I described my dress in front of Justin. I felt like saying, *Believe me, Eden, my wedding-day luck cannot get any worse.*

Once the hair is finished, Eden moves on to my makeup, again with Justin in her face the entire time, and once again this pays off because it is one of the few times in my life that I have had a professional makeup job that didn't look whorish. When it is all finished, Justin whips out his Polaroid and takes pictures of me from all angles to be sure that Eden will see exactly how everything should look on the big day.

We leave Capella and I feel sort of silly with my ultraformal hair and makeup in jeans and a sweater. Justin insists it looks fabulous and treats me to dinner to prove it. It's fun to have a night with just the two of us. We talk about some wedding stuff and we talk about some Logan stuff. In the beginning we got to be such good friends because it was this "us against the world" feeling and because we had this huge secret that nobody else knew. Once we let Logan in on the secret and Justin starting spending more of his time and energy helping Logan through his stuff, I felt grateful but I also started to feel slightly left out.

After dinner, we decide to swing by "our place." With all the insanity over the past few months (and my embarrassment at the attention we get whenever we go there), we haven't had as many of our regular breakfasts as we used to. Tonight it's no more crowded than it is in the morning, but it's a different-looking crowd. On the weekend mornings, it's filled with people in expensive sweat suits reading their papers and eating muffins while their dogs sit patiently at their feet. At night, it's people in trendy clothes stopping for a shot of espresso to keep them going through an active night of clubs and bars. It is also a different staff and nobody realizes that we are the engaged Starbucks celebrities. We squeeze past all the twentysomethings with their caffeine jolts to our table where we sit down with our decaf, nonfat lattes to share a gingerbread man. I insist on treating... now that Justin refuses to take money from me, I feel bad and maintain that I must pay whenever we go out. It's only fair.

Justin and I chat excitedly about all the fun wedding stuff that is finally happening. With our invitations in the mail, many response cards already back, and my bridal shower a few weeks away, our gift registry at Bloomie's has quite a dent in it. Okay, I must admit, I'm that person who cheats and goes on weddingchannel.com to view our registry to see what has been purchased. It's just so exciting, though! Although Justin gets a good laugh from the fact that I've been checking up on the list, he's also excited to hear about the loot that he will be bringing home.

We also laugh about the response cards we've received and the funny things his friends and family have said. He decided to inform most of the important family members and friends that the invitations were for the play he is doing, but then he decided to "shock the pants" off a couple of people, and it is clear by the RSVP enclosures that their pants are definitely gone. Just wait until the wedding day.

I have to admit that mindlessly chatting about all these details helps take my mind off the things that normally torture it. You know what they say about idle hands? The same goes for idle minds. If I can keep myself completely occupied, it's much easier to cope than when I am just open to thinking of all the things I'm doing wrong. I guess it's the upside of having to take care of so many wedding details that I hadn't expected when I began this crazy journey.

46

The Much Anticipated Shower

It's weird how, with all this planning, I hadn't really made myself mentally prepared for what it would be like to be the absolute center of attention. I mean, we've been doing all this work and obviously I desperately want to be a bride or I wouldn't have gone out and hired a fake, gay fiancé, but in all my dreaming of being the bride, I failed to think about how that meant 400 eyes would be on me.

Today, I am a nervous wreck because it's kind of the warm-up to the wedding . . . the bridal shower. Now don't get me wrong—I am insanely excited about the shower. A bridal shower was one of the main events I was longing for that led me to make my fake wedding decision—I mean, by the end of the day I could very well own a French whisk—but now that the day is here and I am getting ready, I am realizing that it's a little scary.

My mom was a complete sweetheart and bought me a new outfit for the occasion. It's an adorable sky-blue dress from J. Crew. The top has a flattering V-neck with an embroidered band around the waist and an A-line skirt to the bottom of my knee. For some reason it's uncomfortably hot in Manhattan today . . . or I am uncomfortably sweaty from nerves, so I put my hair up in a highish ponytail to keep from passing out from heatstroke. Justin approves of my outfit, so at the very least I can rest assured that I look good.

Mom and Jamie are throwing me the shower at the same restaurant where we had Jamie's baby shower (which now feels so long ago). I'm trying not to be a Jamie and feel disappointed that they didn't find a different place for me . . . and the truth is that the restaurant was great and the service was fabulous, so it really is the perfect spot. The biggest difference between Jamie's shower and my shower is that the hostesses today are far calmer than I was. Apparently they both remembered to purchase my gifts before the day of the shower . . . show-offs.

They arrive at my apartment, with Kate, only ten minutes after they said they would and they are both calm, collected, and looking fabulous. How my sister got herself and her baby ready on time and looking adorable amazes me . . . see what I mean about motherhood really bringing out the best in her? Honestly, Kate's outfit is a little cuter than mine, but I am determined not to be jealous of someone who doesn't even have teeth.

Together, the three of us make our way downstairs and into the Explorer, which Mom has semilegally parked. She must have picked Jamie and Kate up on her way to my apartment because Kate's car seat is already strapped in the backseat. I can't help but be amused at how Jamie now leaps for the backseat to sit with her daughter with the same insistence with which she took the front when she was expecting . . . and when we were kids, too—she was the queen of yelling "shotgun" the night before. I kind of suspected she used her pregnancy as an excuse to get the coveted seat.

We all pile in and make our way across town. Because it's the weekend, traffic isn't too bad and we get to the restaurant five minutes before the time on the invitation. We hardly have our purses down when my Aunt Belinda and her daughter Michelle, one of the biggest bridezillas of all time, arrive. Suddenly, I am very shy. I decide to concentrate on what is in front of me, so I greet Belinda and Michelle and ignore that out of the corner of my eye I can see the room filling up.

Once everyone has arrived and has been greeted, I relax a bit and start to enjoy myself. It's so much fun finally being the bride! I tell the story of how we met, our "first date," our engagement . . . everyone wants to hear every story twice, and luckily, I don't mind telling. They ask me about wedding details and honeymoon plans (of which there are none . . . obviously, but I just say he's going to surprise me). Everyone sits down for a lovely lunch and then, the moment we've all been waiting for: the presents!

I joyfully unwrap each package to find the items specifically requested and already adored. All the guests politely ooh and aah as I hold up pink rubber spatulas and three-tiered cookie plates. And as I open, Jamie uses all the ribbons and bows to create an adorable rehearsal bouquet for me, and I secretly save the nicest pieces of wrapping paper and all the gift bags.

I am truly touched by everyone's generosity. Today finally feels like payback time for all the years that it hasn't been my turn. I know I sound so selfish and shallow, but unless you have been miserably single for a decade while your friends were all showered in affection, you can't understand where I'm coming from . . . if you've been there, you know. It's nice to be on this side of things at last.

Then everyone is served slices of delicious chocolate cake with two hot-pink hearts that say Molly in one and

Justin in the other. The whole event feels like it lasts about thirty minutes. When the final guest leaves, I look at my watch and am shocked to see that three hours have gone by. Talk about time flies when you are having fun!

47

The Countdown Begins

Time continues to fly and before I know it, it's June. I have two weeks of school left before summer vacation, so I decide not to stress about any wedding stuff until I am on break. Yeah, right. I stress morning, noon, and night. The kids offer me a small distraction, but it's been warm and sunny out and not a single person is thinking about school.

It's hard to believe how quickly this school year has flown by, and it's crazy to think about how fast my fake engagement period has passed. Besides the obvious wedding-related nerves, I'm feeling really sad that my engagement is almost over. I wish I'd been able to afford to rent Justin for longer. Even I realize how ridiculous that sounds, but being engaged has been so much fun, even if it has been a lot more work than I anticipated. Plus, there is the looming dark cloud that hangs over me, reminding me that at the end of my fake wedding day, I have to go home alone. Once again, I'll be face-to-face with the emptiness of being single.

My days are filled with the trying job of keeping my students under some semblance of control and getting them ready to start the fourth grade . . . no small task. Surprisingly, though, the ten days fly by and before I'm ready, the yearbooks are being handed out and it's the last day of the school year. The last day of school is always bittersweet for me. Like any normal human being, I'm thrilled to be starting a three-month vacation . . . but it's also hard for me to say good-bye to the kids I've grown so attached to over the past nine months.

The kids, of course, are never sad to say good-bye. They run around the room like wild animals, signing yearbooks and eating cake. I am always sure to sign each student's book and present them with their third-grade graduation gift: an erasable pen.

Pen is the preferred writing instrument for the fourth grade and the erasable pen is a helpful segue from pencils. I am always amused by how, at age nine, being given permission to write in ink is so monumental. It's funny how things like that work . . . like in second grade you learn cursive and you can't wait to learn it and you think you'll never print again . . . but almost every grown-up I know prints everything they write. You pretty much use cursive to sign your checks and credit card slips and nothing else.

Finally the end of the day comes and I watch my students walk out the door and prepare myself, knowing that a whole different group of kids will be walking through it next fall. Some parents are kind enough to give "end of the year" teacher gifts and a few others know I'm getting married, so I have a small pile of presents to get home and the sad task of taking down all my classroom decorations. For some reason we have to remove everything over the summer, even though we have the same rooms each year. I'm sad to see the kids go but try to console myself by thinking about what all the coming weeks hold. EEK! I'm getting married . . . well, having a wedding . . . in two weeks!

48

Two Weeks to Go

The next day I find myself at Barney's with my actual wedding dress on my body for the final fitting. It is so much prettier than I even remember it being! My mother, my sister, and Helen all look on in awe. Then Helen takes the delicate tulle veil out and attaches it to my head with a small, pearl crown. Needless to say, my mom and Jamie burst into tears. I have too much on my mind to be my normal, overly emotional self.

Martha's lists have gotten long again and these items are much more hands-on and time-consuming. How ridiculous is it that I now long for the easy days of hiring DJs and videographers? Nowadays, updating the caterer with guest counts as little response cards fill the mailbox and writing thank-you notes for the many gifts already received take up my time.

I am amazed at what an angel Justin is, because really, his role is finished. Once we got engaged I needed him to be at fewer events because our "love" was proven; however, he has remained an awesome friend and partner in all the wedding planning. Secretly, I think he must enjoy doing it, because he's over at my apartment as much as ever.

I take a final look at myself in the dress and try to imagine how it will feel putting it on on my wedding day. Honestly, it's hard to imagine. It's hard to without risking throwing up, anyway. With Helen's help I step off the seamstress's platform and take the dress off, careful not to stick myself with the few pins she put in. All the stress of the past month has caused me to drop a few pounds, so the dress needs to come in a touch. I leave the dress with Helen and join my mother and sister for lunch upstairs at Fred's . . . they proclaimed to be too hungry to wait for me to get changed and went up to secure a table and a basket of bread before I had the dress off.

Mom and Jamie are already sitting at a table when I find them. The wedding stress has really been getting to me, so I am hoping for one relaxing lunch, free from wedding talk . . . too bad I don't get that. They both have "Wedding Day Itineraries" in front of them and a third is lying in front of what is to be my seat.

As soon as I sit down, Mom begins.

"Now, girls," she says, and I silently swear that I will be so glad when Marion is out of her life and the "nows" stop. "Marion has printed up wedding-day itineraries for the bride, mother of the bride, and maid of honor."

"Matron of honor," Jamie corrects her, but Mom doesn't seem to notice . . . she's too focused.

Mom opens up the organized, collated stack of color-coded paper. The first page is pink and filled with all the phone numbers: my home, my cell, Mom's, etc., and, of course, Marion's office and cell. The next page is a green page with a detailed schedule of the wedding day: when I'll be at Capella having hair and makeup done, when I should arrive at The Plaza, exactly what time I will be putting on my dress, etc. The *entire* day is mapped out for me. A wave of sadness washes over me as I read down to the parts that

outline Justin's schedule, on lavender paper, and the ceremony schedule, on yellow paper, because I know it won't be
going down like that.

Honestly, this is getting much, much harder than I'd
imagined it. I thought that concocting the lie would be the
hard part, but now, as the big day gets closer and closer, like
a speeding train, I realize that surviving June 30 is going to
be the hardest part. Suddenly, it's really starting to occur to
me what I am doing. I know you're thinking it's about time.
I was only thinking about myself and how I would deal when
the big day actually arrived and I was not getting married . . .
but now, as I look at my unknowingly excited mother and
sister, I realize how many people are about to get crushed. I
push my food away. Believe it or not, I cannot eat.

I sit through the meal and try to act normal while Mom
and Jamie go through the information in the itinerary and
chat excitedly about the big day. I pretty much feel like the
meal cannot get worse when I catch something out of the
corner of my eye. The something is actually a someone . . .
Claire Reilly. She's having lunch with someone I can only
assume is her wedding planner, Bliss, based on Brad's de-
scriptions of the psycho planner. Of course, Claire isn't polite enough to get off her ass and say hello to any of us, but
I know she knows we are here. I can feel her staring at our
table.

Not being known for my maturity, I sink to her level and
ignore her the same way she is ignoring me. I have every in-
tention of doing this until I am freed from this painful
lunch, but, of course, things don't work out that easily.

My mother catches sight of Claire, and instead of getting
in on the icy game of cold shoulder, Mom warmly calls out
and waves to Claire. I feel like I'm twelve and caught in the
mall with my mom by the group of popular girls . . . utterly
humiliated. My kind and warm mother actually gets up and

walks over to the queen snot's table to greet her. Not wanting to send my own mother alone to face the ice princess, I jump up and follow along.

"Hello, Mrs. Harrigan, this is my wedding coordinator, Bliss Engel," Claire says coolly.

"Oh my, your wedding coordinator!" my mother exclaims like a country schoolgirl.

"Yes, not everyone's mother has the time to plan her daughter's wedding," Claire says in her usual bitchy tone.

"I guess I'm just lucky," I say, jumping in to defend my mother. And, I must say, I really am glad to be planning my wedding with my own loving mom and not some wedding robot with a stupid name.

"Whatever," is Claire's response.

We make the necessary good-bye, nice to see you, pleasure to meet you, remarks and then head back to our own table where I can't help but notice that Jamie seems to have eaten all of the avocado off my unfinished salad. The avocado is my favorite . . . how dare she?

"That poor girl," is the first thing Mom says when she sits down, and for a split second I think she's referring to poor, avocadoless me, until I realize she is gazing toward Claire's table.

"What?!?" Jamie and I command in unison.

"So sad that her own mother won't take the time to do these things with her."

"Her mother probably doesn't want to be around her!" Jamie offers, a perfectly acceptable explanation in my mind and probably the minds of most third-and fourth-graders . . . maybe second and third.

"Or her mother is as evil as she is and so they can't be in the same room together or their evil will destroy the world," I offer, going one step lower than Jamie.

"Please, girls, it's sad that she has to plan her wedding with that Bliss woman."

Jamie and I grumble in defeat. See what I mean about my mother being a kind soul? She never sees the bad in anyone. Feeling sorry for Claire Reilly should prove that to you once and for all.

We finish our lunch and leave Barney's; Jamie and I make obvious efforts to avoid looking at Claire, but of course, Mom goes over to give her one last good-bye and actually offers to help Claire with any wedding stuff if she needs it. Once Mom walks away, do you know what that bitch says?

"Whatever."

Part of me hopes that Mom hears so that she will finally see how awful Claire is; the other part hopes she doesn't, because it might hurt her feelings and she does not deserve that. Jamie and I just turn and give her the stink eye, although I'm not sure she notices, until we are out of sight.

49

One Week to Go

The first thing on Martha's "One-Week-Ahead" checklist is to finalize the seating plan. This is why Justin and I spend most of our free time arranging little Post-its with guests' names around cut-out cardboard circle "tables." This sounds like a pretty simple task, but it's really not. It's like putting together a puzzle.

Actually, it's harder because with a puzzle at least you know there is a correct place for every piece. In this puzzle, you can have eight pieces perfectly placed together and then you remember that piece number four's date slept with piece number two's current boyfriend three years ago and the whole thing gets scrapped.

I'm kind of surprised that Martha leaves this grueling task until the end . . . I guess it's because that's when you have all your guest responses, but still . . . this is impossible! And in our case it's even harder because there is a whole section of guests that we need to keep totally separate in case, God forbid, they decide to stay for the reception and think that they can share their thoughts on the "play" openly.

To make a hard week harder, I get a call from Brad. It's Wednesday night and Justin, Logan, and I are huddled around the coffee table looking at seat assignments and eating huge deli sandwiches when the phone rings. I assume it's Mom with more guidance on where her friends and family members should be seated, so I answer the cordless without taking my eyes off table six.

I'm surprised when it's a man's voice . . . Brad's . . . on the other end.

"Oh, hey, Brad," I say in the friendly manner we've been able to uphold since our last post-blowup talk after the post-office incident.

"Molly," he says numbly, "we need to talk."

"Okay, sure," I tell him, not realizing there is any problem. I cover the phone with my hand and tell Justin and Logan that I will be right back as I head toward my bedroom. "What's going on?" I ask as I stretch my sore back on my comfortable bed.

"Claire told me that you and your sister were very rude to her at Barney's last week," he almost shouts accusingly through the phone.

You've gotta be shitting me.

"You're kidding, right?" I clean up my sentiment a tad.

"I am not kidding, Molly. I thought we'd been over all this. I thought you understood that I am going to marry Claire and you were gonna deal with it."

"I do and I am!" I retort defensively.

"Really? Well, it seems like you don't. Don't you understand how important it is for you to keep peace with Claire if you really want to be friends with me?"

Am I getting this right? I have to suck up to Claire so that she will allow Brad to be my friend? No way!

"That's ridiculous," I reply, getting angry. "If anyone was rude to anyone, it was your bitchy little fiancée being rude to my mother!"

Perhaps adding the "bitchy" description wasn't 100% necessary, but I feel it is accurate.

"How do you figure?" Brad snaps.

"She insulted my mother by saying that she had nothing better to do than plan my wedding."

"That's a lie!"

"No, it's not!!"

"Yes it is, and I know it is because I talked to your mother this morning when she called to be sure I'd be at your rehearsal dinner and she said how lovely it was to run into Claire."

Damn my mother for being the sweetest person in the world.

"My mother is just too sweet to tell you what a two-faced bitch you are marrying," I say with a superior tone.

"Yeah, right. This is it . . . I can't do this anymore. You are a different person and not someone that I like."

"You are the different one, Brad!" I yell as I feel tears start to fall.

"Whatever you want to believe in your little Molly fantasy land. I'll be at your rehearsal and your wedding because I wouldn't hurt your family who has been so wonderful to me, but that is it . . . we are finished!"

"FINE!" I yell.

"FINE!!" he yells back and slams down his phone.

Since I'm on a cordless I have nothing to slam it down on, so I press the "off" button really hard and then throw the phone at the wall as I burst into sobs.

Justin and Logan are at my door in a flash. I tell them the entire story, starting with seeing Claire at Barney's last week. Unlike the last time I came to them with a story about the awful Bradley Lawson, this time they completely agree with me.

"What has gone wrong with him?" Logan asks, and I shrug miserably.

The boys console me, but the truth is that I am just plain

exhausted. Exhausted from wedding stuff, exhausted from Brad stuff, just exhausted from everything. I slip into a hot bubble bath kindly drawn up by Justin and then get into my bed while my wonderful brother and fake, gay fiancé finish the table assignments for me.

50

Another Apology

Brad may be in the process of having his soul sucked out by the human she-devil, but down at the core he is still a good person . . . and still a shadow of the person I knew and loved. And that person has always been very up-front . . . when he's wrong he says it; when he's right he fights for it. I am greatly relieved when he shows up at my door Thursday morning with an apology . . . because that's the right thing and the thing that I would have counted on the old Brad to do.

Logan and Justin are both working today and so I have the apartment to myself and some downtime to try and relax and not think about all the insanity that is going to happen over the next couple days. The ladies of *The View* are doing a good job distracting me with a fashion show of "butt-buster" denim as I enjoy a bowl of Apple Jacks. When the buzzer rings, my heart falls because I am certain that someone or something outside my door is going to destroy the serenity I have been able to create this morning.

I am both nervous and surprised when the voice coming through the intercom is Brad's and he's asking to come up. In the few seconds it takes him to climb the staircase, I straighten up what I can in the room—it's still an overly cluttered disaster, an unavoidable problem in a small apartment with three occupants.

"Hey, Mol," he says when I open the door. "We need to talk."

My first thought is a defensive one—what have I done to upset him now? But then I notice that he seems sad and invite him in and offer him a cup of coffee, which he declines.

"What's going on?" I ask, when we are seated on my couch. We're sitting side by side, but we both have a leg curled underneath so that we can face each other.

"I'm sorry about the way I attacked you the other day."

I can't help but smile—this is the good old Brad. He knew he was wrong and he is admitting it and apologizing.

"We're all under a lot of pressure right now," I say, giving him an easy out.

"I guess that must be it."

It seems like he's gotten off his chest what he came to say, yet he still seems sad and a little distant and distracted.

"Is there anything else?" I gently coax him.

He hesitates for a moment. "I really miss you, Molly . . . we've been like a roller coaster the past few months and it's hard for me to deal with. I hate not having you in my life."

Relief pours over me like floodwater . . . that's exactly how I feel.

"Me, too! I've been miserable."

I look deeply into his sparkling blue eyes that don't seem to sparkle quite as much anymore, and I feel him looking into mine . . . if I were a cheesy person, I'd tell you I could feel our souls connect. I do feel something, though . . . it's like we're caught in a trance.

"I need you in my life," I almost whisper, our eyes still locked.

I've continually tried to deny how much my life sucks without Brad, but the truth is that I *do* need him and was crushed by the feeling that he didn't need, or want, me anymore. Brad opens his arms and I lean across the couch and snuggle into them. It has always amazed me how we fit together like a puzzle . . . it's like we were made to be best friends.

"Me, too," he answers in the same whisper.

When I pull back from the hug, I look into Brad's eyes and something is different. I feel a tingle, or a twinge . . . and an overwhelming feeling of anticipation. With our eyes locked, my breath is taken away. I lean a little closer to him and close my eyes slowly. Before I open them again, I feel his lips on mine. They are warm and soft and I can't help thinking how ironic it is that our lips fit together like puzzle pieces, too.

Then it hits me . . . our lips fit together like puzzle pieces! And I think it hits him at the same time, because we both jump back slightly and stare at each other, wide-eyed. We hold the stare for a split second before mutually grabbing each other and kissing again, this time harder and deeper. It feels amazing . . . but then I remember that these are Brad Lawson's lips that are sending sparks through my body. We jump back again at the exact same time.

"How dare you?!?" Brad accuses me, his voice full of terror.

How dare I what? I was most definitely the one *being* kissed.

"You kissed *me*!" I answer in my own defense.

"Why did you do that?" he questions in a panicked voice.

"I didn't do anything!"

"Damn it, Molly! I thought being friends could work . . . but obviously it can't," he says as he jumps off the couch and moves farther away from me as fast as he can, stumbling over all the stuff filling the apartment since Justin and Logan showed up.

Still in a fog of confusion, I try to replay in my head what happened so that maybe I can gain some understanding. I'm not gaining anything but more confusion, though.

"I gotta get outta here!" Brad yells as he clumsily makes his way to the door.

I stand, but before I can get another word out, he is out the door and heading down the hall. He gets halfway to the stairwell before turning and literally running back to me. His lips on my lips stop him from getting through the door and we have another amazing but confusing kiss. When we pull apart, I see that the twinkle has returned to his eyes.

"Why do I keep doing that?!?" he exclaims. "I've gotta get outta here!"

He heads down the hall again, this time not turning back. Once he is out of my view, I close the door and sink to the floor in front of it. I sit on my floor, my hand on my lips, bewildered and confused . . . what just happened here? The strange thing is that it's almost identical to how our infamous junior-year kiss went down . . . and I let him run off down my hall then, too.

51

The Rehearsal

Unfortunately (or maybe fortunately), I don't have much time to think about Brad or his visit or the kiss (okay, kisses), because the day before the wedding day is a busy day if you do everything on Martha's list. It's an even busier day if you also have to plan how to be left at the altar gracefully, which for me includes learning how to act. It is darn near impossible to accomplish any of these things when you are paralyzed with fear.

Martha's list includes: confirming everything with every single vendor, getting a manicure and pedicure (I know that's enjoyable, but it still takes time and effort), having the rehearsal, attending the rehearsal dinner, getting everything together for the next day . . . it's a lot of stuff. With Justin and Logan's help, I think we are going to manage to get it all done . . . I think. It's funny how in the beginning they were unsure about my plan, but I was positive and gung-ho; now that the time has finally arrived, they are relaxed and ready for "showtime," as Justin keeps calling it (I think he might actually be starting to believe we are in a play), and I am a complete nervous wreck.

Logan and Justin make all the confirmation calls for me while I sit on the couch with my knees bundled up at my chest, rocking back and forth. At least I've been so swamped and stressed with wedding details that I haven't even had time to be swamped and stressed with the Brad thing . . . I'm trying to look on the bright side here.

All the vendors are good to go on wedding day . . . I'm not sure if that is a blessing or a curse. Once all the calls are made, the boys gently unfold me and take me out to get my nails done. We must be quite a sight . . . two gay men flanking a paranoid girl in the whirlpool footbaths. People probably think we escaped from some sort of institution; ironically, the belief that I should be committed isn't completely inaccurate. I must admit, though, that when we walk out of the nail salon we have the thirty most gorgeous toes and fingers in the city . . . and the relaxing spoilage by the manicurist does help to calm my nerves a bit—plus, my nails could not look more adorable. My fingers have a perfect French manicure . . . the manicurist said it is the most popular for brides. On my toes, I did something a bit more fun. They are pale pink with little white flowers to match the ones in my bouquet. Since my dress is long, nobody will really see them, but I will know they are there and, I must admit, they do cheer me up a bit.

Of course, as soon as we get home and I hear the message from my mother on the answering machine with yet another "last minute" list, my shoulders dart right back up to my ears. Logan takes care of calling her back and explains that I am just a little stressed right now. Mom, of course, freaks out, but Logan smooths things out nicely.

Then the boys help me get dressed for the rehearsal dinner. The rehearsal dinner for my wedding—one of the many events in life I felt I was being robbed of by being the only girl placed on this earth without a soul mate. Now that mine has arrived I am feeling like perhaps I was being spared.

I am hardly functioning, so Justin and Logan treat me like their personal Barbie doll and get me perfectly dressed in a stunning off-white silk slip dress that the three of us had chosen a few weeks before. I try to do the yoga relaxation breathing that Justin has been teaching me, and it works a little . . . enough for me to put my own gold strappy sandals onto my blistered feet—thanks to Martha's instruction to break the wedding shoes in around the house. I'm not sure her method for breaking them in includes as much frantic pacing as I've been doing lately.

We are out the door and arrive at The Plaza only fifteen minutes late . . . impressive, considering one member of our party (me) has to be cared for like a child. Jamie and Bryan, with an actual child, only arrived a few minutes before us. Of course, Mom and Marion were close to hysterical that we weren't there at six o'clock on the dot. Oh well, I think they are lucky I made it at all.

In a flurry, Marion ushers everyone to the room where the ceremony will take place and immediately starts pointing us in a hundred different directions—she's like a pastel-clad drill sergeant. She starts the rehearsal with everyone standing where they will be for the ceremony. Justin and I are front and center, looking at each other. Jamie stands at my side and Logan is at Justin's. Once Marion is convinced that everyone will be able to remember their positions twenty-four hours later, we practice the exit. Walking down the aisle on Justin's arm only serves to rub my nose in the fact that tomorrow I will be at this alone . . . my misery increases. After we exit, Jamie and Logan follow, and then Mom and Dad . . . simple enough. Dad actually isn't rehearsing because there is a game in the bar that he is interested in and he insists that since he didn't mess up Jamie's wedding he'll be able to handle mine. I'm not bothered by his absence, because the truth is that none of us needs to practice any of this anyway because it won't be happening.

Marion makes us run through the whole walk-in, stand-in position, and walk out twice more before she is satisfied that we are prepared for the big day. After the wedding party has been dismissed, Mom and Marion take me upstairs to show me the room where I will be getting ready for the big day. When we arrive at the room, I'm surprised to see that it has double doors leading into it . . . in my experience, only suites have double doors. I am certain we don't have a suite and just chalk it up to how classy The Plaza is . . . until Marion opens the doors to a room, actually rooms (plural), bigger than my apartment . . . it's not just a room, it *is* a suite. My breath is taken away. The room is amazing. Not only is it huge, it's . . . well . . . grand. "Grand" is the only way to describe it.

A knot instantly forms in my stomach. Reserving a regular room at The Plaza was a splurge, given the pittance left in my wedding fund, but I felt like it was crucial to the day. I mean, what feels splendid about getting dressed for your wedding in your own apartment? And then what would I do . . . take a cab here in my gown?? It felt worth the money to be able to get ready in the very hotel where my (fake) wedding would be taking place. Now I am panicking because clearly there has been some sort of a miscommunication with Marion and I am going to have to pay for this suite, which is surely beyond my budget.

I look to my mother, who is beaming at me, and I feel bad that I am going to have to let her down with the information that we are not going to be able to spend the morning in this amazing room. Don't ask me why this riddles me with guilt and the rest of the fake wedding is okay. I am about to break the news when I hear my father's voice behind me.

"Surprise, baby! What d'ya think?"

It takes me a second to catch on, but I finally piece together my mother's beam and my father's words. This suite is their gift to me ... on my wedding day. I whirl around and throw my arms around his neck. "Oh, Daddy! It's so beautiful. It's wonderful!" I exclaim as I start to cry and wrap my arms around my mother as well.

It really is the perfect room to put on the perfect dress for the perfect wedding ... my tears of joy turn into sobs of sorrow when I remember that tomorrow will not end perfectly. It might end perfectly according to my plan, but that certainly is not a perfect storybook ending. Mom and Dad, and Marion, don't realize my sobbing is anything more than happiness and excitement, so Mom and Marion cheerfully continue the tour of "your suite," as they call it.

It has a dining room with a large enough table that Mom has arranged for the seven of us (me, her, Dad, Jamie, Kate, Bryan, and Logan) to have a room-service breakfast. After that, I will be moving to the large dressing area in the huge bathroom, which includes a whirlpool tub, to have my hair and makeup done ... another surprise, the gang from Capella will be coming to me. The suite has a comfortable living room with a big TV and a view of Central Park for me to relax in and have friends come by, if I choose. The final room is a large master bedroom with an enormous king-sized bed where Mom drops another surprise on me ... Justin and I will be spending the night in this room! I'm going to vomit—without a doubt. The emotional cost this will have on my parents is bad enough, but now they are actually enduring monetary costs as well. My deceit sickens me.

Of course, I'm not actually given time to go to the bathroom and heave up the nonexistent food in my traumatized stomach, because Mom and Marion whisk me out of the suite as quickly as they whisked me in; it's time to get to the rehearsal dinner. These women are sticklers for their schedules.

52

The Rehearsal Dinner

We hurry down to a private room in one of the hotel's nicer restaurants where Justin and Logan are already warming up the bar. Justin rushes to my side, as a good fiancé would, and I joyfully—well, I try to make it joyfully—tell him about our amazing wedding night suite. I am impressed with his acting skills, because he puts on a reaction for Mom and Dad that seems like a normal amount of excitement for a man to have the night before his wedding. Once we are alone, though, he checks to make sure that I am holding up all right. So-so is the most positive answer I can give.

Slowly, our . . . okay, *my* closest friends and out-of-town guests arrive at the dinner and I put on my happy face to greet everyone. I am holding it together for old family friends and relatives. I'm even okay when Lauren and Alex run up to me, screeching with excitement. It's when Brad walks in that my "okayness" is challenged, once again.

Claire is clinging tightly to his side and I can tell right away that she is in one of her "moods." Whenever I say "moods," I mentally make little quotations with my fingers because "moods" are what Brad has referred to them as, even though I am convinced that they are actually just her personality. Needless to say, Brad and I haven't spoken since the kiss and his completely freaked-out exit.

They politely approach me as soon as they walk in, but there is something strange. Brad seems totally preoccupied and confused . . . and he seems to be avoiding looking at me. When he says hello he looks at his feet; when he says good-bye he looks across the room. With my wedding one day away, his being eight days away and the obvious conclusion that his future wife and I will never get along, he has become utterly uncomfortable around me. He is polite, but I feel like the familiarity and warmth are gone. I feel like he wants it to be there, but he doesn't know how to make it happen. Of course with Claire it was never there, so I'm not completely shocked when her greeting to me is:

"So, you really are getting married at The Plaza. I figured I would just believe it when I saw it."

My jaw drops open and I stare at her for a second before shifting my gaze to Brad, who just laughs, stupidly, as though this were a funny joke, and stares intently at his shoes. Is he blind? Is he deaf? Does he still think I am the liar about Claire's horribleness?!? I honestly don't have the strength for this tonight, so I just turn and walk away from them. As I make my way across the room I can hear Claire making a snotty remark and Brad not responding to it. My heart breaks in two that such a wonderful person will be vowing to stay with a complete bitch 'til death do them part.

Except for the Brad/Claire run-in, the rehearsal dinner is lovely. Like the shower, it's a good preparation for how the big day will be. I manage to put out of my head the knowledge that the next day will be one of the worst of my life, rather than one of the happiest, and end up enjoying the evening . . . as much as I can.

I'm still an emotional wreck, but that's not anything completely new for me. I cry when my dad gives a toast, I cry when my mom gives a toast. I cry when Justin and I get up and give a toast to Mom, Dad, Jamie, and Logan. I cry so much that there is a chance I can get in a boat and row myself away from this awful situation I've created on a river of my own tears. Jeez, have I become melodramatic or what?!?

Aside from me, the mood for the evening is festive. I take time to look around the room and see that everyone, except Brad and Claire, of course, is having a great time. In typical Harrigan fashion, the wine is free-flowing and the food is plenty. I'm exercising enormous amounts of self-control at the bar, although I am aware that getting smashed might be the best thing for me. I have to stay focused and keep my energy up because I have a ton of work to do tonight, plus tomorrow will be hideous enough without a hangover. After this rehearsal, Justin and I have a rehearsal of our own . . . we have to rehearse how things are *really* gonna happen tomorrow.

53

The <u>Real</u> Rehearsal

Justin, Logan, and I finally get home after about two more hours of roasting and toasting than I would be up for under the best conditions. We are all exhausted but we know how much work still lies ahead of us. We walk in the apartment and Justin immediately puts on a pot of coffee as I feed Tiffany some leftover salmon I'd swiped from The Plaza for her.

We each fix ourselves a cup and sit down around the living room coffee table to plan things out. The morning—for me, at least—will go pretty much according to Marion's schedule. I'll arrive at The Plaza on time, with Logan, and we will have breakfast with the family in the amazingly beautiful suite. Then I will get ready as planned and be downstairs for the ceremony at the appointed time. Justin's morning will be completely different.

Justin will be free . . . once he leaves my apartment tonight, our contract will have come to an end and he will no longer be indentured to me. It's strange to think that he won't "have" to hang out here anymore, because it always feels more like he wants to. Although we agreed in the beginning and all the way through that we want to remain friends, we've realized that Justin does need to get out of the picture for a little while to let the wedding fiasco blow over and to make it seem like he legitimately broke my heart.

Once we have the outline of our game plan in order, it's time to get to the trickier part. I need to learn how to act . . . specifically, act shocked and shattered that Justin is abandoning me at the altar on our wedding day. We had originally thought that perhaps he should actually be there on the wedding day and announce that he has realized his homosexuality and can't go through with the marriage . . . but I changed my mind and decided that I don't want him to show up at all. The ceremony is going to be difficult for me regardless, but I don't want Justin to have to be a bad guy in front of all my friends and family since he is anything but. Obviously his "side" will be enormously confused about why he invited them to a play he isn't in, but we both agree that chances are they will just leave when the "ceremony" doesn't happen, and it will be my friends and family who stay at the reception to cheer me up.

"So," Justin starts, "you will be standing at the end of the aisle, and there will probably be uncomfortable rumblings that I haven't shown up. You need to act confused."

"Okay, confused," I repeat as I write down, *step one: confused*, on a little spiral notepad. "Like this: 'What do you mean? Is he late?'" I rehearse.

"Yeah! That's perfect," Justin coaches.

"Logan, this is where you come in," Justin snaps Logan to attention. "You will be the one to tell Molly and Larry that I'm not coming."

"Okay . . . what should I say?"

The story is simple: Justin cannot marry me because he has realized that he doesn't want to be with a woman. Like always, we're sticking as much to the truth as possible. Justin forges a little breakup note explaining his absence; Logan will "find" the note (he'll find it inside his coat pocket, but nobody else will know this) and give to me.

The note is simple and to the point. He simply writes, "Molly, I'm sorry I cannot go through with it. I've realized over the past year that I am gay. I love you, but I cannot marry you. Justin." It's completely true . . . it just leaves out the whole part about me hiring him to pretend to want to marry me in the first place.

"Molly," Justin turns back to me, "after Logan hands you the note, read it slowly, two or three times, like you can't understand it, then look up at your dad and hand it to him."

"Are you sure about that?" Logan cuts in. "What if Dad figures out it's a fake?"

"How's he gonna figure that out?" I ask.

Logan accepts the good point and we keep on going.

"Okay," Justin continues, "after your dad looks at the note, you are going to be shocked and hurt."

"Should I cry?"

"You can start a little," he advises. "You really have to almost play it dumb here . . . this has to be a complete shock to you."

"Okay, like 'Daddy, I don't understand?'"

"Yes! Exactly."

"How long do I do that for?"

"A little while, and it's okay to get really upset."

"Okay, so I'm confused, shocked, hurt . . . got it. Then I put on my strong face, right?" I ask as I practice the "strong face" that Justin had shown me a few days before. My bottom lip should be quivering, my chin up and my eyes wet, but without falling tears.

"You got it."

The three of us run through the plan a few more times, with Justin playing the part of Dad, before we feel comfortable with my performance. After that, we move on to what will probably be the hardest moment of the day . . . when I address my guests. Justin was kind enough to write out my monologue, as he calls it, this week since I've been so swamped with last-minute wedding stuff. The monologue is the moment when I am really going to need strength.

The plan is for me to compose myself at the back of the room, and then walk to the front and announce to our guests that the wedding will not be taking place. I will say that I am not sure what happened to Justin or to "us," because, as Justin has emphasized many times, it is crucial for me to maintain my complete shock and surprise. Then I need to put on my strongest strong face and invite the guests to please join me at the reception that my family and I have worked so hard to plan. If I can get through the monologue as planned, I think I will be home free.

I rehearse it a few times with Justin and Logan critiquing me as I go. Finally, they are satisfied and the coffee is all gone, which means our work is done. Justin collects the few items left around the apartment . . . he has been taking stuff with him for the past two weeks. Once he has all his stuff, he starts toward the door.

"Are you sure you don't want to stay over just one more night?" I ask, hopeful that he will because I am sad to see him go.

"It's bad luck for the groom to see the bride the day of the wedding," he reminds me playfully.

I look at my watch, it's almost 2:00 A.M. . . . it *is* the day of the wedding. I show him this as I remind him that the wedding is doomed anyway.

"No, I've gotta go. What if your family comes to surprise you in the morning?"

I know he's right . . . it sounds like something my parents would do, but there is still something awful about watching him sneak off in the still of the night.

Before Justin steps out of my apartment for good, he gives me a huge hug, then one for Logan, and then another one for me. Nobody really says anything; I guess because it's all been said or we know it all already. Logan and I embrace each other as we watch Justin walk down the hall.

"I'll call you tomorrow, secretly, and tell you how it all goes!" I quietly yell after him just before he reaches the stairs.

"I'm counting on it," he says as he turns down the stairwell.

We close the door and I cry in Logan's arms for a few minutes before I ask him what I have done. He promises that it will all work out, which only makes me feel slightly better.

"Hey, what is it you always say? Eyes on the prize?"

I nod wearily. My vision is blurry from exhaustion and tears . . . I don't think I can see the "prize" right now, I tell him.

"This is the finish line, Molly . . . look around this apartment and think . . . your dream is going to come true tomorrow."

I look around the apartment at all the beloved registry gifts that have been pouring in. Thinking back, going through with all this for gifts and attention seems so ridiculous. I know what I wanted was the experience of being a bride, and I must admit that some things have been completely wonderful . . . but I am really coming face-to-face with the fact that having a wedding without having a real groom really isn't much of the experience at all.

I'm exhausted . . . exhausted by all of the planning, but more by all of the lying and covering. Part of me is relieved that tomorrow it will finally be over. Logan and I climb in our respective beds but sleep doesn't exactly come easily. I toss and turn, a bundle of nerves, until sometime around sunrise when I finally doze off. What feels like minutes later, Logan is shaking me gently, telling me that it's time to wake up.

"Good Golly Miss Molly, it's your wedding day."

54

The Very Much Anticipated Wedding Day

I am so tired that I feel sick as Logan gently shakes me and tries to get my eyes open. A split second after I regain consciousness I remember what today is and I bolt upright, then I quickly shove past him to the bathroom to throw up. We're off to a great start.

Thank God for my brother; he is a saint. He's right behind me, holding my hair back and reassuring me that today is going to be great . . . just how I planned it. Didn't I tell you he's the sweetest kid ever born? When my stomach is empty, he runs a bath for me and even brings me a 7-Up, which I sip miserably as I sit beneath the bottle of bubble bath he poured in for me.

I must admit that after the bath, the soda, and a marathon session of relaxation breathing, my nerves and misery are replaced with just the tiniest bit of excitement. Today *is* my wedding day, and the only one I will ever get, so it's time to keep my eyes on the prize, as Logan reminded me last night, and get the show on the road.

I pull out my copy of Marion's schedule for the big day and check that I am supposed to be at The Plaza at 9:30 A.M. to meet the family for breakfast. It's 8:45 now, so I only have a short time to get myself dressed and head over to the hotel with Logan. I manage to dress myself and am in the process of triple-checking my bags to ensure that I have everything I need ready to go when the front door buzzer goes off.

Before I have time to think about who could be ringing my bell the morning of my wedding, Mom and Jamie are charging into my room in a tornado of excitement. I have a quick flashback to Justin's premonition the night before that my family could surprise me in the morning . . . I owe so much to him. Sure enough, they do have a great surprise for me . . . a limo waiting downstairs to take us all to The Plaza to get the day started. A rush of excitement washes over me as I grab the bags and follow them to the door, where Logan is waiting with a huge grin. Logan and I confirm with each other that we both have everything we need before giving Tiffany a super-large breakfast and dinner-sized portion of kitty kibble and heading out the door.

In front of my apartment is a gleaming white stretch limo. Logan opens the door and I stick my head in to find Dad, Bryan, and Kate a mile away sitting in the very back of the car. I climb in and hug all three before joining my younger brother and sister in playing with every knob, switch, dial, and button in the car. We play all the way to the hotel, turning music on and off, opening and closing windows and sunroofs (that's right, there are two), and generally annoying everyone else.

Our troop reaches The Plaza without Dad threatening to "turn this car around!" the way he would when we were little and acting like we are today. To be honest, even Dad played with a few switches . . . this family is in a mood too good to be destroyed, and it is contagious. Marion is waiting for us in the lobby in what I think must be her casual outfit . . . stiff-looking khaki slacks and a crisp, button-down blouse tucked in. She looks different when she isn't in her pastel power suits . . . almost motherly. She'd probably impale herself on her enormous ring if she heard me describe her like that.

Marion escorts us all up to our suite where breakfast is already waiting. The tears begin as soon as I see the breakfast. Besides my favorite eggs Benedict and hot chocolate, there is a plate of pumpkin scones from Starbucks. For a split second my mind jumps back to Justin and what will happen this afternoon, but a squeeze on my shoulder from Logan helps me return it to the back of my mind. We all dig into the feast that awaits us and, in typical Harrigan fashion, don't stop until there isn't a speck of food left on the table. Then we all drape our bodies over the numerous couches, plush chairs, and, of course, the king-sized bed, trying to ward off food comas. Having my whole family around me and so happy makes me happy . . . moments like this are when I feel like my whole plan is worthwhile.

After we do some digesting and get some energy back, the boys are shuffled off to their room (not suite) to get ready. Since it doesn't take them nearly as many hours to get ready as it takes us girls, I think they make plans to hit some golf balls or see a movie. The girls definitely don't have time for that kind of playing around. Moments after the food is wheeled away, Eden shows up with a suitcase of hair and makeup supplies to get started on us.

Jamie is in the middle of feeding Kate and Mom is going over some last-minute details with Marion, so I am the first one to head to the "vanity area," as Marion calls it. I try to relax and enjoy it as Eden sets up her equipment and starts pulling, curling, and spraying my hair. As she works, I'm reminded of the day of our run-through when Justin was supervising. There have been some fun times during all of this wedding insanity.

Before I know it, my hair and face are perfect replicas of the Polaroids taken by Justin weeks ago. Everything looks exactly how I dreamed it would, and I am relocated to the

comfortable couch in front of the window overlooking
Central Park while Jamie moves into the vanity area. As I sit
there alone, well, Kate is with me, but she is napping, I stare
out the window at the people in the park having a regular
old Saturday while I have the biggest day of my life. It's a
strange feeling . . . like I am somehow detached from the
rest of the world today. I stare, stalker-style, at the families
with children and the couples holding hands . . . for some
reason, I am mesmerized.

Jamie returning from Eden's clutches, and beckoning for
Mom to get in there, finally breaks my trance. Jamie looks
stunning . . . I am constantly amazed at what motherhood
has done for her. She was always beautiful, but since becoming Kate's mother, her Jan Brady tendencies have signifi-
cantly lessened. Her hairdo is a low and loose chignon. It
almost looks like a haphazard bun, except for the sweeping
side part and the intricacy of the hair knot. It looks absolutely beautiful.

"Do you have your something old, something new,
something borrowed, and something blue?" she asks me as
she casually beams at her sleeping daughter.

Yikes, with all of Martha's lists and Marion's orders, nobody had specifically reminded me about this old tradition.

"Let's see . . . my dress is new, and my garter has a blue
bow on it . . ." I trail off as I search the room for some old
stuff I can borrow.

"Your engagement ring is old," Jamie reminds me.

I feel a twinge as I look down at my hand where Nana's
ring sparkles as brilliantly as ever. Being able to wear this
special ring for a year has been a true gift . . . but I cannot
look at the ring without thinking about what Nana would
think if she knew what I was doing. Nana was a true romantic. She loved weddings because of the romance—not the
flowers, dresses, and cakes, but what they symbolized. It is
now painfully clear to me that she would not approve of my

great plan, and every time I look at her ring—the ring that my grandfather had made especially for his true love—I have to acknowledge this.

"So you just need something borrowed," Jamie continues as she walks toward me. She stands in front of me and holds out her hand. "I want you to borrow the diamond earrings that Mom and Dad gave me as a wedding present," she says as she opens her palm to show the sparkling studs.

"Really?" I ask.

"It would be my greatest honor as matron of honor," she says with a giggle.

I stand up and we hug as tightly as two people can when they are being protective of hairdos and makeup jobs. We also blink furiously to prevent tears from streaking our faces.

Once Mom is finished with Eden—and looking amazing, I might add—we begin to get ready. It's crazy how fast the day has flown by. Around noon, room service revisits our suite with tiny finger sandwiches that we nibble while trying not to mess up our makeup. We have a short time to relax, but my mother's sister Belinda comes by to wish us well and deliver two dozen long-stemmed roses for me. A short while later, Alex, Lauren, and Maggie come up, bearing a plate of my favorite chocolate chip break-and-bake cookies.

Too quickly, it is time to put on our dresses, which also means that the hardest parts are getting closer. First, the three of us together put on the flower girl dress we got for the still-sleeping, six-month-old Kate. The dress is the same hydrangea blue as the sash on Jamie's white maid-of-honor dress . . . the exact dress that Justin had proclaimed would be perfect when we selected our flowers with Iris so long ago (thank goodness for the Internet).

Kate could not look more adorable in her blue dress with a white bow around her chubby middle and another white bow around her bald head. Next, Mom and Jamie get dressed. Jamie looks stunning in the white dress, thanks to a visit to the Mystic Tan and some blond streaks in her sandy hair. She looks like she has spent the last six months jogging on a beach, not nursing an infant. Mom also looks her best in a stunning mother-of-the-bride suit. It's champagne-colored silk with a beautifully beaded jacket and knee-length skirt. Finally they are ready and I am the only one left in my regular clothes.

Getting me into my dress is no small feat. Once I carefully remove my tank top by pulling it down over my hips, I have to be hooked into my special, girdlelike bra. It sounds more uncomfortable than it is . . . it is actually the first strapless bra I've ever worn that hasn't slipped down, and it makes me look like I have a good amount of cleavage. Once the foundations are in place, I step into the dress and try my best to stand still while Mom and Jamie button up the back. When the dress is on, I steal a look in the mirror . . . it looks as beautiful as I'd remembered it. Finally my feet are slipped into my white satin sandals and my little crown and veil are attached around my up-do. It's showtime, as Justin would say.

Just as we finish, the phone in the room rings. It's Dad telling us it's time to get down there. Mom and Jamie head for the door with Kate and me to follow.

"I just need one second alone," I tell them.

"Okay, are you sure you want to be alone?" Mom checks.

"Yes, I'm okay—I just want a second. I'll meet you down there."

They agree and head out the grand double doors, leaving me alone in the suite.

I stand in front of the room's full-length, three-way mirror, feeling almost paralyzed. I can't believe that it's really me draped in white satin and tulle. I feel like I'm playing dress-up. I guess the fact is that I am . . . and I can't shake the feeling that any minute now, the real bride is going to burst through the door and show me for the imposter that I really am.

This is how I am feeling when there is a knock on the door, and so I jump, startled that my neurotic fear is coming true. I don't respond to the knock, silently praying that whoever is there will go away, but instead the door opens. Without moving my feet, I turn and steady myself for the wrath that is to come. Instead of a bride on the rampage, it's Brad standing on the right side of the suite's double doorway. I honestly think I would have been less surprised if it had been a psychotic Bridezilla.

"Brad?" I ask, thinking there is a chance that my eyes are deceiving me.

"Molly, I need to talk to you," Brad says with great urgency.

"Now?"

"I can't wait." He rushes in and then he pauses for a second. "You look amazing."

I suddenly remember where I am and what the day is. I turn back to the mirror and look down my body at the white gown and then back up. When my eyes reach the top, they land on the reflection of Brad's eyes.

"Thank you," I say and neither of us shifts our gaze for another beat.

"I need to talk to you," Brad repeats.

"Okay," I tell him, easily ignoring the fact that I am supposed to be staging my fake wedding any second now.

"You can't go through with this," Brad states matter-of-factly.

"What?" I ask weakly, positive and mortified that Brad has gotten wind of my insane plan.

"You cannot marry Justin," Brad states, this time sounding slightly desperate.

He doesn't know about the plan. He thinks that I am

moments away from saying "I do," on the happiest day of my life and he is trying to stop me. My head spins for a moment. How dare he?

"How dare you?" I say out loud.

"Molly . . ." Brad starts, but I cut him off.

"I can't believe you're trying to ruin my happiness!" I say, getting louder.

"I love you," Brad says in his normal voice. "I'm in love with you," he says, a bit quieter.

I don't hear him, though. I am so wound up and angry that I only hear myself scream, "Get out!"

Brad opens his mouth to say something. Maybe to protest the exile I have demanded, but before he can get a word out, I scream "NOW!" so loud that my guests downstairs probably hear.

Brad looks down at his shoes as he turns and walks out of the suite. He doesn't say another word or look back. It feels like forever before I finally hear the suite's door close and I exhale . . . I hadn't even realized I'd been holding my breath. I turn my full attention back to the mirror. My face is as red as a cherry.

Anger surges through me. I am in disbelief that Brad would make yet another attempt to ruin my wedding. All the times he tried before were bad enough, but to try on the actual day of . . . and just minutes before the ceremony!!! His nerve is truly unbelievable.

I look in the mirror again and take a deep breath. I have to compose myself. I cannot let him ruin this for me. I have put too much into this day; I have made too many sacrifices. It is literally taking all my strength not to let this minor setback completely derail me. I shake with anger as I try to take deep, relaxing breaths. Just for the record, they aren't working.

Eyes on the prize, I remind myself. This is it . . . the finish line . . . the final frontier. Today is the day I've been dreaming about and working for. It is SO like Brad to try and ruin it, but I will not let him. All the anxiety I was feeling is overtaken by this anger and I take that anger and use it to fuel my confidence. I'm ready for showtime, as Justin would say. Let's get the show on the road.

55

The Big Moment

This is where we met.

"Today is my wedding day . . . it should be the happiest day of my life. It should be the day that at long last all my dreams are realized and I embark on the love boat to the island of happiness and bliss that everyone else has already been living on. That couldn't be farther from the truth. Instead this day is worse than I ever imagined it could be. I'm standing in a suite at The Plaza hotel . . . no expense has been spared in pursuit of matrimonial perfection. I am wearing my dream, white (at last!) Vera Wang strapless wedding gown. My fantasy wedding is minutes away from beginning and I'm finally realizing what I have done."

Sound familiar?

I look in the mirror once more, still trying to catch my breath and calm myself down, and then I look around the beautiful suite and remember each second I've had in it—from yesterday when my parents surprised me, to today. My whole family has been beyond generous and loving with everything to do with this wedding and I have lied, hugely and blatantly, to them. My selfishness has been monumental. As I stand here, ready to go play the part I rehearsed all night, I am finally appalled at myself for concocting such a plan and going through with it. Don't get me wrong . . . I recognize that I have had many happy moments and I could even stretch things so far as to say that I've given my family joy through the planning of this wedding . . . but when it comes down to the cold, hard, truth . . . I've fucked up.

My mind is still racing when there is a gentle knock on the door. I jump slightly, my confidence wavering as I fear that it could be Brad again. I feel another surge of anger before calling to whoever is outside that they may come in. It is Ashley, Marion's assistant. She looks more like a member of the secret service than a wedding coordinator today with her headset and clipboard.

"Molly? Are you ready?" she asks gently.

"As ready as I'll ever be," I admit, and start toward the door.

The walk down to the ceremony is surreal, to say the least. As I walk through the halls of the hotel, people stop and stare at me, and they whisper to each other or wish me congratulations. One little girl even tugs on her mother's skirt as she points at me in awe. They all think they know what today holds for me . . . they are wrong.

I finally get to the room where my dad is waiting to escort me down the aisle. I take a peek inside and am surprised to see both sides of the aisle almost equally full. At the front of the room is an amazing arch of pink, blue, and white hydrangeas . . . it's stunning. Logan is standing underneath it with the minister. I can tell from all the way back here that he is nervous. Mom is sitting in the front row and Jamie is about to push Kate down the aisle in a beautifully decorated pram. I give her a tight hug before watching her walk down the aisle to "Canon in D." Then I turn and look at Dad, trying to run through what is going to happen in my head one final time. He doesn't seem to notice that anything is wrong.

Just as the "Wedding March" begins to play and my dad reaches for my arm, Marion rushes up to us in a flurry. Finally somebody realizes the groom is missing! She is more unkempt than I have ever seen her, despite wearing one of her more beautiful Chanel suits . . . her hair is messed up from pulling her headset on and off and she is sweating a little around the brow. The disheveled look definitely doesn't suit her. As she screeches to a halt in front of us, she gulps to catch her breath and regain her composure. Marion pauses for a split second before opening her mouth to speak to us, then holds up one finger, turns around and hisses, "Stop the music!" into her headset, then turns back to us and takes another deep breath.

"Now, Molly," she begins, never missing a chance to slip a "now" in, "we are having a tricky time locating Justin."

I almost have to giggle at the way she phrases Justin's absence, but I focus and remember what I am supposed to do: step one: confusion.

"What do you mean?" I ask her with only a little panic in my voice. The truth is, I don't need to fake the panic because I do feel a bit anxious.

"We're sure he's around here somewhere . . . relax dear, this happens all the time. A groom will go to get a breath of fresh air or a drink of water right before ceremony time without realizing how long he is gone. Just relax for one more minute and we're going to find him in a jiff." She smiles at me sympathetically before hissing into her headset, "Ashley! Find the groom! STAT!" She then turns back to us with another smile before she slips away.

I turn and look at Dad, maintaining my confused look, and see that he looks completely alarmed. Oh my God, I hate myself for putting my family through this.

"It's okay, Daddy—we'll get started in just a minute."

My dad takes a deep breath and turns to look at me with sorrowful eyes, "Molly, I don't want you to panic, but I want you to prepare yourself." Dad pauses and takes a deep breath. "I haven't seen Justin all day."

"What do you mean? Are you sure?" I ask, almost impressed with how confused I seem.

"Let's just wait and see . . . I'm sure Marion and Ashley will find him," Dad tries to reassure me.

I could not feel more awful about the pain I'm putting my dad through . . . I try to catch Logan's eye to get the show on the road, but I can't because he is giving confused looks to Jamie and Mom.

What feels like half an hour later . . . and may well be, Marion and Ashley have recruited Logan to help with the search, so I know the note will materialize any minute now. Finally, the three of them approach Dad and me.

"Molly," Marion begins as Ashley stands behind her, looking only slightly less miserable than Logan, "it would appear as though your groom has decided not to join you today."

For a split second I have to stop and be impressed with the kind and gentle way Marion has developed to say, *You've been dumped on your wedding day, kid*, but before I can control it or remember what step two is supposed to be, tears start falling. I knew he wasn't showing up, I knew I wasn't getting married today, but now that it's actually happening, I am in disbelief.

"He left a note at the front desk," Logan pipes up, taking the note from his coat pocket where he carefully placed it the night before. He unfolds it and hands it to me.

As planned, I read it—slowly, three times—before handing it to Dad with my confused and hurt face.

Dad reads the note, then crumples it up and throws it on the ground as his face flushes crimson. Logan and I glance nervously at each other . . . I'm suddenly completely blank on what I am supposed to do next . . . so I sob. Dad holds me tight as I wail, and I don't even worry about my beautiful hairdo or perfect makeup job as I hiccup for air.

Thankfully, Logan remembers what to do and quietly says, "Should someone tell the guests?"

Right! The guests . . . "I'll tell them," I say bravely, collecting myself and putting my strong face on.

"No, Molly, you don't have to," Dad interjects.

"It's okay," I tell him, "it's my place. They are here for me."

"I'll be with you, Molly," Logan says, taking my hand.

With Dad, Marion, and Ashley staring at us from behind, and the room of guests turned and staring at me from the front, my brother and I walk up the aisle in stone silence. When we reach the front where Father Roberts is standing, I turn and take a deep breath before beginning my prepared monologue.

"I am not sure what happened to Justin or to us," I begin slowly, "but we will not be getting married today," I say as a small weep escapes from my chest. I close my eyes for a second and take another breath before opening my mouth to continue. I can't continue, though, because from the back of the room Dad yells, "It's okay! He's here!! He must have changed his mind!"

What? Now I am really confused. What is Dad talking about, and what is Justin doing here?!? I squint to look down the long aisle and I do in fact see someone, presumably Justin, running toward the room. I look at Logan, whose face looks as alarmed as mine must.

Just as Justin enters the room, my mother stands up and shrieks, "Everything is okay! Justin wants to marry you!"

I hear four voices yell, "NO!" and the only thing I am certain about is that one of them is my own. I look around the room . . . the second one definitely came from Justin, the third I believe from Logan. I scan the room and see the

only other person standing and the voice of the fourth "no":
Brad.

"No?" my mother repeats; now it's her turn to be confused.

"Justin can't marry me—he's gay!" I blurt out, and immediately hear an enormous, collective gasp from the room, but I continue to stare right at Brad. His visit to my bridal suite is starting to come back to me.

"Molly is right," Justin explains to the room of wide-eyed wedding guests, but I'm not listening to him, I'm looking straight into the eyes of Bradley Lawson and something is different.

I flash back to the way Brad looked at me when he walked in the room and the way he said I looked amazing. That was the word he used, wasn't it? "Amazing."

I hear Justin start to explain his arrival. "I'm here today because I'm in love with Logan and I can't let him out of my life."

Another collective gasp from the room and everyone, including Brad and me, turns to look at Logan, whose eyes are already filling with tears.

"I love Molly, I love your family, but I am in love with you," Justin says to my brother.

"I'm in love with you, too," Logan whispers to Justin before running into his arms. Half the room (the half that thinks they are at a play) bursts into cheers; the other half looks even more surprised and confused.

My mouth turns into a smile, but before I can truly be happy for them, I turn back to Brad. It seems that throughout all the Justin and Logan hoopla, he hasn't taken his eyes off of me. I flash back to the pleading in his voice when he told me I couldn't go through with marrying Justin.

"Why did you say no?" I yell to Brad so that he can hear me above the cheering half. My yelling gets everyone's attention and there is once again a pregnant silence, and once again all eyes are on me.

"I had to try," Brad says.

Suddenly my mind is flooded. The crazy afternoon at my apartment and the electrifying kiss Brad and I shared on my couch—and in my doorway. Then the rest of his visit earlier today washes into my head. Brad said he loved me . . . he said he was in love with me. Could that be right? I must not be remembering correctly . . .

"I couldn't let you go without trying," he goes on.

Huh?!? Really? Is it true?

"What?" is all I manage to say.

"Because I love you."

And then the strangest thing happens. When Brad says he loves me, it just FEELS right and I realize that it feels so perfect because I love him, too. How could I have never realized before? And suddenly what happened in my apartment two long days ago makes perfect sense . . . we do fit together perfectly, and it's for a reason—we're meant to be together. My eyes are finally open.

"I love you, too," I tell him, and it is the most natural, simple thing I have ever said.

The entire room breaks into applause with a few whistles and hoots as Brad and I head toward each other, but before we can, there is a screeching.

"What the fuck?!?"

Another gasp, more silence, and everyone turns and stares at the most outraged Claire I have ever seen. She has her hands on her hips, her mouth hanging open in disgust, and her little foot tapping away.

Before Brad can say anything to her or offer any explanation, the entire room boos her and someone yells, "Kiss already!"

What else can we do? We kiss, and it's the most amazing

kiss I've ever had. There are fireworks from the tips of my toes to the top of my head. It's like the way people kiss in movies, only better. The only thing I can say to slightly describe it is: imagine spending your whole day looking at the most amazing chocolate cake but thinking it's not for you and then you realize it is and you take a big bite . . . no, that doesn't even do it justice. Let's just leave it at amazing . . . and when something is so amazing, you want more . . . so I kiss him again.

We pull apart and look into each other's eyes and it's like coming home. Our gazes are broken by someone yelling "Encore!" from the back, and I can't help but giggle. This has turned into a pretty entertaining play.

56

Getting Things Straightened Out

Once the crowd finally settles down, my dad makes his way up to where Justin, Logan, Brad, and I are standing at the front of the room. The poor guy has gone from looking very red to very white.

"Okay, lemme get this straight," he says, scratching his head, which I notice for the first time looks a little balder. "You are also gay?" he says to Justin.

"Yes," Justin confirms.

"And you love Logan?"

"Very much," Justin answers as he squeezes Logan closer to him.

Dad nods and then turns to Brad and me, but before he says anything he turns back to Justin. "Did you know you were gay when you proposed to Molly?"

Uh-oh . . . my heart skips a beat . . . how much truth is going to come out here today?

"I had a feeling," Justin admits, and then he steals a glance at me and gives me a quick wink, which I return with a heartfelt smile. "But as the wedding day got closer I realized I couldn't be with her, especially since I had fallen in love with Logan."

Phew . . . yet another exemplary job of using vague truths to cover our lie. Well done, Justin.

"Okay." Dad nods with the slightest understanding before turning back to Brad and me. "And Brad, you love Molly?"

"With all my heart," he says, and my insides completely melt.

"And you're sure you're not gay?" Dad says with only the slightest hint of sarcasm.

"I'm positive."

"And what about Claire? Aren't you supposed to marry her next week?"

Brad hangs his head in shame, "I was supposed to, but I can't. I'm in love with Molly and I can't spend the rest of my life denying it."

Dad smiles warmly. "I always thought you two belonged together."

There is a loud, almost animal, grunt from where Claire is standing, tapping her foot.

"Screw you!" she screams at Brad, and maybe at me, too. "You pathetic twerps deserve each other!!" she screams before turning and storming out of the room. Once again, the wedding guests erupt into cheers.

"Well," Dad says as the room quiets back down, "I couldn't agree with her more. You twerps do deserve each other," he says. "And as for you twerps," he continues, turning toward Logan and Justin, "we've grown to adore Justin over the past ten months and I'm glad that this means he'll be staying in our family."

All the new couples are hugging and glowing, all the wedding guests (especially those who believe they are play patrons), are clapping wildly until Brad lets go of me and gets down on one knee. My heart literally stops beating.

"Molly Rose Harrigan," he begins, "you have been my best friend for twelve years, you are my soul mate, you are my other half, and I want you to be my wife. Will you marry me?"

Needless to say, the answer is yes, but I'm crying so hard at this point that I can't get it out; instead, I resort to frantic nodding. He seems to get the picture, because he stands up and grabs me in a tight embrace, twirling me around and tangling us both in my train sash.

"I love you!" I manage to get out through the sobs, as there is mad cheering once again, and Brad lays another of his amazing kisses on me.

"So," my mom breaks in, interrupting our kiss, "you know, we could have a wedding here today if you want."

I pull back from Brad and look around the room . . . I'd practically forgotten where we were and what else was going on. Brad and I look at each other and shrug.

"If you want to," Brad says.

Wow . . . my heart is racing as I look around the room and think, and finally, I decide. I take a deep breath, "No." The crowd groans. "I want to be engaged! I want the experience of planning the wedding with the person I love," I explain, and I steal a quick glance at Justin, who is nodding in agreement.

"Well, then," Dad announces, "join us today for an engagement/coming-out/falling-in-love party!" The room goes completely berserk as the newly-in-love-and-engaged couple and the newly-out-and-in-love couple kiss, again.

Epilogue

One Year Later

I remember a year ago, on my first wedding day, I read Martha's *"Your Wedding Day"* list. The only item for the day was "Relax and enjoy yourselves!" Yeah, right, I thought to myself, and I began to wonder if Martha herself had ever even had a wedding. I had seen a Cybill Shepherd made-for-TV movie about Martha's life (rather unflattering, I might add), and I know she was married but never remember her actually having a wedding. I bitterly cursed myself for spending all those months blindly following the advice of someone who may have never actually been through it; proof that she had no clue what she was talking about was the suggestion that a girl could possibly relax on her wedding day.

Today I get it. Today is my *real* wedding day, and I honestly am completely relaxed. This whole year has been totally different. The year has been how I always thought and dreamed wedding planning would be. Brad and I have had a wonderful time doing everything together. Nothing has been stressful, nothing has made me miserable, and I haven't cried anything except tears of joy. This is how it should be.

My marriage is minutes away and I am in my old room at my parents' house, looking down into the yard where our most loved family and friends are happily drinking champagne. I am wearing the same dream white, strapless wedding dress, but I have had it hemmed to the middle of my calf and I have retired the crown and veil. The dress looks fantastic. Although Helen, at Barney's, was terrified to carry out my alteration request, she stuck by her "customer is always right" mantra, and in the end, she even admitted that she almost liked it better. My hair and makeup have been done by me . . . and Jamie, and Justin, and a little bit of input from Logan.

Jamie is wearing the same beautiful bridesmaid's dress, but instead of a professionally polished hairdo, she has her hair up in a comfortable ponytail. Kate, of course, has outgrown her perfectly matched dress, but that's okay . . . Jamie and I had tons of fun shopping for a new flower girl dress . . . and this time around she is actually going to walk—well, toddle—down the aisle.

There is no fear today, there is no stress, only happiness and love. I take one more look down at the people in the yard, and turn around when I hear my mother knock softly on the door.

"Come in," I tell her.

Mom slowly pushes the door open and takes one look at me, sitting on the window seat, looking down at the yard like I always did as a child, and the tears start falling. "Good Golly Miss Molly," she whispers. Then she pauses, wipes her tears with the back on her hand, and looks at me again, "That's the last time I'll be able to call you that."

"Why?" I ask.

"Because, tonight you'll be Mrs. Molly."

Now it's my turn for the waterworks. I'm going to be Mrs.—Mrs. Molly Lawson.

"Let's go," Mom says, taking my hand. I grab the bouquet of wildflowers Iris has made for me and walk downstairs with Mom. Dad is waiting for me on the deck. I stand with him and together we watch Mom and then Jamie with Kate walk down the aisle. The best part is that at the end of the aisle I can see Brad, standing and waiting for me . . . and looking more handsome than ever.

Dad gives me a final hug as the "Wedding March" begins to play and we follow the rose-petal-strewn path that the others have already walked down.

All the guests are crowded around the ivy-covered arch at the end of the yard. Brad and I decided not to have official seats with "bride's side/groom's side" because we are on the same side. Everyone smiles brilliantly at Dad and me as we walk, but I can only see Brad . . . and I think Brad can only see me, because his twinkling blue eyes are locked on mine.

Today just feels right. Getting married to Brad, in the backyard of the house I grew up in, surrounded by friends, family, and love all around, is how it should be. This whole year, in fact, has felt right. Justin was exactly right when he said that the experience of being engaged and having a wedding would be better when shared with someone I love.

I do not, however, have any regrets about hiring Justin. Okay, well a few regrets about all the lies I had to tell, but when I think about what a wonderful friend I have made, and when I think about how happy in love my little brother is and how he may never have had that if not for my insanity, it feels worth it.

Brad and I exchange vows that we have written to each other and rings engraved with our wedding date and the infinity symbol before we are pronounced husband and wife and Brad is given the go-ahead to kiss me with one of his amazing kisses that a year later still weaken my knees.

Then we run down the aisle like two kids on a playground and into our future . . . which is much more romantic than into the sunset.